The Dark Well
of
Glastonbury

The Dark Well of Glastonbury

Phillipa Bowers

CRONE

CRONE

ISBN; 978-0-9929516-0-3

Cover art: Phillipa Bowers
Designed and typeset by Rhiannon Hanfman
Printed and distributed by IngramSpark/Lightning Source

Crone Press,
25 Bere Lane
Glastonbury
Somerset BA6 8BD

www.phillipabowers.co.uk

CRONE

For all the Guardians of the Dark Well, past, present and future

Phillipa Bowers.

Chapter One

London, January 1903

Louisa could hear the Vicar's voice echoing in her head, 'Ashes to ashes, dust to dust; ashes to ashes, dust to dust,' in time with the clippity-clop, clippity-clop, clippity-clop, of the horses' metal shoes on the cobbles. When the carriage pulled up outside the house and the sound stopped, she glanced at her cousin and seeing her head hanging forward in a doze, turned to look outside.

The coachman was standing on the running board ready to open the door and his black coat covered most of the window. She saw her reflection in the dark glass and pulled the black mourning veil up then raised her hand to pinch her white cheeks, until, seeing the pale image overshadowed by a dark shape, she gasped in surprise. The picture vanished as the man jumped down and opened the door, but she could still see in her mind's eye the silhouette of a large bird with its wings outstretched.

Her companion awoke with a start and said, 'I do apologise, my dear. I had so little sleep last night, I am embarrassed to say I gave in to tiredness.'

'Of course I understand, Emily,' Louisa replied with a smile. 'The work you do at the hospital must be exhausting.'

They alighted from the carriage, stepped through the ornate wrought iron gate and walked along a stone path through the garden towards the house.

As she passed an emerging clump of snowdrops Louisa paused to admire the tiny shoots of her mother's favourite flower. If only her mama were still alive she could tell her of the strange apparition in the dark glass; the dear woman would have insisted privately it was a portent of the future. With a smile Louisa recalled how she would have given a cautionary wag of her finger and whispered the warning, 'This should never be mentioned to anyone and especially not in polite society.' When Louisa had asked the reason for this, her mother had always shaken her head in a despairing way and shrugged, then after that she would have proudly added, 'My Grandmama used to say, "The second sight is accepted by few and understood by none." Just remember, my dear, you have the gift and it comes from my side of the family.'

Hearing the horses' hooves clattering, she looked up and watched the black plumes on their heads waving as they pulled the carriage away then wondered if they were already on their way to pick up other mourners and take them to the cemetery. Another daughter burying her father perhaps, a husband parting with his beloved wife, or worst of all, parents watching a small coffin being lowered into the cold dark earth.

Once inside the house and having asked the maid to bring a tray of tea, Louisa ushered her cousin into the sitting room and invited her to sit down. She then unpinned the large black veil draped over her hat and with slow deliberate movements, tore it into two, then four and finally into eight pieces, all of which she threw on the floor and jumped up and down on them vigorously. Turning breathlessly with flaming cheeks to face her astonished cousin, she said, 'My mother used to say trouble comes in threes and that's the third funeral in six years: first my son, then my husband and finally my father. I think that's quite enough, don't you?' Then she sank to her knees and gave a few dry sobs, but was unable to shed any tears.

Ten minutes later, feeling refreshed after tea and cake, she turned to her cousin sitting beside her on the chesterfield and said, 'I'm so grateful to you, dear Emily. I don't know how I could have coped today without you.'

Putting an arm around Louisa's shoulders, her cousin said, 'I would like to help you in the future, my dear. I promise to do so in any way possible.'

'Perhaps you could find useful employment for me in your hospital,' Louisa suggested. 'I've had a great deal of experience in caring for the sick these past ten years as you know.'

'Do you really need to earn money, my dear?'

'I do. The solicitor explained the situation to me yesterday and I'm afraid it's not good. My father did not manage his affairs well. He was a gambler, as you probably know, but he was also foolish in other ways: I knew he had sold the house in Chiswick after making unwise investments, but now I've learned that he also loaned someone a lot of money that was never repaid and has been living on credit for several years.'

'Do you know to whom he lent the money?' Emily asked.

'No. When I asked the name of this person the solicitor simply shook his head sadly. I have to accept the past is over and done with, and the debt to him will now never be honoured.'

Emily shook her head and gave a sympathetic sigh.

'Unfortunately there is a complication which affects me now.' Louisa gestured around the room. 'When my father gave us this house to live in after we married I did not realise his name remained on the deeds. I don't know why he did not transfer it into my name at the time; I suppose he thought I would inherit it anyway after his death.'

'Which you have,' Emily said with a perplexed frown.

'That is so, but once the house has been sold to pay the recent gambling debts my father incurred while living with me, I shall be almost destitute; so you see—'Louisa smiled at Emily '—that is my reason for mentioning nursing, which does seem to suit you, dear cousin.'

'It does indeed. Much to my mother's horror, it suits me very well. I'm afraid my poor dear Mama cannot understand why I would choose to live as I do, working amidst the filth and degradation of the worst areas in London. It's my vocation and my whole life.' Emily gave a sad smile. 'I wish I thought being a nurse in the hospital would be suitable for you, Louisa, but I fear you're not used to scrubbing floors, nor are you strong enough to struggle with violent drunks, or to lift portly gentlemen when unconscious after being operated upon. I know you have nursed both your husband and father; but there's some very unpleasant things to deal with in a hospital, including rather unsavoury characters at times, even, I'm sad to say, ladies of the night who are injured or ill.' Emily smiled benignly. 'I think you need to find an occupation that is more fitting for you and your talents.'

Louisa shrugged. 'I have no training or experience other than thirteen years of marriage, during which I managed a house and servants and cared for my husband and my—' she gripped the arm of the chair '—my son and latterly, my father. As far as I can see, my only way of earning a living, apart from—' she gave her cousin a roguish grin '—as a lady of the night, which I really wish to avoid, would be to go into domestic service. I think I could be a lowly maid if I was given simple tasks and good instructions, but definitely not a cook.'

She took a sip of tea while wondering what other means of employment might be possible. 'I am proficient at sewing and embroidery, therefore seamstress is a possibility and a shop assistant is also possible, although I know my father would turn in his grave at the thought, as would my dear husband. I had thought of teaching piano and was really excited about the prospect of helping little children learn to play; until I realised it was an impossible dream.' She gave a hopeless shrug and explained, 'Apart from the necessity to sell my beloved piano and therefore having no instrument on which to teach; I shall also be renting, as impecunious widows do, a small room intended for servants at the back of someone's house, usually up a dingy staircase and not the sort of place to which respectable people would send their children.'

Emily looked thoughtful then suggested, 'You could become a paid companion to a gentlewoman. You would live in nice surroundings, chores would be done for you by servants and you would be well fed.'

'Yes,' Louisa agreed. 'I think that would be acceptable. I would enjoy reading to her and if she had a piano could play to entertain her.'

'There are several wealthy benefactors that come to visit the hospital, ladies of good family, who may have an elderly relative in need of a companion. I will make discreet enquiries on your behalf.' Hearing the clock on the mantelpiece chime twelve times, Emily said, 'Unfortunately, I must go soon.' She gave a slight frown and added, 'I regret my sister did not attend the funeral.'

'Edwina wrote and sent her condolences. She explained that since your mother's recent illness she is staying with her in Glastonbury. The duties involved in running the household and caring for Aunt Agnes made the journey from Somerset impossible.'

Emily gave another slight frown and looked out of the window for a moment before saying, 'I believe your mother's sister lives in Glastonbury.'

'Oh yes, indeed. Aunt Rosemary sent a very kind note explaining that she is no longer quite so able to travel far.'

'I heard from my mother that Aunt Rosemary and your mother were not ...' Emily paused searching for the right word. 'I think they were not on good sisterly terms for many years. Was there ever a reconciliation between them?'

'Sadly not,' Louisa replied with a shake of her head.

'My mother was fond of them both, having known them from childhood, and was sad when they fell out. She tried to ascertain the cause of their disagreement but without success.'

Louisa nodded. 'I also failed to understand. My mother refused to speak her sister's name, or have it said in the house.'

'Your Aunt Rosemary is known for her forthright manner; perhaps she spoke her mind at an inappropriate moment. I know my father did not approve of her and thought she was not suitable company for his wife, but my mother kept up their friendship despite his opinion. I fear my sister has very little time for her too and I must admit, my dear, having heard about the reading of tea-leaves and other forms of divination with which the old lady is involved, I do have some sympathy with Edwina.'

Louisa wanted to avoid any further criticism of her mother's youngest sister, whom she had loved dearly and therefore enquired, 'Is cousin Edwina enjoying her stay in Glastonbury?'

'I believe my sister finds it dull and countrified, as indeed, I must confess, do I, but then I love the hustle and bustle of my busy life in the hospital. Edwina and I are very different; she misses her friends and her dressmaker in Brighton. I suspect she would find Glastonbury agreeable if replacements for them both could be found.'

'Glastonbury is very dear to my heart; I was sad when we no longer went to stay with my aunt or visited your parents' house when we were there.'

'I remember you came to stay with us as a young girl, just you and your father.'

'Yes, my mother never went there again after the falling out with Aunt Rosemary. I think my father was sad about that. He was very fond of his 'little brother' as he called your father.'

'That's true, the two brothers were very close, which is the reason we came to visit you in Chiswick, after you no longer came to see us. I recall some lovely times at your house by the river. In fact, now I come to think of it, I am working at the hospital because I met a lady involved with it at one of your parents' dinner parties.' Emily stood up. 'And now, my dear, I must take my leave in order to get back to my patients.' Emily kissed her goodbye and having promised to keep in touch, left the house.

Louisa wandered from room to room, touching treasured ornaments and vases that had been wedding presents or gifts from her husband and running her hands over much loved furniture with which she must soon part. Everything held memories. The chair her husband had sat in each evening brought reminders of many hours they spent sitting by the fire reading or talking together.

The piano held pleasurable reminiscences of playing his favourite music for him and also of the dear father who had bought it for her sixteenth birthday. Stroking the polished lid she recalled his excitement when it arrived and her mother teasing him, saying, 'You are still a child at heart, my love.'

While in her bedroom and holding a silver-backed hairbrush in her hand, she caught sight of her reflection in the dressing table mirror and was horrified. When had the pretty young wife with fair curls framing her face been replaced by this tired, pale and really rather plain woman? She moved closer to the looking glass and inspected the familiar blue eyes. How long ago had those dark smudges formed under them? And the lines on her forehead, when did they appear? She watched tears of dismay well up until her face was a blur before dabbing it with an embroidered handkerchief and hurrying out of the room.

She walked across the landing and opened the door of the room that had been a nursery for three years and was now completely empty. She knew her husband had meant well when he had ordered everything to be removed one day while she was out and yet it had seemed so cruel at the time, when all she had wanted to do was sit with the mementoes of those three golden years with her boy.

Now at last she could look at the barren space and understand her husband had also suffered and not only that—he could not bear to see her sitting day after day in the room that had become a shrine to their dead son.

Turning away she closed the door and, hoping her husband could hear her say she regretted the things she had said at the time when he was already frail, she whispered, 'I forgive you and hope you will forgive me.'

She went downstairs to the kitchen and knocked on the door. Hearing the scrape of chairs on stone floor, she smiled, knowing a teatime break was being interrupted, before entering to find the cook and the maid standing, waiting for her.

'As you know,' she paused, swallowed and began again, 'as you know, I have agreed to sell the house to our neighbour. I am so very sorry to part with you both after the years you have worked so well for me.'

The cook said, 'We both found new situations, Mrs Wendon, thanks ter the references yer given us. Yer don't need ter worry about us.'

'Working for yer's been a pleasure, Mrs Wendon.' The maid dabbed at her eyes with her white apron. 'Life's never going ter be the same again, not fer me.'

'Nor me,' the cook declared.

'And it's certainly not going to be the same for me,' Louisa said with a wry smile.

Six weeks later Louisa looked at the sleeping baby in her arms and feeling the train slow down, knew she must reluctantly part with him at the next station. Holding him for a short time had brought back memories and also awakened a deep longing for another child to love. Raising her eyes she saw the mother, who looked barely more than a child herself, struggling with the buttons on a small boy's coat. It was clear that another baby was waiting to be born in a few weeks and she wondered how the young woman would manage when there were three offspring needing her attention.

'Got a real gift with children you have, lady,' the young woman said, smiling at her across the gap between the seats. 'I thank you for helping me mind 'em—' she gave helpless shake of her head '— dunno what I'd 'ave done without yer.'

'It was a pleasure,' Louisa replied. Then, as the train came to a stop and the door opened, she handed the baby to his mother and waved to the older boy while saying, 'Goodbye Edgar, I hope you will look after Mamma in your new home.'

The flustered young woman said breathlessly, 'I hope you have a lovely holiday in Glastonbury,' before struggling out onto the platform.

Louisa watched a young man in khaki uniform run to her and after kissing her cheek, scoop up the boy and sit him on his shoulders, then lead his family away. While the doors were banged shut and a whistle blew, she wondered what life would be like for them now he had joined the army.

The young woman had tried to hide her nervousness about the new life ahead without the support of her mother in London. She had explained with enthusiasm how good it would be to have a regular wage and how happy she would be to live in the home near the barracks, but she could not disguise her anxiety about the future. When Louisa had said, 'We must be thankful the Boer war is over,' the young woman had looked suddenly older. With a sigh she had replied, 'My Dad says the army's a good reliable occupation, 'cos there's always trouble somewhere in the empire.'

A fly on the outside of the window attracted Louisa's attention and while focusing on the glass, she suddenly caught a glimpse of a man with dirty bandages around his head walking in a line of others, each with similar bandages and all with one hand on the shoulder of the man in front. With a gasp of horror she quickly turned her head away and rubbed her eyes to erase the terrible image.

Her mother instantly came to mind and she smiled at the memory of her looking flushed after two glasses of port wine while reminiscing about her psychic grandmother in Somerset.

Thoughts of her mother brought up memories of earlier trips to Glastonbury and visits to her mother's sister, Rosemary, in an old stone house behind the wall of the ruined abbey. During the last of these reunions, when Louisa was fourteen, the two sisters had fallen out—the reason for this terrible screaming argument had never been explained and there was no contact between them for the remaining two years of her mother's life.

Aunt Rosemary had sent a birthday card every year and a letter of condolence on receipt of each notification of death, but they had not met in the intervening years, which had seemed sad, but unavoidable. She had considered warning her aunt of this visit, but having realised the once spritely woman must be very old by now, had decided to contact her when established at her destination.

The train moved out from the station and gathered speed through green fields dotted with cottages and farmhouses, very like the tiny ones in the toy farmyard she had played with as a child and for a while she enjoyed memories of her privileged life in the house by the Thames in Chiswick before she married.

When her mind returned from dancing at parties and rowing her boat across to the island for picnics, to worrying about the young wife and her children, she remembered how her husband used to tease her in the early days of marriage for taking on the worries of those around her. 'Other people's lives, my dear, other people's lives,' he would say with a shake of his head. Adding as he lit a cigar, 'You can't live it for them, Lou, just worry about us, my darling, we have enough vexation of our own.'

With a wry smile she acknowledged he was right—not that he could ever have imagined at the time how overwhelming those worries would be one day: first with the long, slow wasting disease that had eventually killed him, then for her son struck down with scarlet fever, and finally for her father who came to live with her after losing his house to creditors and died a broken man in the home she had now sold to pay his gambling debts.

She had told the young mother that she was travelling to stay with her cousin, giving the impression she was going on holiday, but this was far from the truth. She had been invited by Cousin Edwina to act as companion to Aunt Agnes, Edwina's mother. Although no mention was made of Edwina's sister, Emily, Louisa felt sure it was she who had suggested this offer should be made. The letter had made clear she

would not be a guest and had been couched in terms of patronising delicacy, avoiding any words such as employment or money, suggesting that she would be welcome to visit and act as companion to her aunt, who was rather frail after a stroke.

Louisa knew she had no option but to accept this generous offer. She realised that a widow aged thirty-one, who had no home and only a small amount of money, would be foolish to refuse, despite her doubts as to the wisdom of the venture. One concern causing her to hesitate, even while writing the letter of acceptance, was her scant acquaintance of Edwina since they had grown up; in fact their only meetings of late had been at family funerals.

She remembered Edwina's wedding twenty years earlier when George, the groom, having obviously drunk too much, had patted Louisa inappropriately while passing behind her. She was talking to Aunt Agnes at the time, while holding a glass of punch and when she reacted and jumped with shock, this drink somehow landed down the front of her aunt's silk frock which caused a great deal of consternation to everyone, especially her aunt who, she was sure, had seen the reason for the accident.

Now, on her way to take up the offer, Louisa wondered how frail her aunt had become in the four years since they last met at an aged great aunt's funeral. At that time Aunt Agnes had been a gentle, sweet woman living contentedly in the shadow of her large and jovial husband, Uncle Wilfred, who unfortunately died a few months later. Louisa had been sad when unable to attend her uncle's funeral, due to both her husband's rapidly deteriorating condition and her father's deepening melancholia. She would have liked to comfort Aunt Agnes, of whom she was very fond, and to represent her incapacitated father at his brother's burial.

As the train pulled into the station she stood up and reached for the door, wondering if she would be met and taken to the house. After alighting she saw a porter waving while bringing her trunk and hatbox

on a trolley. She walked with him to the pavement outside where a groom was waiting with a small carriage.

While riding along she recalled making the same journey with her father when they had come on one visit without her mother. Remembering his exuberant brother, Wilfred and his sweet wife, Agnes, she smiled and thought how different the two brothers were. While Uncle Wilfred was a loud, charming and slightly flirtatious man with the ladies, her father had been quiet, gentle and unassuming; until her mother's death, when the occasional game of cards and a glass of whisky he had once enjoyed escalated into the destructive addictions of his last melancholic years.

The journey to her aunt's house was through narrow lanes that she recalled were made even smaller in summer by the drifts of white cow parsley interspersed with bright pink foxgloves and campion on either side.

Seeing the Tor reminded her of walking up the green slopes with her father who had said the tower on its top was all that remained of a church that had been destroyed by an earthquake. She had been fascinated by this fact and also that long ago there had been a monastery on the slopes. With a smile she recalled how they had chased her panama hat when the blustery wind lifted it off her head and played with it, carrying it in leaps and bounds just out of their reach until it was eventually caught in a thorn bush. When they had retrieved it they lay on the grass and laughed and laughed until she had the hiccoughs.

On arrival at the wide gates she was transported around the curved drive to see her cousin standing on the wide steps of the imposing house.

Edwina, who was elegantly dressed in a tea gown of pale green silk, raised one eyebrow very slightly while glancing at Louisa's black mourning outfit, but was pleasantly welcoming as she ushered her into the large hall. 'I thought you would like to refresh yourself

and see your room before meeting Mama,' she said, beckoning to a maid who was hovering under the curved staircase. 'Brown will take you up. I have asked the housekeeper, Mrs Thorne, to come and explain mealtimes and Mama's routine.'

After a pause, Edwina gave a gracious smile. 'I have to leave now to go for tea with friends. I suggest we meet tomorrow after breakfast for a little chat.' With a relieved look on her face, as though thinking that all had been explained, she waved her hand in a gesture of dismissal.

Knowing this was how she would be treated in future Louisa felt a momentary pang of resentment. Then, resolving to make the best of her new situation, she followed the maid up the stairs.

Her room had obviously once been a dressing room with a door leading into, she assumed, her aunt's bedroom. She thanked the maid and waited for her to leave before sitting on the narrow iron framed bed to survey the tiny windowless space. Although tears were forming in her eyes she was determined not to show weakness and took several deep breaths to stem the flow while waiting for the housekeeper to arrive.

Mrs Thorne bustled in a few moments later and smiled as she welcomed her warmly. 'We'll all be so glad to see the mistress, beg pardon, the old mistress I should say, cared for. We've had a succession of nurses who really were not—' she paused to search for the right word '—suitable, as you might say.'

Hearing this Louisa realised her duties would be far more onerous than those of a companion and her heart sank even further. She smiled politely on hearing that she could take Monday afternoons off if she wished and listened as mealtimes were given and was told her food would be brought to her on a tray in order that she could eat with her aunt.

A few moments later the housekeeper opened the door and led the way into the bedroom. Louisa went and stood looking down at the tiny body under the bedclothes beneath a head on the pillow that

19

seemed out of proportion to it, as if either one had shrunk or the other had grown bigger. The old woman's face bore little resemblance to that which she remembered, apart from the slightly hooked nose protruding above the now sunken toothless mouth.

'She had a stroke a few months ago and hasn't spoken since, well, not in words that make sense, more like grunts if you see what I mean,' Mrs Thorpe said with a sad shake of her head. 'Poor dear Mrs Govern; she'd be so upset if she could see herself. Such a proud lady and so fastidious about her appearance, it breaks my heart to see her so.'

'I'll do my best for her. I looked after my father and my husband for several years, so I have some experience,' Louisa said, thinking she must immediately wash the old woman's matted hair and cut the fingernails curving around her fingertips like claws. She also wondered why her younger daughter Emily had not come to care for her mother until, recalling Emily saying that her mother disapproved of her career, assumed there would be too much friction between them for a relaxed recuperative atmosphere.

Mrs Thorne interrupted her thoughts, saying, 'Please don't mind my asking, Mrs Wendon, but I think I might know a lady who's related to you. I believe she is your mother's sister …'

'You know Aunt Rosemary?' Louisa asked excitedly. 'Oh how I would love to see her again! I had intended calling on her as soon as possible. I expect she is frail now.'

'Such a dear lady—' Mrs Thorne smiled '—and frail is not a word I would use to describe her even now at her advanced age. She lives close to my sister; they are good friends and look out for each other.'

'That's wonderful news,' Louisa said, she almost added that her aunt and her mother had fallen out many years ago, but decided this was family business and there was no need for such explanation. Also, she thought with a wry smile, in this small town where everyone knew everything about everybody the housekeeper would probably already be well aware of this story.

Having been informed that the old lady could neither hear nor speak she tended to her basic needs with just a minimum of caring expressions. Once, hearing her aunt make a sound that might have been, 'I thank you,' she thought it was merely coincidence, but nevertheless responded with, 'It is a pleasure, Aunt Agnes.' When the same sound was made the following morning after breakfast and again after luncheon, Louisa began to wonder if a change was taking place. She had heard of people recovering from a stroke, but not actually experienced this herself and wondered if she should mention the possibility to Edwina.

The following afternoon a maid came to Louisa and said she was wanted in the sitting room. Feeling apprehensive, she went down and found her cousin lying languidly on a chaise longue with one arm resting along the back of it. 'I've been meaning to ask you for a chat,' Edwina said, indicating with a wave of her hand that Louisa should sit on the small upright chair facing her. 'But I've been so busy with engagements recently. I am almost as occupied as I was in Brighton. Already I have been asked to sit on the committee of two charities and now that George has been invited to join the local lodge, I shall have to mix with the other Freemasons' wives I'll meet at Ladies' Nights here.' She simpered and dabbed her nose with an embroidered handkerchief. 'One needs to find out what to wear on grand occasions. I believe the fashions are changing now the royal family are out of mourning for the dear queen and one does not want to be behind the times. It's so important to support one's husband, don't you think?'

Louisa opened her mouth to agree, but closed it again on seeing her cousin was in full flow and not expecting a response.

'I have yet to find the right dressmaker. I suspect some of the local ladies travel to Bath....'

Louisa stopped listening and looked around the room at the beautiful plaster border around the edge of the ceiling and the central rose from which hung the crystal chandelier. There were too many patterns on the walls for her taste and also too many pictures, nevertheless it was delightfully designed with French windows opening onto the terrace at one side and a large bay looking out to the abbey ruins on another.

She wanted to ask if Edwina and the pompous oaf, as her father used to call George, sometimes returned to their own home in Brighton, or were now living permanently in her mother's house, but it was clear from her cousin's attitude towards her that such questions would be seen as presumptuous from not only a poor relative, but one who was little more than a servant at that!

Suddenly realising her cousin was saying her name, Louisa smiled in what she hoped was an appropriate manner.

Edwina gave a small wave of her hand. 'I'm so glad we had this little chat, I wanted to know you had settled in satisfactorily before I leave. I shall be going to our home in Brighton in the near future for a few weeks to settle things there before moving here completely and I wish to be sure I can leave my mother safely in your hands.'

Louisa opened her mouth to say she would be delighted to care for the old lady, who would most certainly be safe in her hands, but knew from the turn of Edwina's head that the interview was over and she was being dismissed.

At that moment the door burst open and George Prior strode in. He nodded perfunctorily at Louisa, who wished him a good afternoon before she left the room and while closing the door behind her, heard him say, 'What is that woman doing here? I thought I told you....'

Not daring to listen any longer, she hurried across the hall and began climbing the stairs. She glanced absentmindedly at the ancestral portraits lining the wall beside her while thinking that his antipathy towards her was due to the glass of punch spilled on his mother-in-law's frock almost twenty years ago and felt laughter bubbling up inside her. Then, recalling her cousin's autocratic manner, anger overwhelmed any sense of humour and for a moment her mind would not let go of the resentment seething inside it. She wanted to scream at the top of her voice, 'How dare that silly woman talk about being fashionable like the new Queen Alexandra or Princess Mary, while I was sitting there obviously poor as a church mouse in my outdated mourning clothes!'

On arrival at the landing and deciding to be amused rather than outraged, she made a face at the picture of a portly gentleman with a curly wig before walking to her aunt's room.

Louisa soon established a routine for each day and made her aunt look more attractive. She fed the old lady soup at mealtimes and sat watching her sleep during the day, or possibly lie awake with her eyes closed; she was unsure which was the case, because the breathing did not seem like the steady rhythm of slumber. When reading to her she felt sure from the flickers of her eyelids and tiny smiling movements of her mouth that the old lady could hear.

On the morning she found some false teeth in the bedside cupboard, cleaned them and put them in the old lady's mouth, she was astonished to feel her hand grasped. Seeing her aunt's one-sided smile and hearing her say slowly and indistinctly, 'Thank—you,' was astonishing and, most amazing of all, was a word that could have been her name, or might not, but Louisa chose to believe it was and while stroking the pale forehead assured her, 'It's a pleasure, Aunt Agnes.'

Louisa now felt sure the old lady could hear perfectly and speak with some difficulty, which was contrary to her cousin's insistence that her mother had lost all methods of communication. Although longing to tell Edwina this good news, she was wary of speaking too soon having noticed how her aunt always lay apparently comatose whenever anyone else was in the room.

On the first Monday after her arrival, she cleared away the luncheon tray and made the old lady comfortable in readiness for a sleep then said, 'Aunt Agnes, my dear, I should like to take in some fresh air. I remember going to the old abbey ruins when I was here as a girl. Do you think I may go there for a walk?'

'Yes,' was very clear. The name that followed was not easily understood, but there was no mistaking the slowly enunciated, 'will—allow—if—say—my niece.' Feeling uplifted by this exchange, Louisa bent and kissed her aunt before hurrying downstairs to tell housekeeper she would be out for an hour or so.

She knew from the earlier visit as a young girl that the ruined abbey was behind the house and on leaving the front door went around to follow a path down the back garden to a wrought iron gate set in the tall stone wall. After opening the gate she surveyed the stone ruins of the abbey set in the bare January landscape with skeletal trees in the distance.

Remembering the wild flowers she had picked there as a child, she thought of the floral wallpaper of her aunt's bedroom and wondered if it had been designed to remind her of spring throughout the year. Having decided this would be a good topic of conversation with which to ascertain the old lady's level of understanding, she set forth through the wet grass.

There was a small narrow path where either an animal or human had regularly walked to the ruined abbey and following it she held up her skirt and petticoat to keep them dry. Remembering how she had removed her shoes and stockings when young to experience the fresh sunlit grass under her bare feet, she felt a sharp pang of sadness for the lost freedom of childhood.

A few minutes later, standing before the majestic stone arches, she gasped in admiration and knew she must bring a sketchbook on the next visit and draw them with a view to making a water colour painting during the many quiet hours she would sit beside her aunt.

She walked slowly around the outside of the walls, avoiding occasional lumps of stone and following where others had obviously trodden through the grass. On finding an old wooden bench in a sunny spot with some wooden planks between it and the solid stone of the wall, she sat down and looked around her.

After admiring the building that she felt sure was the abbot's kitchen, she tried to remember the whereabouts of her Aunt Rosemary's cottage and thought it might be the other side of the boundary wall facing her across the tangled brambles, bushes and undergrowth. She was determined to visit the elderly aunt soon, despite feeling anxious and wondering if she was being disloyal to her mother in doing so.

The sun was bright and she closed her eyes. A pattern of lights formed behind her lids that suddenly took on the shape of a girl in a cloak…

Chapter Two

Willow straightened and raised her head, causing the hood of her cloak to fall back and reveal the auburn hair waving around her pale face. She lifted a hand to push a loose curl over her forehead then, remembering there was no longer any need to hide the purple mark above her eyebrow, lowered her arm and placed it on the small boy leaning against her.

'I don't want you to go, sister dear' he said gripping her hand with both of his.

'I have to, little brother —' she bent and kissed his forehead '—I must go and do my duty....'

'But I want....'

'We can't always do what we want—' she heard the intake of breath behind her and longed to look around, but dared not lest her resolve should weaken '—sometimes we have to be strong. That's what I'm asking you to be now, dearest boy.'

Hearing the mournful sound of a horn, she gently prised his fingers from hers then walked to a wooden jetty and stood gazing into the mist swirling over the water. When the prow of a boat nosed its way towards her, she took a deep breath and swallowed. The time had come, just as she had known it would. Indeed, just as her mother had foretold when they last looked into the dark pool together.

The barge came fully into view and was soon beside her. A broad shouldered man standing in the bows raised a horn to his lips and blew long and loud. A small woman and an old man, both of whom she knew to be highly respected elders of the clan, were seated on board and beckoned to her. A familiar figure appeared beside her and she felt his strong fingers take hers. She squeezed his hand, but dared not look into his face while he helped her onto the boat. They had made love for the last time. Now, she must leave him to fulfil her destiny. She would neither look back at him, nor at the couple who had sheltered her during these years in waiting, nor at the brothers and sisters she could hear calling a tearful farewell. They had all known she would leave one day and now that day had come. They all knew she loved them. They would follow her to the island for the celebrations and in future would not call her by name, using instead the title Lady of the Dark Well when they came for guidance.

The mist rose while they travelled through the water and she could see the huge dark shape of The Great One silhouetted against the pale morning sky. The earthwork dominating the landscape appeared from this vantage point to be gigantic kneeling man with his head crowned in a circle of tall stones, but she knew that, had she been coming from the other side, it would clearly be a voluptuously curved woman.

Her mother had told her that many seasons ago the ancestors had worshipped only the female side of the divine because, back in those days, people had not learned that both female and male played their part in procreation of everything, including themselves. When they understood, then they created this wonderful manifestation of the divine balance in their world wherein the suns rays shone between the two and appeared to impregnate the female side each spring when the seeds of plants sprang into life.

Ever since that time, generation after generation had revered the sacred symbol of oneness in creation, calling it The Great One, and had used it to celebrate the seasons and all the important times in life including, as they were now about to do, death.

A bird swooped past as it skimmed the water looking for fish. The beauty of it made her smile. Some birds formed patterns in the sky as they travelled in groups, but this elegant creature was usually alone, except when breeding; and, seeing another flying a short distance away, she knew the season was about to change. The air would soon be warmer and the wonder of spring would begin.

On arrival at a small wooden jetty, she stepped onto the land and gasped in awe. Although she had visited the sacred island many times before to spend days with her mother by the dark pool, everything was somehow changed; the grass seemed greener, the huge yew trees at the entrance to the processional way appeared taller and The Great One rose above her more majestically than ever.

The two women who tended the white and the red springs were waiting for Willow by the yews. Both stood erect with hands on hearts and eyes downcast at the figure lying on a bier at their feet.

She had attended burials before and seen many dead creatures, both animal and human, but the sight of the form wrapped in a familiar cloak caused an involuntary shiver nevertheless. That small bundle was all that remained of her mother, the dear woman whose place she must now take as guardian of the dark well, the most sacred of waters on this, the most sacred of islands.

Two men went and lifted the bier. The guardian of the red well beckoned Willow and indicated that she should lead the way to the mound. She walked slowly and purposefully between the yews and followed the winding path through the trees of the densely wooded lower slope of The Great One. On arrival at the lowest grassy slope she paused to look down at the shining waters below and then up at the rounded shapes above. The beat of a single ceremonial drum dominated all sounds, even those of the birds in the trees and she wondered if her mother, who loved their songs, might have preferred to hear them on her last journey. Continuing on the path she led the way round and round the sloping grassy terraces until, reaching the entrance to the cave, she stood and waited, hearing the drum beating in time with her heart, until the rest of the long procession had joined her.

One of the men lifted the corpse and held it out to her. She pulled back the cloak and kissed the thin hands and pale forehead of the wasted body. 'Farewell,' she said, adding in a whisper, 'I will do my best.' Then she walked with the man to the rocks beside the gaping hole and together they threw her mother down into the darkness.

She stood quietly whilst the people behind her left to begin retracing their steps and smiled on hearing a child exclaim, 'Look, look Mother, look down at the gathering grounds. The fire is alight! Can we go to the feast now?'

Memories filled her mind. Her mother's moans when giving birth to a dead baby: her tears when throwing the tiny corpse into the heart of The Great One. Her mother's face lighting up as she said, 'Willow, my daughter, you have the gift and shall take my place by the dark pool.' Adding with a wry smile, 'There may be times when you will regret this gift and wish you had not the honour, but it is your destiny and cannot be denied.' That was a wonderful memory one to keep in her heart during the lonely days and years ahead.

She turned to find the two guardians of the red and white springs.

'We will be of support to you—' She of the Red inclined her head questioningly '—that is, if you wish us to be.'

'Oh yes, my lady.' Willow bowed to her. 'I shall be grateful for your guidance.'

She of the White gave a slight sniff of disapproval. 'Your mother was not always so appreciative.'

Willow smiled, remembering her mother's irritation with some of their comments—usually about the men who came to visit her. 'She always respected you both; of this I'm certain. And please be assured I intend never to give you cause for complaint. I shall live quietly alone and….'

'That, my dear child, is neither likely nor possible—' She of the Red smiled benignly '—you are as beautiful as your mother and will be desired by men just as she was. In fact—' she glance sideways at her companion '—I believe there is already one who loves you, is there not?'

Willow felt the colour rise up her neck and over her face. 'You are well informed, my lady. There was a close friendship with a young man in the village, as you evidently know, but I have foresworn him. He understands that I am now dedicated to guarding the sacred water of the dark pool and can therefore never be his wife.'

She of the White looked hard into Willow's eyes. 'Do not forget that any child you bear must be taken to live with your kin in the village until your death when one of them, if a daughter, may be chosen to take your place. Only the guardians of the sacred island may live here.'

'I'll not forget, my lady.' Willow bowed her head in acknowledgment, thinking as she did so that at least her mother had left one living daughter to follow on, thereby avoiding the backbiting and competition that would ensue when either of these women died.

'We have both stayed virgin,' She of the Red said, gesturing towards She of the White.

Knowing this was both a boast of their superiority and implicit criticism of her mother's renowned love of men, Willow replied, 'I am filled with admiration for you both and will do my best to abide by the laws of this island. I promise to …' she hesitated, wondering how to avoid swearing to remain virgin when already no longer in that state. 'I promise I shall never take a husband.'

The mouth of She of the Red widened into a smile before she said, 'You are your mother's child, my dear.' She held out her hand, 'Come, let us walk down together, the three guardians of the sacred waters, the red, the white and the black.'

As they walked along the track away from the cave of the after world and towards her new life, Willow imagined the twists and turns her feet followed to be representing the path of her life to come. It would not be easy, but then living was always hard. The years ahead would be no more difficult than those she might have spent in the village with her man and their children working to get enough to eat; they would be lonelier years, definitely, colder at night, no doubt, and just different, that was all.

On arrival at the foot of The Great One the three of them stood at the place where the red and the white waters met and flowed down into the valley below.

'Never be afraid to come and ask for my help,' She of the Red said, holding out her hand.

She of the White sounded less sure, less convincing as she echoed the other's words, adding, 'You are so young, so very young to take on the responsibility of guardian of the most sacred place on this sacred island.'

'I thank you both, my ladies.' She took the hand of each one. 'I hope you will put me to the test soon and come to consult the dark pool.'

'When the moon is full?' She of the Red asked.

'That was my mother's favoured time, I know, but I have no preference. You may come at any time of the moon and I will do my best to read what is shown for you.' Hearing the sounds of singing and drumming, she said, 'The festivities have begun. Shall we go together to join the clan in their celebrations?'

They each thanked her in turn and declined her invitation then walked away to their respective huts, one by the white spring and the other by the nearby red spring.

Willow continued alone to the two great yew trees where she stood watching the figures silhouetted against the fire as her kinfolk danced to the sound of the drums beaten by a group of young men and women. She had never been fond of the drums, finding them intrusive at ceremonies and not conducive to raising the spirits of the dead, as was the accepted wisdom: now however, seeing the gay abandon of the dancers, she longed to jump and twirl with them, but instead, remembering her new and respected role, she merely clapped her hands in unison with their beat.

She felt his presence and immediately ached to feel his touch, to smell and taste him.

She turned and found him standing an arm's length away.

'My love,' he whispered, 'I saw you here alone and could not resist '

With open arms she welcomed him into her embrace, saying, 'Just one last time, love of my life.'

They sank down behind the trees and made love while uttering low murmurings of pleasure and gentle endearments to one another. She knew as his seed entered her body that it would take root and gave such a cry of ecstasy that he placed his hand over her mouth to drown the sound.

'I feared someone would hear you and find us,' he whispered while holding her as they lay in the torpor after love.

She laughed quietly against his chest, revelling in the languid release of tension in her body and knowing that his child would bring comfort to the life lived without his love.

After a while, hearing the sound of voices, they quickly arranged their clothing and stood up. Each placed a hand on the other's heart, but said nothing before he walked towards the dancing throng, while she remained, standing beside the great yew.

'What a wonderful celebration of your mother's life!' A deep voice said beside her.

She turned to find the head of a neighbouring clan, with whom her own people had recently agreed to live in peace after generations of warfare; a large man with sheepskin around his shoulders and a huge carved stick in his hand. She noted with relief that there was neither a sharp flint tied to the stick, nor a flint axe in his belt and, determined to show respect while controlling her fear of him, she bowed her head before saying, ' I wish you well, Eagle, father of your people.'

'And I wish you very well, Guardian of the Dark Water.' He fingered the soft fleece on his shoulder. 'As proof of my goodwill to you and your clan I shall bring gifts to your mother's.... I mean to your hut.'

Unsure how to respond to generosity from one outside her own clan, she gulped and stammered, 'I ... I thank you, sir.'

'I've heard tell of your mother's wise counselling—' he inclined his head towards the dark pool '—I trust you will honour me with your wisdom?'

'You are welcome to come to the well, sir. But remember it is not my wisdom, sir. I can tell only what I see, no more and no less.'

He laughed. 'Well done! You have proved yourself wise already.'

She was uncomfortable under the glittering gaze of his pale blue eyes and longed to escape. 'I must go now to sing the lament for my mother. I wish you farewell, father of your people.'

He nodded and turned away before striding towards the fire and throwing himself into a frenzied dance.

She walked around the revellers, stepping over several sleeping children and a couple locked in embrace, then reached the hut that would now be her home.

All her life so far she had lived in close, very close, proximity to other people. Now, looking at the small thatched hut built up against an outcrop of rocks, the reality of her new life became clear. Although she would have this child newly placed within her, once born the baby would be taken to live with her family and her life would be solitary.

There would be no small children snuggling up to her on cold winter nights, no man snoring and no woman singing to a sick baby; she would be alone, completely alone. Her mother had always assured her that she was safe because men of the clan respected the guardians and came only for guidance, or, as in her mother's case, by invitation. Her mother had never been afraid and she must emulate her and be brave, or appear to be.

Seeing gifts placed by the door she went and admired three clay pots filled with food from her kin, a leather cup from one of the elders, a pair of shoes from another, a fleece for her bed that she knew was from her lover and a beautiful green and grey blanket that could only be from the guardians of the red and white springs, the former of whom was renowned for the rare colours from secret recipes she used

33

to dye the yarn she span and the latter who was known for her fine weaving.

Picking up the fleece she walked inside the hut across the rush-covered floor to her mother's sleeping corner and placed it on top of the sweet grasses lying there. Later she would fetch fresh grass and dry it in the summer sun, but for now it would be comforting to know her mother had slept upon the bed before her.

She moved around the small space, touching the walls lined with woven willow stems and admiring the hooks cleverly fashioned from them, on which were hanging dried herbs and all manner of useful items, including feathers, lengths of animal gut and the sharp flint axe her mother had used for cutting plants or stripping a pelt of meat.

Just inside the door, attached to the central beam supporting the thatched roof, was a larger hook from which hung her mother's favourite clay cooking pot. Reaching up, Willow took down the blackened bowl and carried it to the small fire-pit at the back of the hut in readiness for heating food when she had lit the fire. Then, knowing that before eating she must consult the dark water, on this, her first day as guardian, she turned and went outside.

The light was fading as she walked the few steps to the pool hidden beneath an overhanging rock and knelt on the largest of nine flat stones laid in a circle around the motionless black water. Sounds of revelry and drumming wafted across from the meeting ground as she allowed her eyes to go out of focus. A momentary thought of her beloved man dancing with one of the village maidens distracted her and then, in a flash, the vision was there.

She saw herself lying curled up asleep in the hut. In the dim light from the burning embers of the fire she saw first one baby, and then another, both girl-children, snuggled in her arms. The scene touched her heart, and she ached with longing to hold the dear babes. Then the picture changed, and she was horrified to see herself, looking older and weary, picking the poisonous plant growing by the riverbank. This could mean one of two things; either she intended to end her life or, worse, much worse, wished to take that of another.

Staring into the pool after the picture had vanished, Willow shivered in horror. This was no ordinary sight. The two daughters were to be expected because, as she now recalled, her mother had seen them long ago when she was very young and said that she must be strong and remain true to her destiny no matter how hard this might be. This had not seemed very portentous at the time and the thought of two daughters had delighted her, but now, knowing poison would be linked closely with the babies, she was filled with foreboding.

So deeply engrossed with this vision was she that no sounds reached her ears and she was unaware of a person approaching until a large shadow fell over her. Without looking up she knew who had come to see her and felt a shiver of fear.

The leader of the neighbouring clan placed a bundle beside her, saying, 'Here is a cloak for you. I need your guidance, my lady.'

She looked at the yellow and brown pattern of the wool, knowing that, no matter how finely woven nor how warm it was, she would never wear such a garment; everyone knew those colours were woven in that particular way by the women of his tribe and all would be aware how she came to own it. Some kindly folk might assume she had received it as reward for scrying in the pool, but many less generous-hearted people would laugh and say she was her mother's daughter and soon all her clan would think she was this vile man's lover. In a calm, controlled and very cold voice, she said, 'I will tell you what I see, Eagle, father of your people.'

She waited for him to sit on a rock nearby and then peered down at the dark surface of the water. The picture was a long time coming and she was about to admit failure when it briefly appeared in crystal clarity. He was holding a baby and laughing. It only lasted for an instant, but it was long enough to recognise the child as one born of her.

She was gripped by ice-cold terror paralysing her whole body. It was clear to her that this man wanted control of the island and would use any means, including her, to get it. For many heartbeats she was unable to move, then, taking a deep breath, such as she would before diving into the lake for a swim, she turned her head to look around for help, but there was neither sight nor sound of any living soul.

She looked around for a loose rock or a stick with which to fight him, but there was none. Remembering her mother's favourite flint axe was hanging just inside the hut, she rose to her feet and took one step, but it was too late. He dived forwards, grabbed her around the waist and carried her into the hut then kicked the door shut behind him with such force the building shook and pots hanging from the roof beam rattled.

He was so tall he had to stoop in the small hut and his hands were so strong she was powerless in their grip. Once he was on top of her she knew he would knock her teeth out or disfigure her if she resisted any further and therefore, with a heavy heart, she closed her eyes and let her mind float away while he forced himself on her.

She remembered lying in her lover's arms just a short while ago behind the yews and also in another hut with similar low light from embers of the fire. Such tenderness he had shown in his sweet, sweet caresses. How wonderful to love and be loved! He had made sure she enjoyed the height of love before he experienced his own. Such a lover! How lucky she was to have known such true passion and sharing of ecstasy!

On coming back into consciousness she opened her eyes, saw his silhouette standing over her and closed them again, thankful the ordeal was over. She heard the rustle of rushes on the floor as he walked away towards the door, then the thud of his head banging on a low beam and a muttered curse. A moment later, just when she was expecting him to open the door, she heard the clank of clay pots falling to the ground followed by a highly pitched scream.

She could see him huddled on the floor holding his face and moaning.

36

While hoping he would go and leave her alone she lay very still, but the longer he remained on the floor of her hut, the more she realised he must be badly hurt. Eventually, unable to bear the sound of his moans any longer, she went cautiously to investigate.

He lay resting on his elbow and looked up at her with one eye, while covering the other with his free hand.

In the dim light Willow could see dark smears between his fingers and knew they were blood. From the pieces of pottery strewn around him she assumed he had caught the side of his face on either the cooking pots or the hook on which they were hanging. Seeing him lean on his free hand as though about to stand up, she feared he would attack her again and ran outside.

There was only one place to seek sanctuary. She continued running to the hut beside the red spring and banged on the door.

The guardian was surprisingly kind and gave sympathetic sighs while listening to her story. 'The elders will be angry if they hear about this and what's worse, I fear we will have war between the clans again if your kin know...'

'If?' Willow interrupted. 'Are you suggesting I should not tell them?'

The other woman shrugged and looked at the rushes on the floor. After a few moments she said, 'I suggest we go together and see if he is still in your hut. If he's there we can go in search of help, but if not —' she put a hand on Willow's shoulder '— I think we could hope he'll be too humiliated to admit how he came by the wound on his face and will not trouble you again.' She gave a dismissive sniff. 'Men like Eagle boast of the scars inflicted by wild boars or warriors' axes, but not cooking pots.'

'Those hooks of my mother's are sharp at the end and may have cut deeply into his flesh—' Willow screwed up her face in anxiety '—What do I do if he's died of the wound?'

'Let's worry about that if we find his corpse, which I doubt.' The guardian of the red spring picked up a woollen cloak and put it around

Willow's shoulders, saying, 'We don't want anyone to see your torn skirt and bodice.' She muttered, 'Beastly man! I knew no good would come of letting him visit the island.' Then taking her hand, she added, 'Come, let's go and see if he's still there and in need of my healing powers, in which case—' her grip tightened '—he will also feel the lash of my tongue!'

As they walked through the deserted gathering grounds, Willow wondered what her mother would have done in the situation. Suddenly tears streamed down her face; and whether she wept with grief or the horror of violation, she did not know, while stumbling blindly along the familiar path.

On arrival at the pool she hung back while her companion looked inside the hut and was relieved to hear there was only the bloody rushes on the floor to show for his presence.

'He's run home to lick his wounds, like the cur he is,' said the guardian of the red well.

Willow walked inside and sank to her knees. 'I was so proud to take my mother's place. So happy to be here with a wonderful destiny set out before me.' She groaned remembering the two babies in her arms and the plant by the river and slumped forward. 'And now that vile man has ruined everything! What shall I do? I have nowhere to go. I can't return to the clan and admit I've failed in my duty already, when I've barely begun.'

She could hear the rising panic in her voice, but was unable to stop. 'I have seen this is my destiny, but maybe it is just a possibility and I could change it. Yes, that's it. I saw myself gathering the plant with which I could end my life. Could this be the destiny I should choose?'

'You will not take your precious life, my dear.' The older woman knelt beside her and took her hand. 'I don't scry in the pool as your mother did, therefore I have no knowledge of what will transpire in the future, but I do know you must fulfil your destined task. It's hard, my dear, but you will prevail and I will help you live the life you've been given.'

'You would help me?'

'I most definitely would. I may not have agreed with everything she did, it's true.' The old woman's smiling face looked young, despite the wrinkles and sagging skin along her jaw. 'Young enough to be my daughter she was and I loved her as such.'

She stood up and raked the ashes then began adding small pieces of wood to rekindle the fire. Once the flames were flickering she added some larger logs and turned back, saying, 'I'll love you as a granddaughter, if you'll let me.'

'Yes, indeed, Grandmother.' Willow stood up and hugged her. 'But I warn you there will be trouble from the happenings of today—' she placed both hands over her belly '—I know there was a child placed within me by a good man, but this vile bully may have replaced it with his offspring and we cannot know which will be born. I am destined to have two daughters, my mother told me of this long ago and now I have also seen it, but that is all I know.'

'I have heard of two born together,' said She of the Red. Adding with a shake of her head, 'Although it's rare for both to survive.'

'I could take the plant that will free my womb of any child, as you know, my lady and then the events of today would be of no consequence. But if I do not take it and fulfil my destiny, then the violation may impact greatly on our people. This is my dilemma!'

'We shall face the future together,' the old woman said, 'maybe there'll be blessings for us all too, my dear. Now you lie down and sleep awhile. I'll sit by the door and keep watch. Whatever betides from now on, you can rely on me.'

Willow curled up on the bed and fell instantly asleep. In dreams of childhood she ran in sunlight amongst the flowers and played hide and seek with other children in tall waving grass. She swam in the lake and caught little fish in a net. She learned again to move a small boat through shallow water with the aid of a long pole and screamed with laughter when it broke and she fell backwards, almost turning the little craft upside down. She ached with love on seeing her mother sitting in sunlight by the pool, combing her long red hair and, catching sight of an admiring man also watching her, felt a familiar pang of jealousy.

Awakening with the image in her mind and the painful hurt in her heart, she resolved that her daughters would not suffer the same fate; her children would be welcomed with open arms when they visited her and no man would ever be more important than them.

During the following days she tried not to dwell on the dreadful experience with Eagle and it slowly receded from her mind while receiving visits from members of her clan, who came for readings of the pool and brought food in payment, as well as much wanted news of her kin. Spring was in the air and she felt optimistic for the future, although missing her family and the man she still loved.

The seasons changed. Willow's belly grew through the summer season and the time of harvest, then, when the days were short and cold, her time had come.

Fewer people came for guidance when the weather turned and although it meant less food was brought as gifts, she was glad to be undisturbed while giving birth. The guardians of the two springs, who both now treated her as a beloved granddaughter, took turns to come each day and so it was She of the Red who was with her to help deliver the babies.

'My word, this is a big one!' exclaimed the old lady, wrapping the first girl in fine woollen cloth. Then, when the second one slithered into the world a few minutes later, she gave a sob. 'Oh poor little soul! This one may not stay long with us. She's very small but she does have the mark on her forehead like yours.'

When both babies were in her arms Willow looked down wondering who had fathered them. Were they born of the gentle man she had loved, or the evil one who had forced himself upon her? Either way she would have to give them to her kinfolk to mind, just as her mother had done and her mother before that; that was the way of it. One day, one of them would take her place—probably the bigger of the two, the old woman was right: the little one was unlikely to survive. Realising this, Willow was horrified — what if they both lived? Would they dispute who should be the guardian? If only one could read the water then that would settle the matter. But suppose both had inherited the gift, what then?

Thinking she might find the answer in the pool, she laid the babies side by side on the bed and stood up. Hearing the smaller one give a whimper she picked her up and, feeling she might not have her for longer than a few hours at most and wishing to keep her warm for as long as possible, tucked her securely inside her bodice. Then, wrapped in a warm cloak, she went out to the pool.

Kneeling on the cold hard stone in the twilight, Willow looked down into the still, dark water and saw the man who had raped her throwing back his head and laughing as he held aloft a small girl with long dark hair.

Sitting back on her heels she felt warm tears trickle down her cold cheeks. His plan to gain a foothold on the island was clear. No doubt once his daughter had replaced her, he would become respected as an elder and after that might find a way to impose women from his clan at the other two wells.

Willow felt very cold, but also very clear. A man like that did not understand the peaceful ways of her clan. He had made a truce with them in order to take the island and gain power over all the people who revered and respected it. Now she knew the reason she had seen herself picking the poisonous plant; the babies must die in order to save her clan from the harm the evil man would do to them.

Her heart thumped painfully in her chest as she stood up and walked back to the hut. Suddenly, just as she approached it, the door opened to reveal a hooded figure. She stopped, rooted with shock. Before she could make a move the intruder pushed past her, knocking her off balance. Feeling herself falling, she twisted her body to avoid landing on the baby and fell backwards onto the path.

Her only thought was for the tiny child and she anxiously put her hand in her bodice. Once sure the baby was still breathing and had sucked at her finger as though asking for milk, she struggled to her feet and walked to the open door of the hut. Fear gripped her for several heartbeats. Someone could be waiting there to kill her.

When no one appeared she walked inside and saw with relief it was empty, until, looking at her sleeping corner, the truth became clear; the intruder had taken the other baby.

In blind panic and despite feeling weak and dizzy, she walked across the gathering grounds and banged on the door of the dwelling beside the red spring. The guardian opened her mouth in greeting but, seeing the wildness in Willow's eyes, said, 'My dear child, I fear you may have childbirth fever. You should not be out and about so soon after deliverance, come in and lie down, my dear.'

Willow found the room was going round her. Fearing she was about to faint and possibly hurt the baby while falling, she sank to her knees with her arms protecting the child. 'My child has been taken from me,' she said.

The old woman knelt down and hugged her. 'I thought she was too weak to survive, my dear.'

At that moment there was a whimpering sound. Willow immediately uncovered the baby and held the child close to her heart. She was suddenly weeping uncontrollably and unable to explain that, not only had one precious baby been stolen by their vile father, but she had thought to kill them both in order to save them from him and now she knew in her heart that this would have been impossible. The tears kept flowing and seemed as though they would never end as she faced the reality that she could not have given them the poison, not even to stop his evil plan.

The other guardian arrived and took up the baby while She of the

Red held Willow in her arms until the terrible weeping eventually subsided. Then the two older women listened in horrified silence while she described in faltering words how the intruder had taken the other child.

'I came to you two dear friends for comfort—' Willow spread her hands in a gesture of helplessness '—there is no one else I can turn to.'

'Oh yes there is,' said She of the White.

The two old women looked at each other and nodded before they said in unison, 'The elders must be told.'

The following day, when the sun was high, Willow walked with the other two guardians to the gathering grounds where the elder men and women of her tribe were sitting in a circle waiting for her.

'We have talked at length,' the oldest woman said then shook her head sadly, adding, 'but we are not of one mind. Although this is a rare and terrible violation of our sacred island…'

Hearing the word although, Willow knew there was little likelihood of getting her daughter back and stopped listening. When the tiny baby stirred in the shawl slung across her chest, she felt a powerful wave of love sweep over her and knew what she must do to keep her alive.

'And so you see,' the elder woman was saying, as though summing up the decision of the meeting, 'that while the council is sympathetic to your cause, many of us feel, with great regret, that our people should not be asked to fight the neighbouring tribe again—' she paused and looked embarrassed '—and some of our number feel we cannot be certain it was they who took your child.' She gestured at the other eight elders, who were looking intently at her. 'I have the great burden of the casting vote—the power to call our people to fight or to keep the peace we so enjoy.' She walked over to Willow and taking both hands in hers, said, 'My Lady, Guardian of the Dark Pool, whom we all love and honour greatly, please help me with this heavy burden.'

Willow took a long deep breath and stood erect. She looked into the elder woman's eyes and at each of the other eight in turn around the circle, then said, 'I remember the dead warriors carried up to the cave in The Great One and I have no wish to be the cause of any more such loss. If I am to give the casting vote whether I am to be avenged or not, then I must state my case plainly.' She swallowed and went on. 'I will accept that no action be taken—' she heard the sigh of relief from the circle and held up her hand '—on one condition.' She dared not look at the circle of elders. 'That I be allowed to keep the remaining baby with me.'

The old woman gaped at her then frowned and asked, 'You wish the child should not be brought up by your kin?'

'I do. I will leave you to make your decision.' She turned and walked away to join the other guardians waiting by the yew trees.

Voices could be heard as the group debated. One man sounded angry as he exclaimed about a break with tradition and another argued against him, demanding, 'Surely this is a small price to pay for peace?'

When her name was called she returned to the centre of the circle and, looking at their relieved faces, she knew their decision before the elder woman said, 'We accept your condition, My Lady, Guardian of the Dark Pool.'

As though hearing this, the baby made a little chirping sound and the elder smiled, adding, 'Go, take your little bird, my dear. I hope the joy you find in her will ease the pain of losing her sister.'

Little Bird, as she soon became known, was beloved of all who knew her, especially the guardians of the red and white springs. When old enough she skipped merrily between the springs and the dark pool helping all three women fetch wood and water. She learned to spin and dye the yarn with She of the Red and how to weave the yarn with She of the White and most important of all, she showed great aptitude for scrying in the dark pool—even greater, so her mother said, than herself.

Willow kept her resolve to remain celibate and did not take lovers as her mother had. The man she had loved before coming to the pool was a frequent and pleasant visitor in her dreams, although, in reality, he kept his distance at the seasonal celebrations and ceremonies for the dead.

The vile man who had raped her also entered her sleeping mind, but he appeared in nightmares from which she awoke weeping for the child she had lost and sweating with the fear that he might also take Little Bird from her.

From time to time she remembered the vision of collecting the poisonous plant by the river and wondered anxiously if it would ever come to pass, but the more time elapsed without such a situation arising, the less she worried about it.

And so it was that many seasons passed contentedly with much happiness and laughter.

❖   ❖   ❖

Before dawn of the day when the rising sun would touch the heart of The Great One, Willow stood in the moonlight with the council of elders as they awaited the arrival of visitors from the neighbouring tribe. She guessed that Eagle had a reason for arranging this official visit after a long absence and when the boat drew up alongside the landing stage she was not surprised to see the silhouette of a girl standing beside the chieftain's huge bulk.

When Eagle helped his daughter alight from the boat, leaving his wife and other children to fend for themselves, Willow was aware of several elders glancing towards her. She knew that although four of the council members who had sat in judgement after her child was taken had now died and been replaced, the other five remembered her case and they, like her, would know the significance of this gesture and also that they were meant to see it. The message was clear: sooner or later he was going to establish his daughter's right to be the next guardian of the dark well.

Little Bird, who had been lurking behind the official welcoming party at the landing stage, hurried to her mother's side and whispered, 'Her name is Swan. Isn't she beautiful?'

Willow felt her heart thumping as she nodded agreement. The girl was indeed very lovely, but there was also a haughtiness about her that was troubling in one so young.

When Little Bird tugged at her hand urging her to keep up with the procession, Willow said she must keep her promise to call on the other two guardians, adding, 'I will see her soon, my dear. First I must go to our dear grandmothers and bide a moment with them. They are too frail now to walk the path to the heart of The Great One.' In fact she needed time to think. One half of her was longing to be near her newfound child, while the other needed to pause and assimilate the information gained from seeing her.

Swan, as she now knew was the girl's name, was indeed beautiful: she had the look of Eagle's tribe, tall with their dark colouring. Whereas Little Bird was made in her own image—apart from her nose, which was like neither hers nor Eagle's, but was exactly the same slightly hooked shape as that of the man she had loved and foresworn. These girls were indeed sisters, born from her womb, but it was clear that different men had fathered them.

On reaching the hut beside the red spring she found the other two guardians eager to hear news of the arrival they had been anticipating for two full moons. 'It's as we thought,' she said, after greeting them. 'He gives her special respect and is going to make great show of her.'

'Has she inherited a mark on herforhead from you like Little Bird?' She of the Red enquired.

'I couldn't see in the darkness,' Willow replied. 'And I must admit to being frightened of finding she does have the mark, for then we will have a battle to decide which one can follow me and I doubt our council is strong enough to stand up to him.'

She kissed both old women and passed through the yew trees to follow a group of her clan as they walked along the ceremonial path. Most of the men wore horns on their heads and the women carried flowers. Many were young and already paired with their chosen one in anticipation of the revelries to come. She could hear them giggling as they talked about the neighbour's arrival, admiring the beauty of the girl and the handsome looks of her brothers. When one of them said something about their father, 'Eagle One Eye', she realised with a shiver how seriously wounded he had been that day and this might be the reason he had not returned until ready to show off his daughter. With a wry smile she wondered if perhaps he had told another version of the wounding—one that was more heroic than walking into a hook hanging from a beam in a hut after raping the occupant?

The celebrations were joyful as usual after the sun had risen and kissed the melded figures, male and female, of The Great One. Willow watched happily as the women and girls put flowers in one another's hair before walking back to the meeting ground where they formed a great circle.

When everyone was dancing to the beat of a drum, Willow slipped behind one of the yew trees and watched them. She could soon see that, while every young male looked admiringly at Swan, the girl ignored them all, except for one young man of her tribe with whom she exchanged several glances.

Willow could see the men were not the only ones to be enthralled, Little Bird was transfixed by the beautiful stranger and so she was not surprised when her daughter came breathlessly to ask, 'Please, please, My Mother, I beg of you, allow me to invite Swan to visit us soon. We have so much in common, we love all the same things and—' she opened her eyes wide '—we both have a mark on our forehead. That is so amazing! Please may she come to stay?'

With mixed feelings of dread and excitement, Willow agreed and watched the girls ask Eagle who laughingly gave his permission. The sight of the girls hugging one another with joy brought tears to Willow's eyes and for a moment she ached with love and longed to hold them both in her arms.

A short while later, when the dancing had resumed, she watched with consternation as Eagle suddenly broke the circle and grabbed hold of Swan's arm with one hand while pointing menacingly at the young man beside her with the other. The rest of the dancers kept moving, but all eyes were on Eagle as he marched his daughter away, followed by the rest of his family hurrying after him.

When Swan arrived four days later with two protective henchmen Willow welcomed her, but was soon appalled by her arrogant manner towards these guards. Also, seeing dark bruises on the girl's arms, she felt a deep unease and wondered if the scene in the circle dance was but one example of Eagle's bullying.

She watched with delight as the two girls collected flowers and chatted together. The thought that Eagle had told Swan to endear herself to Little Bird constrained her from showing too much affection, but when in close proximity she nevertheless longed to stroke her long dark hair and kiss her rosy cheek.

The visits became a regular occurrence and Willow delighted in the presence of both daughters. While watching them as they talked together she revelled in Little Bird's happiness, but still had reservations regarding Swan: firstly she was sure the mark on the girl's forehead was a scar, not a birthmark and secondly, and more importantly, the girl showed no sensitivity towards the dark pool and had to be stopped from throwing flower petals into it. The explanation that the surface must be kept in readiness for anyone who might come seeking guidance seemed meaningless to her.

Little Bird continued to dote on her new friend and on the fifth visit ran eagerly to greet her as usual then walked off arm in arm with her towards the meeting ground, while the two henchmen relaxed in the shade of some rocks a short distance from the pool.

When a woman of her clan came to ask for guidance from the pool, Willow agreed and went with her to sit on the stones beside it. The picture was slow to form, as sometimes was the case, then, to her delight, she was able to tell the woman that the longed-for baby would be born to her and would live into old age.

After the woman had left she retreated into the shade by her hut and drank from the skin of water hanging there. Then, thinking the girls would soon be hungry, she went to fetch herbs and green leaves to cook with the fish the woman had brought her in payment. She was bending over a clump of leaves growing by the nearby stream when Little Bird appeared looking troubled.

Willow immediately thought Swan must have fallen or caught her hand on a thorn bush and had opened her mouth to ask what had befallen when a young man ran past, closely followed by one of the henchmen. A few moments later, Swan and the other guard appeared; both gave a curt nod to her before walking away in the direction of the jetty.

Little Bird burst into tears and took a long time to explain between sobs that the two lovers had met twice before during the visits and spent time together while she kept watch. On this occasion however, the guards had become suspicious and arrived at the scene before she could warn Swan and her young man. She buried her head in Willow's lap and wept again.

There were no more visits from Swan and little was heard of her after that day. For a full turn of the seasons, Willow waited, knowing Eagle would one day make his case to the elders, and so he did during the following summer.

On being informed by an elder that he had asked for a hearing and there would be a council meeting the following day to make a judgement, she was almost relieved to have the long wait over; despite the certainty of her name being besmirched in his determination to win and also the possibility of his triumph. She knew another two elders had died during the long cold winter and they been replaced by younger people who would not have been present at the time Swan was taken from her and they might well believe his version of events, no matter how untrue it might be.

She explained the situation to Little Bird and for the first time told her the full story of both hers and Swan's conception. To her surprise the girl listened calmly and then said, 'My Mother, I have heard a different tale from my sister. She believes you beguiled and entrapped her father and then viciously attacked him to make it appear he had forced himself upon you. I know this version of events is common knowledge in the clan, it has been told to me recently by a young woman who heard it from one of the boatmen when she returned from a visit to her family across the water.'

Willow was devastated and stared speechlessly at her daughter.

Little Bird took her mother's hand and continued, 'I have never believed this story and knew that one day you would tell me the truth of it. Now we must face the fact that the rumours will have been heard by the elders as well as the people here.' She shook her head sadly before adding, 'I know this is terrible for you and you must be prepared for the worst imaginable lies to be told against you, but, oh, My Mother, this will also be hard for Swan, much harder than for either of us.'

When Willow gasped in surprise, Little Bird went on, 'I know her heart. She has not the gift of sight and only pretended to see in the pool because her father told her to. The poor girl only wishes to live a normal life with the man she loves, but she is too terrified of her father to disobey him.'

Willow put her arms around Little Bird and kissed the red mark on her forehead. 'We have our destinies, you and I, we can only do our best to fulfil them honourably.'

With a heavy heart Willow left the hut saying she needed to be alone in order to think. In fact she walked purposefully to the river in search of the poisonous plant growing at the water's edge. She was

50

determined to make the future easy for both her daughters and reasoned that if the judgement went against her she would have the poison readily to hand in her house. She could quickly eat the root and die content in the knowledge that Little Bird, if ousted from the pool, could make a new life in the village with the clan and might even assist Swan, the new guardian of the dark pool, with advice.

Walking back to the hut carrying the plant, she remembered the sight in the pool long ago and was relieved it had not been a warning she would kill her children, as she had feared. She even smiled to herself, thinking that, in comparison with such a devastating possibility, the thought of taking her own life seemed quite simple.

When the sun had waned a little she went to see the two guardians of the red and white springs. Both old women, on hearing the news, were determined to bear witness for Willow, despite painful joints and fading sight, and nothing she could say would deter them.

The following morning, with their heads aching after a sleepless night, mother and daughter walked through grass laden with dew to the springs and then, each supporting one old woman, they slowly, very slowly indeed, made their way to the gathering grounds.

The grass was dry and the ground warmed by the sun when they joined the elders who were sitting on nine of the stones in the circle with Eagle on the tenth. Looking at the council, Willow's heart sank. Not only were they looking irritated by her tardy arrival, most of them had not been present when she had been allowed to keep her remaining daughter after the one now named Swan, was taken from her. Of the three who had been present at the earlier hearing, one was almost blind and two were deaf; all three might well have forgotten about the abduction of her baby.

When Eagle was invited to put his case he walked to the centre of the circle and began a spellbinding performance in which he argued that, after being enticed into her hut and seduced by Willow, he was attacked by her to look as though he had forced himself on her. At this point he touched his blind eye and then after a shake of his head, added, 'So is it any wonder that I arranged for the removal of my child from such a wicked and dangerous mother?' He went on to explain that he had only been informed the wicked woman had given birth and had no knowledge of a second child, but had he known— he put his hand on his heart at this point—he would have wished to save both his children from the clutches of a woman who was capable of blinding an innocent man.

Willow watched the faces of the elders and could see from their sideways glances that they had heard the rumours about her, but also from their respectful, almost reverential manner towards Eagle, they were afraid to challenge this powerful and charismatic leader.

Eagle evidently felt he had them in the palm of his hand and spoke of the beautiful daughter, so virtuous and so gifted a seer, who would be robbed of her birthright as guardian of the dark pool by this wicked, dangerous woman who was was capable of blinding a man to protect her honour as Seer of the Sacred Island and hide the fact she had enticed and bewitched him into sexual congress.

One of old women elders evidently recalled the earlier version of the story and asked the reason he had not come forward at that time.

Placing both hands on his chest he replied, 'I was too ill, both in my heart and in my eye.'

Willow stopped listening and only heard the occasional word being emphasised, such as banished, duty and sacred. She could see the elders gazing at Eagle intently and guessed they were weighing up the situation. None of them would want this dispute to fester and develop into a war between the two clans. All the elders wanted a peaceful solution and all of them knew he had many henchmen eager to be warriors with axes in their belts, whereas their own men had no interest in fighting anyone. She felt certain he would triumph. Once Swan was installed he would gradually take over the island. She stopped speculating when one of Eagle's henchmen arrived outside the circle and gesticulated at his master.

Eagle, who was in full flow, frowned as he stopped in mid-sentence and demanded angrily to know the reason he was being interrupted.

The man shifted uncomfortably. 'It's a private matter, about your daughter, my lord.'

Eagle looked towards the landing stage. 'Is my daughter here at last?'

The man looked agonised. 'I must speak with you, sire.'

Eagle gave a polite bow to the council, saying, 'I beg your pardons for this ill-mannered interruption. I fear my daughter has been delayed for some reason—a good one I'm sure. She is the most respectful and responsible of young women.' He walked outside the circle and listened to the henchman in silence for a few moments, then, with a great roar of fury, he felled him with one mighty punch of his right arm and, without looking back, he strode away.

Little Bird ran to the unconscious henchman and knelt beside him. Willow joined her and held his hand until he opened his eyes and said, 'Wasn't my fault, My Lady. They must've planned it for days. I think they took a boat when we were bringing the chief here. One person says they went towards the South, another says North and another says West. They could be anywhere by now.'

Willow wept with the joy of knowing Swan would be happy with the man she loved, Little Bird would be happy as the future guardian of the dark pool and she had no need of the poisonous plant.

Chapter Three

Louisa blinked and rubbed her eyes. Looking at the place where Willow and Little Bird were kneeling beside the wounded man with the elders sitting in a circle around them, she was surprised to see only undergrowth and bushes.

Focussing her eyes to the present outlook, she saw the abbot's kitchen, which now seemed so out of place, although she had difficulty in remembering what had been there at the time of Willow's guardianship of the dark pool.

As the memory faded, much as dreams do, she wondered if the guardian's house had stood there and tried to take her mind back to that time, but to no avail. She could only see the beautiful stone building where the Abbot's feasts would have been prepared.

She wondered how the kitchen had survived the vandalism suffered by the abbey church behind her and tried to imagine what the monastery would have looked like in the days before King Henry's men took possession of it.

A movement and a cough caused her to look around anxiously.

A man wearing a wide-brimmed and misshapen panama hat, sitting on a block of stone a short distance away, leaned forward and said, 'I apologise if I startled you, madam. I was concerned because you cried out a few times. I hope you're not unwell or suffering in any way.'

She frowned. 'I don't understand.'

Taking a large white handkerchief from his jacket pocket he held it towards her. 'You were weeping, madam.'

She put her hand up to her face and felt the wet cheeks. 'I'm so sorry. I have had an extraordinary experience. I must have been crying when I thought she might take the poison...' She broke off and took the handkerchief from him, then breathed in the scent of lavender while drying her face.

Feeling his greenish grey eyes watching her speculatively, she realised he might be a member of the family that owned the estate and explained, 'Oh dear. You must think I am an intruder. My aunt, Mrs Govern, is acquainted with the owner and said I should say I am staying with her and ...'

'Fear not—' he held up his large square hand '—I had not assumed you were trespassing. I, too, am a friend of the owner and it is for him that I am dowsing the area.'

'Dowsing?'

'Some call it divining. It's a hobby of mine.' He reached for a forked stick lying beside him on the stone. 'This hazel twig never fails to find water. One can find energy lines by the same method, so I'm told, but I am presently mapping the watercourses. In the absence of anyone to do so for me, please allow me to introduce myself, Edward Francis, at your service,' he removed his hat revealing a shock of auburn hair glinting in the sunlight. 'I have not seen your aunt lately, not since before my departure to Africa from whence I have recently returned. My father and her husband were good friends and I have known them all my life.'

Louisa wondered if his family would be known to her parents who had both grown up in the town, when he leaned forward and asked, 'You did say somebody might take poison, did you not, madam?'

'I did.' She replied feeling very foolish. 'I must have fallen asleep and had this very vivid dream.'

'Not a pleasant one.' He stroked the bushy moustache beneath his strong straight nose, while adding thoughtfully, 'If someone might take poison.'

'It wasn't like normal dreams. It was very real. I think ... I don't know how to explain, it seemed to be something that happened here a long time ago.'

'My aunt sees the future in things—mainly in the tea-leaves, but also palms, cards and that sort of thing. Was it like that?'

'In a way, I suppose.' Although longing to explain she had the gift of second sight, she was aware of his being a complete stranger to whom she had not been formally introduced and therefore held her tongue.

'It sounds to me as though you tapped into a past experience.Perhaps you were here in another lifetime.'

His acceptance of her behaviour in such a calm, matter of fact way made her relax and without stopping to think, she said, 'I'm not sure, but I might, well actually I'm almost sure, I've just seen something that could, as you say, have happened in the past.'

'How long ago would it have been?'

'I don't know.'

'What were the people wearing?'

'Clothes made from wool they had woven. In the winter they had animal skins and big cloaks.'

'Any guns?'

'No, definitely not.'

'What about knives or swords? '

She visualised Eagle with his axe in his belt and shook her head. 'Stones sharpened to make knives or tied to sticks were the only weapons I saw.'

'Flints,' he said nodding. 'So, before metal was discovered. Certainly was a long time ago.' He took a silver cigarette case from his pocket and offered it to her. She was surprised to be offered a cigarette in public and after thanking him, said, 'I used to have one after dinner with my husband when there was no one else to see me. Smoking in the open air feels rather bohemian!' She bent forward to reach the match he held towards her and, seeing a livid scar on the side of his face that was nearly, but not quite, hidden by his moustache, almost gasped but managed to light the cigarette and inhale the smoke.

'Boers,' he said, evidently knowing she was looking at him.

'I'm so sorry.'

'Don't be.' He gave his lopsided smile. 'I'm alive and I'm here—' he touched the cigarette case '—which is more than the chap who gave me this.'

'Are you still in the army?' she asked, thinking of the young family on the train and the vision in the window.

He blew the smoke from his lungs and replied thoughtfully, 'No. I've had my fill of fighting farmers, and of wars that don't make sense.' He grinned and pulled out a pocket watch from his waistcoat pocket. 'I won this off a Boer. When they captured me they didn't know what to do with me. I'd gone out looking for a scout who was missing and they caught me—a fine officer I was!'

'That sounds terrifying!'

'They were just men like me with no appetite for killing. We played poker while they waited for their reinforcements and when they hadn't come after a day and a night, they took my uniform and my hat and sent me back to my unit.'

'Why would they do such a thing?'

'I think it was a magnanimous gesture to send me back alive and also a humiliating one for me to be seen in such a state by the soldiers of my unit. Anyway, after a while one of the Boers came riding after me and gave me his hat because the sun was so hot.' He smiled cheerfully. 'I decided there and then that if I survived I would wear it to remind me of his kindness. And what's more, I would never try to kill anyone ever again.' He grinned like a small boy. 'Fortunately for me, managing my father's properties for him now he is elderly does not involve either wearing a uniform or shooting an enemy.'

She looked at the camera on a tripod nearby and asked, 'Do you also take photographs?'

'I do. The owner of the abbey ruins asked me to take some pictures of them; that is what I was doing when I saw you. In fact you are in one photograph, not close up you understand, but from afar so that you and the ruined wall make a delightful composition. I'll develop it and give it to you.' He reached into his waistcoat pocket and pulled out a small white card, saying, 'Please give my regards to your aunt and remember me to her.'

She looked at the beautifully engraved name, Edward Francis, Great Yews, Glastonbury, Somerset and recalled seeing the entrance to a house a short distance from her aunt's. Also a picture flashed into her mind and she smiled while remembering Willow making love behind a huge yew tree.

Although lacking the introduction by a respectable person of her acquaintance, she nevertheless felt compelled to ignore convention and said, 'I'm Mrs Louisa Wendon. How do you do?'

With a solemn bow he shook her hand. 'I am very pleased to meet you, Mrs Wendon.'

'You seem to know a great deal about history, Mr Francis.'

'That's another hobby of mine—especially the history of this area.' He pointed to the wall behind her, 'There's a crypt down there that was dug out early in the last century. I remember seeing some engravings my father owned of the work being done, I haven't seen them for years, but I'm sure they're still in the house somewhere. I will search for them—one of the attics would be the most likely place to start looking.'

'A crypt.' Her heart was beating faster than usual as she asked, 'Is it possible to get down there?'

'No, I fear not. There are planks of wood across any possible way in. If you look behind the bench at the back of you, you'll see what I mean.'

Louisa turned to look and then, hearing the church clock in the high street chime four times, she exclaimed, 'Heavens! I had no idea it was so late. I must get back.' She stood up and started to walk away.

He raised his hat. 'Maybe we'll meet again, Mrs Wendon and you can tell me if you have any more interesting visions.'

'Good Heavens! Do you think I might see more stories like that?'

He shrugged and replaced the hat. 'Who can say? There's a plethora of local legends and history. Joseph of Aramathea is believed by many to have brought his nephew the young Jesus here when he came to buy tin and also he came back after the crucifixion to build the first wattle and daub church. Then there was Saint Patrick and Saint Dunstan and a few hundred years after that, the monks found the tombs of King Arthur and Guinevere in the grounds of the abbey.' He spread his arms expansively. 'So there's plenty more for you to see—I'm sure I would be very curious if I were you.'

'Yes, you're right, I would like to know if such an experience could happen again, but I may not get the chance very often. I'm caring for my aunt who is unwell and I have only one afternoon off a week.'

He bade her goodbye and doffed his floppy hat again.

Louisa ran along the narrow path through the wet grass to the wrought iron gate and paused to catch her breath before walking sedately along the path to the front door.

That night, after getting into the narrow bed, she thought about the experience at the abbey and wondered what her husband would have said about it. He had always laughed at any suggestion of her mother's psychic ability, which, when she came to think about it, was the reason she had never mentioned the possibility of her own gift. Now that death had intervened and prevented her from finding out how he would react to her recent extraordinary experience, she felt a familiar wave of hopelessness washing over her.

As always, when suffering this deep yearning for her lost life and love—so unbearable it was beyond tears, she determined it must never happen again; she must not let emotion take control, but with a sad sigh she knew grief would lie in wait, ready to pounce when least expected.

She reached out to the small chest of drawers by the bed and pulled from it a small photograph of her wedding day. Then, clasping it to her, she yawned and snuggled down into the lumpy mattress. As a young girl she had never doubted her destiny was to marry and raise children. But life was like a desert of shifting sand in which anything could happen, or, indeed, nothing.

She fell asleep telling herself there was still life to be lived without a husband and baby, and although not happy, she would make her own way somehow.

Very soon she dreamed of standing at the heart of The Great One and looking out over a vast expanse of water gleaming like beaten silver in the moonlight.

Over the next several nights more dreams followed with many different images of The Great One; sometimes it was dark lilac in the distance silhouetted against the paler tinted sky, at others it was an eerie grey-green rising from pale clouds of mist, while often it was large and looming over her, either bright green in sunlight or dark green under leaden sky, but always a powerful presence, almost, it seemed, drawing her gently, but firmly towards it.

>ᗰᐧ >ᗰᐧ >ᗰᐧ

Each day, while moving around the room, Louisa had been aware of the old lady's eyes following her as she bustled about with clean bed linen and nightclothes. Several times she saw her open her mouth, as if to speak, then close it again and was intrigued, but said nothing. She wanted to see if the few words spoken before her walk in the abbey grounds had been simply an aberration, or if the old lady was regaining her speech.

When the maid brought in the supper trays two days after her vision experience, it was clear to Louisa, from the way her aunt's eyes moved and flickered, that she could hear and probably understand what was being said, which was perplexing when Edwina was so sure her mother was deaf and had lost her senses.

After the maid had left the room, Louisa picked up the spoon and said, 'I think you could start trying to do it yourself tomorrow.'

The old lady lifted her left hand and said slowly, 'Why—not—now?'

Louisa was careful to show no surprise and gently helped her to hold the spoon and dip it into the broth then carry it to her mouth. When the small bowl was empty, Louisa cut up some of the vegetables and chicken from her own plate and gave it to her.

After the old lady had slowly eaten the food and given thanks for it, Louisa said, 'I am sure you need more food than you've been getting. I shall ask for scrambled eggs for breakfast tomorrow.'

'Kedgeree,' her aunt said firmly. Adding with a lopsided smile, 'Kedgeree—please—Louisa.'

Louisa said, 'Edwina will be so delighted when I tell her about your progress...'

'No!' The old lady's voice was strong and although her right hand moved only slightly, her left one rose up from the bed with surprising force. 'No—one—must—know. It's—our—secret.' She fussed with the bedclothes with the good hand, then added, '—want—to—surprise—her—when—I'm—ready.'

'Very well, Aunt Agnes, I'll keep the secret.'

Their eyes met as they smiled and held hands. 'Tomorrow—I—should— like—to—sit—by—the—window,' the old lady said.

'It will be a pleasure to get you up from that bed, but for now, would it be acceptable to settle you for the night, Aunt?'

'It—will—dear—Louisa.'

The following morning, when the kedgeree had been eaten, Louisa encouraged her aunt to limp, very slowly and carefully, a few steps to an armchair, which she pushed across the room to the window overlooking the garden and the abbey ruins. She then sat on the seat beside her and listened to reminiscences about her childhood.

When the maid brought a lunch of chicken and asparagus that her aunt had asked Louisa to order for her, the old lady ate it with relish, saying, as she sat back in her chair, 'That—was—a—good—deal—

better—than—the—dishwater—I —had—before.'

Louisa laughingly said she was happy to see her enjoying her food. Then, seeing how bright the old lady's eyes shone and wishing to keep her talking she decided to broach the subject of her experience in the abbey, 'I met a man on Monday who said he knew you and Uncle Wilfred. His name is Edward Francis, do you remember him?'

'He—is—the—son—of—Wilfred's—friend—Arthur—Francis. A—delightful—lad.'

'He sent his regards to you.' Louisa smiled, and added, 'He is more than a lad now.'

'Yes—of—course—I—remember him—at wedding—with—Bishop—in—the—cathedral—forget—bride's—name.' She paused for breath and then continued. 'A great—beauty—from—good—family—in—Bath.'

'He was very kind to me after I had a strange experience in the Abbey ruins …' She hesitated, wondering if her aunt would be sympathetic.

'Strange —How—strange?'

'I had a kind of vision or dream of….'

'Tell me—my dear—pray—tell me.'

'It was a very long time ago, when this was an island with water stretching for miles.'

'Yes—called—the—Isle of Avalon—before—the rhynes—were dug —to drain — the land—by the monks—I believe.'

Louisa looked at her aunt's animated expression and into her shining eyes and knew she must tell her the whole story. 'There were three sacred springs here in those days, the red and white were springs that ran constantly and the black was an extraordinary pool of still water. The guardian of each one was a highly respected woman: She of the Red and She of the White were healers, and the most respected of all was She of the Black, or the dark pool, as it was known …'

'Wonderful!' the old lady said. 'Was—the dark pool—for scrying?'

Louisa was astonished. 'How did you know that, Aunt Agnes?'

'Don't know—my dear. Please—continue—story.'

'As you clearly know, the guardian of the dark pool was a seer and people came to her for guidance. She looked into the still water …'

An hour later, Louisa reached the point where Swan had run away with her lover and Willow would continue as guardian of the dark well with Little Bird as her successor and said, 'I hope I have not exhausted you, Aunt.'

'Oh no! You—awakened me, Louisa—with your—experience—from the past. Your mother—would love—this! We used to have—such wonderful—talks when we—were young. She—and her sister—were both more gifted—than I, but I was—always interested—and loved to—hear them read—the cards, or—the tea-leaves—or in other ways—your mother—was fond of dowsing—I recall.' She gave a chuckle. 'We kept such—things a secret—from our husbands—once we married—both brothers—did not approve—of such things—only Rosemary—who remained a spinster—continued, and—still reads the tea-leaves—to this day.'

'Does Aunt Rosemary come to visit you,' asked Louisa.

'She has not called—of late—which is unusual—in fact—I have not seen her—since my illness. If you—see her—send my love to her.'

Louisa agreed and said she would visit her mother's sister on her next afternoon off.

The old lady was quiet for a while. Louisa was thinking her speech had improved that day and was expecting her to fall asleep with exhaustion when she was surprised to hear her say even more clearly than before, 'I would so love to go—with you to the—abbey, but …' and looked down at her legs while shaking her head.

Louisa wanted to take her there and said, 'I will see if a Bath chair can be found, but in the meantime we must get you stronger and then perhaps we can tell Edwina how well you are.'

'No!' The old lady's face was red and her head and hands shook with agitation.

Seeing again her aunt's reaction, Louisa promised to keep silent. She waited until the old lady had fallen asleep and then sat at the small Davenport beside the window where the accoutrements for writing were arranged. She stared at the white sheet of paper lying on the leather inlay for a few moments then dipped the steel nib of a pen into the cut crystal bottle of black ink and wrote, *Dear Aunt Rosemary*. After this she sat looking out of the window at the abbey ruins directly ahead with the parish church of Saint John to her left and wondered what to write next.

When no further words came to mind, she laid down the pen and imagined the three friends, Aunt Agnes, her mother and her mother's sister Aunt Rosemary, doing together all the same things she had done as a young girl. Going to church on Sundays, learning to read and write with a governess, learning to dance and then attending parties under the close supervision of a chaperone and also, unlike her, somehow, finding a way to experiment with their psychic gifts.

Picking up the pen again, she wrote, '*I have come to stay with Aunt Agnes who has been unwell. I would like to visit you one Monday afternoon and hope you will let me know when would be convenient.*' She wanted to say so much more: how she had longed to see her for years and that she felt sure her mother had also felt the same and ached to be reconciled, but had not known how to begin. Instead, hoping these feeling might be expressed at some later date, she signed her name, '*Your loving niece, Louisa.*'

On the following Monday the sky was overcast and by eleven o'clock the rain was falling heavily. She had already checked to see if there had been a reply from Aunt Rosemary and found no post had arrived for her, therefore, although disappointed, she hoped the weather would improve enough for her to visit the abbey ruins again. This time she would take a sketchbook and make some drawings of the abbot's kitchen.

By two o'clock the rain had subsided into a steady drizzle and seeing her aunt had fallen asleep after eating lunch, Louisa decided she would return to the abbey regardless of the weather. She called on Mrs Thorne the housekeeper who supplied her with a long mackintosh cape that would protect her clothes and some galoshes to fit over her shoes, then made her way out of the house and garden to the bench beside the wall.

The sky soon cleared and the rain stopped while she waited hopefully, until, after several minutes during which no vision had appeared, she took out her sketchbook and a pencil. She was drawing the outlines of the abbot's kitchen when the strong smell of acrid sweat caused her to look around, expecting to see a person nearby.

On seeing no one, she turned back again, whereupon a sudden burst of sunlight caused her to close her eyes. In the darkness behind her eyelids several silhouettes formed…

Chapter Four

A group of people were standing by the water's edge waiting attentively while a man, wearing many metal ornaments and bracelets all glistening in the sunlight, stepped from a boat onto the landing stage.

The young girl hiding behind a tree watching them could see some of the elders were wary, while others, mostly the men, were eagerly anticipating his arrival. Her mother, who was the guardian of the dark well and therefore one of the dignitaries welcoming the visitor, was affecting indifference while buzzing with excitement.

Guessing the introductions would be both long and dull, the girl slipped away and ran to the old watchman's hut nearby.

'Greetings, Windflower,' the man said, emerging from the darkness. 'What news do you bring?'

'A shining man has come. He is the handsomest, most magnificent...'

'Shining did you say?'

'His body gleams in the sun; indeed it is as though its fire has touched parts of his arms and his chest. You must come and see for yourself.'

'He must be the powerful shaman I heard of who has come to show us the way to make blades harder than flint—' the old man rubbed his white beard '—I fear no good will come of it.'

'My mother is excited, I can tell.'

'I daresay she is, dear child, but though she be full of wisdom for others when looking in that well, she's empty when it comes to herself.'

Windflower nodded. Her mother was the vainest, the haughtiest and often the silliest, person she knew. 'She'll speak for him if they have a moot, I know she will.'

The old man shrugged. 'She'll want what he makes—' he grinned revealing broken yellow teeth '—probably want him an' all I expect.'

Despite knowing the man was right, she was now overwhelmed with loyalty and stopped listening while he continued talking. She thought of her mother, who was renowned for her weakness for young men, but was so clever at looking into the well that everyone, including Windflower, smiled and forgave her. Also her mother had reclaimed her when the foster family she had grown up with died after a strange fever struck their village the previous summer; admittedly there were frequent reminders that she need not have made this generous gesture, usually when wanting her to perform some useful task, but nevertheless she had brought her here to live and that had made a bond between them.

Being the daughter of a guardian of a well meant she was often alone and she missed the companionship of other children, but it also gave her great freedom to run around the sacred island. She knew all the good places to hide, the best trees to climb, the best tasting springs and where animals lived in their burrows or hides.

The other guardians were both kind to her. She of the Red had a grownup daughter in the village with daughters of her own, one of whom was destined to follow her grandmother, and also she had a son who often visited when the moon was full and he could come across the water by night to spend a day with his mother; although friendly towards her, he was older and she was shy in his company.

The old watchman was now talking about the hard knives and she stopped thinking in order to listen.

'I reckon there'll be trouble if that Degan clan get 'em.'

She was intrigued and asked why this might be.

'Long ago they were our enemies. Always wanting to get on the island. My old mother told me one of their leaders forced himself on a guardian of the dark well and put out one of her eyes. Long ago it was, but I've never trusted 'em since I heard that.Can't trust people who put out women's eyes. Never know what they might do with a knife. Did enough damage with flints, that's what I say.'

She heard the sound of voices drifting from the meeting ground and left to go in that direction, intending to stay out of sight and hear what was taking place.

Having climbed a tree nearby she peered through the branches and watched the shining man gesticulating while talking to the elders who were seated on the circle of stones listening intently. Now she could see the visitor wore wide bracelets made of the same golden metal as the small finger ring that had been a gift to her mother from a stranger several seasons earlier and knowing how highly prized this was, she understood the reason for her mother's excitement.

The man was handing objects to each of the elders and the three guardians, and although too far away for her to see what they were, she could tell by each person's reaction that these things were frightening in some cases, worrying in others and fascinating in most.

When the tally of hands was taken it was clear from the delight on her mother's face and the way she sidled up close to him that the man, who had won the approval of the elders, was welcome to spend the night with her.

Knowing she should avoid the dwelling until morning, Windflower wandered through the woods until darkness and then slept in the branches of a huge oak tree. On her return to the hut at daybreak she found her mother and the man standing in the doorway. She backed away to let him pass as he emerged and was horrified when he pinched her unformed breast, saying, 'Your turn next, little maiden.' Then he strode away laughing loudly.

Her mother sounded angry as she said, 'Next time, be sure to stay away until I am alone again.'

Windflower was too embarrassed to respond. No man had ever behaved towards her in this way. Even the boys of the clan, who teased her unmercifully, had never said or done anything so offensive.

When the shining man came the following night and the night after that, Windflower fetched wood and made a tiny shelter next to her mother's hut. During the following cycle of the moon she heard the man and her mother talking and making the sounds of love in the hut each night while she was snug and warm in her own bed.

To the great consternation of the watchman and several others, the man was given permission to make a dwelling of stone on the far side of The Great One and with the help of eager young clansmen from the village he began cutting down trees with his big, hard knives.

'No good will come of this,' the watchman said.

'This will come to no good,' the guardians of the red and white wells said in unison.

'It's progress,' said the son of She of the Red when he visited the following full moon. 'But you're right, Mother. Bad things will happen once men have bigger and sharper weapons to fight.'

Windflower, who had been sitting quietly in the shadows beside the red well asked, 'To fight who?'

The young man shrugged. 'Any one they see as a threat and every one who has something they want.'

She thought of the small boys in the village rolling around in the dust as they bit, hit and clawed at one another and nodded, 'Or just for the fun of it.' She looked at him, adding, 'I don't mean you, Tall Oak. You're not like that.'

He grinned. 'I'm a peace loving man. Mind you—' he looked side-ways at his mother '—I think I got into a few scrapes when I was little.'

'You did, My Son. But I'm pleased to say you weren't much good at fighting and I'm even more pleased you didn't take after your father Bloodaxe.' She of the Red shook her head sadly. 'Never happy unless he was getting into a skirmish with one of the Degan clan, silly fool!' She looked at Windflower, saying, 'I think Tall Oak should walk you home, my dear.'

'I'm used to walking alone …'

'I don't care what you may have been used to doing. There are men all over the island now, cutting down trees and burning them to make charcoal in readiness for the making of the knives.'

'There's no point in arguing,' her son said, holding out his hand to Windflower. 'Come, I'll walk you home on the way to my boat.'

They walked along in silence until, stopping a short distance from the dark well, he said, 'You are beautiful, Windflower. When you are old enough may I offer you my bed to share?'

She was too shy to admit he had been in her heart of late and feared he had thought her merely an ugly child. All she could do was whisper, 'Yes,' before running away to her little hut. Once there she remembered her duty was to follow her mother as guardian and was deeply worried until she remembered her mother was much younger than She of the Red, who showed little sign of dying and was expecting one of her granddaughters to take on the guardianship of the well. With the hope that her mother would live long, she fell asleep wondering how many babies Tall Oak would father for her.

❖   ❖   ❖

Three winter, three spring and three summer seasons passed in which many trees were burned and the 'shining man', as Windflower had named the newcomer, mixed the beautiful golden metal beloved of her mother with another metal and, to everyone's amazement, produced strong knives.

The sacred island was no longer the place of tranquillity, now it was crowded with people from the villages who had only been there before to celebrate the seasons or their joining of hands and, on occasion, to bury their dead in the heart of The Great One. Every member of every clan that could reach the island by boat wanted a knife for one reason or another; most of the women wanted one to cut the herbs, the grasses, the yarn and everything else they had previously cut with a flint, while the men needed to cut wood, gut a fish and all manner of things. And everyone knew, but no one admitted aloud, that they wanted to have a weapon in order to defend themselves now that everyone else had one.

Windflower, who had become a woman, knew Tall Oak would soon ask that they should walk the processional way up The Great One and join their hands. Although longing for this day when she would go to live in the village with her man, she was anxious about leaving her mother whose behaviour had become worrying since the shining man had stopped visiting by night.

One day when the sun was sliding down behind the land, Windflower went walking through land where the forest had been cleared at the far side of The Great One. On reaching an area of woodland as yet untouched and finding a tree she had loved to climb when younger, she pulled herself up onto a well-remembered perch.

Sitting on a branch with her back to the solid trunk of the old oak she wondered how long it had taken to grow and how soon it would be cut down. With tears in her eyes she stroked the gnarled bark of the ancient tree and felt sure that too many beautiful trees were being destroyed in order to make more metal than was needed by her people.

Remembering a vain attempt to explain this concern for the trees to her mother, when the only response had been a dismissive wave of the hand and a loud jingling of many metal bangles, she sighed despondently.

At that moment the guardian of the dark well appeared in the clearing below followed by a group of local women. Windflower opened her mouth to announce her presence, but before a word could be uttered one of the women produced a shiny circlet and placed it on her mother's head. She could see it looked like a garland, such as a maiden might wear for the coming of spring ceremony, or the joining of hands with her husband, but it was not soft green leaves that would wither and die, it was bright shiny metal.

When other women bowed down and called her mother the living embodiment of The Great One, she reacted with such a loud gasp of shock she feared the group below might hear it. Seeing a woman look up for a moment before lowering her head again in obeisance, she held her breath for several heartbeats and then kept absolutely still until the group walked away singing a song in praise of The Great One.

She had always known her mother took her superior position in the clan very seriously and assumed such behaviour was normal for a guardian of the dark well, but this episode had left her with a feeling of deep unease.

Feeling the need to talk with a trusted friend, she ran down the slopes to the hut of the old watchman and found him sitting with his back to a rock and his eyes closed.

'Greetings, my friend Windflower,' he said.

She grinned, knowing he could tell one person's step from another without seeing them. 'Greetings, my friend Brown Fox.'

'Come, sit and tell me what troubles you, maiden.'

'You know I'm troubled?'

He opened his eyes and peered at her, 'I may not have the gift of seeing in a well, but I know a worried young woman when I see one.' He patted the ground beside him, saying, 'Come join me. Are you anxious about joining hands with your beloved?'

She shook her head then sat down and described the scene in the clearing.

He waited for her to finish and then asked, 'You're sure about all this?'

'Yes.'

'The bowing down and all?'

'Yes.'

'I see.' He scratched his white beard thoughtfully. 'I'd heard rumours of such goings on for several seasons now. I know many members of the clan are very worried; only the other day I heard a couple discussing her as they walked past me. When the husband said that she'd let power go to her head, his wife defended her saying the men are biased because she is a powerful woman.' He shook his head sadly. 'I wonder now if the man was right.'

'I don't want to make trouble,' Windflower said. 'I just wondered why she's acting like the Queen of Spring when it's not yet time and without …'

'The King?'

'I didn't see a man wearing horns, in fact I didn't see any men at all.'

'This confirms the worries of several elders. May I tell them of your concern?'

Knowing this would be treachery in her mother's eyes she groaned. 'She is my mother. I love her …' she spread her hands in a gesture of despair.

'Perhaps we might share the problem with Tall Oak and the other guardians.'

She was aghast. 'Have they talked with you about this?'

He nodded sadly. 'Most of the elders are anxious, but no one wishes to confront her. We don't want a dispute on the island. There has been nothing like this is living memory and none of the tales of old tell anything of the kind.'

'She would have the shining man on her side,' she said.

'And also some of the men who want the weapons he makes.' The old man held his head. 'I fear they would be only too glad to use them to support her.'

Windflower went home to the dark well feeling overwhelmed with the weight of this great problem. She found her mother sitting outside talking with a group of women and after greeting them, slipped quietly into her own small hut where the steady drone of voices reached her. With a sad heart she heard the reverential tone of the women as they called her mother Oh Great One and her mother's authoritative tone as she replied to their questions.

When a woman began singing a song in praise of Spirit of The Great One, which she guessed was addressed to her mother, Windflower knew she must speak with the other guardians, with Tall Oak and with all the elders of the clan.

The following morning, after a night of anxious wakefulness, she went and sat by the dark well. Although able to see and understand its mysteries, she rarely looked into it, knowing her mother believed this was her prerogative. Now, however, she felt impelled to do so.

With a horrified gasp she watched as men disembarked from boats onto the shore in a culvert close to the place where the shining man worked his magic with fire and metal. The picture disappeared quickly leaving her staring open mouthed at the blank surface.

'Can you not wait for my passing, Daughter?'

Feeling a cold shudder of fear shake her body, Windflower turned to see her mother standing nearby with clenched fists and face distorted with rage.

Without waiting for an answer, the guardian of the well went on, 'Have I not explained enough times that while I live, I am the guardian, the sole and only person with the power to read the well?'

'Yes, Mother, but …'

'Don't "but" me, insolent creature.'

Windflower said, 'I saw the Degans arrive in boats, they looked hostile and....'

'Don't be ridiculous. If they did come, which I doubt, it would be in peace. There has been no war between us for a long time.'

'I tell you they looked dangerous, Mother. They were near the shining man's dwelling…'

'I know you have always been jealous of me, but you must also be simple minded if you imagine such stupid stories would frighten me.'

Windflower stared at her mother in speechless astonishment.

'There! That hit the spot didn't it? You can't deny you were jealous, can you? First you made that hut next to mine in order to spy on us. Then you ignored him, in fact you were downright rude to the poor man when he offered you a beautiful bangle.'

Windflower felt anger and panic rising. 'None of this matters now. I tell you we are in danger.'

'Don't talk rubbish. I know what you are planning, you scheming little traitor. You will not take my place before I die, do you hear me? I won't allow it and nor will my followers; they know I am the living spirit of The Great One. You, however, sneak around watching us, hiding in trees to see what we're doing. Do you really think I don't know what you're up to?'

'I only want to help, to …' Windflower heard the jangle of bracelets and then felt the slap across her mouth. She saw the wild anger in her mother's eyes and knew there was no point in trying to reason with her.

'Get away from me, go— ' the bracelets clattered in a sweeping gesture of her mother's arm '—go back to the village and bear a child fit to take my place. Go back and take the hand of any man who will have you. Go! Get out of my sight.'

Windflower turned and ran down to the watchman's hut and told him what had taken place. His lip quivered as he listened. 'Something should be done. I'll fetch the elders and the other guardians.'

'No. I beg you, do nothing. We don't want the argument and strife that would ensue if I complain to the council. That would only serve to prove I do wish to take her place while she still lives.' She licked her lip, tasting the salty blood. 'I'll go and live with Tall Oak and hope to bear the girl child worthy of being the next guardian of the dark well …'

'But that should be you!'

'I love Tall Oak and want to be with him, you know that, my friend.'

He held both her hands. 'You will be sorely missed by me and the guardians of the red and white wells.'

'I beg you tell them my reason for going. I think it best if I go quickly and quietly. When you speak to others of this, please warn them to keep vigilant. I fear there will be trouble with the Degans.'

Brown Fox nodded and gave his word. They walked to the landing stage where he watched her climb into a small boat and then untied the rope attached to it.

She took the long pole and pushed the craft away from the bank, waved to him, then turned her face away from the sacred land she loved.

The sun was glinting on the water as she travelled towards the village. Several men and women waved and shouted a greeting as they passed in their boats carrying freshly caught fish. She knew they wished to go as fast as possible and get their catch on land before the sun was too high in the sky, while she wanted to take her time and savour this journey to her new life, in much the same way as she had walked the path from the heart of The Great One on the day she became a woman.

A heron landed on a floating log and watched her for a moment then took off and flew elegantly away across the shining reflection of pale blue sky. She saw a white cloud in the distance and was reminded that this season would soon end; then the days would shorten and darker clouds would colour the water grey, but, she smiled at the thought, there would be a warm man to snuggle up to on the cold, dark nights.

A young girl paddled past in a very small and flimsy craft reminding her of similar escapades in childhood and the eventual, predictable sinking of such fragile creations. She dipped her pole into the water and measured the depth before and aft of her own boat, then having ascertained it was no deeper than the height of the child's shoulder and also that she was now in sight of the village, she waved cheerily to her.

Soon she was approaching the huts clustered together on an island so low they appeared to be floating on the water. She could see thin wisps of smoke snaking up from the thatched roofs and hear children calling excitedly to one another. A sudden feeling of fear gripped her — what if Tall Oak had changed his mind? What would she do then? There was no hope of returning to the sacred island and she knew of nowhere else to go.

She took a deep breath to calm herself and, seeing a group of figures standing on a landing stage, knew the fisher folk had already arrived and spread the word she was on her way. Also, looking back and seeing the girl was following in her wake, laughing and waving, she realised the child was one of Tall Oak's sisters, the youngest daughter of the guardian of the red well, who had come to welcome her.

Tall Oak waded into the water to pull the boat up to the wooden landing stage and then took her hand as she stepped ashore. He touched her swollen lip and asked who had done this. When she described her banishment he put his arm around her shoulders, saying, 'I know you must be distressed, but I have been fearing your mother would prevent you from coming to live with me. Now she has sent you to me and I am grateful to her. I have long since made a dwelling to share with you.' He waved his free hand and shouted to the people around them, 'This is a wonderful day, everyone. Please come and celebrate our joining of hands.'

Children whooped with joy, women laughed and wept at the same time and the men slapped Tall Oak on the back and kissed Wind-flower's hand. The couple stood in the centre of the small dusty meeting place and then the villagers formed a circle around them. The oldest woman came forward with a long rope and asked if they wished to be tied together for as long as they lived. When they both agreed and held out their hands towards each other the woman wound the rope around their wrists, saying, 'You are joined as one, just as the earth and sky flow one into another. So shall you be.'

Windflower and Tall Oak said in unison, 'So shall we be.'

All the people said, 'So shall they be.'

There was a moment of stillness while the newly joined couple stood tied together looking into one another's eyes and then, with great shouts of delight the children came running into the circle to untie the rope and claim a piece of it for good luck.

A fire was lit, fish was fetched to eat and fermented honey and water was brought to drink. The party went on until the fire died down and all the food and drink had been consumed. When the last sleepy child had been carried away and the last neighbour had brought a small gift to put in their home, they went into the dwelling and were soon on the bed of sweet grasses making love.

The following morning, on rising at dawn, Windflower opened the door and gasped in awe. Before her lay shimmering water lapping against the ground below her feet and in the distance, dominating the landscape, dark as violet flowers and silhouetted against a paler sky, stood The Great One, majestically towering above the sacred island.

Although still sad to have parted from her mother in such a way and also worried about the threat in the future, the following days were happy. She joined in with the other women making preparations for the cold season to come, storing dried berries, fruit and roots and making the cheese from goat's milk that would be a treat in the darkest days. During her life on the island she had relied, as her mother had, on the generosity of the people who came for guidance from the dark well and now she found pleasure in remembering and relearning the ways of her childhood.

The season of darkness was soon upon them. During the short hours of daylight she worked to fetch fuel to keep the fire alight and cook any fish or creature that Tall Oak could catch. Then, in the dimly lit dwelling, she would relish being alone with him.

The days and nights passed. One season led to another. From time to time she heard news of her mother from the villagers who made the journey to the sacred island to consult the dark well, to bury their dead, or to celebrate the changing seasons. Most people kept their eyes averted, when reporting, 'The guardian of the dark well is strong,' or 'in good health' or some such vague response and when, as was usual, no one showed any willingness to say any more, she had not the heart to press them further.

On the day Tall Oak reported that his mother, the guardian of the red well, was becoming increasingly worried about stories being told regarding Windflower's mother, she knew the time had come for her to return and see for herself what was happening. They decided to join the other villagers in celebration of the spring at the next full moon a few days hence when they could also give thanks for the baby growing within her.

In order to arrive at daybreak for the marriage of the male and female sides of The Great One, it was necessary to embark in their boats by moonlight. No one spoke, not even the children, as they slowly moved through the gleaming water to the sacred island. The absence of sound, other than that of the pole pushing the punt along, heightened the feeling of anticipation; in this silence Windflower could hear her heart beating while she wondered if reconciliation with her mother could be possible; and, if so, whether a blessing from the present guardian of the dark well might be bestowed on the unborn child who might one day follow in her footsteps.

The old watchman met them at the landing stage and was clearly overjoyed to see her again. He took her to one side and after congratulating her on the child she was carrying, told her how worried he was about her mother.

It transpired that most of the women who had revered the guardian of the dark well had now backed away, leaving only one follower who guarded her by night and day with a metal spear.

Windflower was appalled. 'A spear! Are you sure?'

'I'm sure. Ask anyone, they'll tell you it's true.' He stroked his beard and shook his head. 'I'm afraid things have gone from bad to worse. She's fallen out with the metal maker and with the other guardians and with most of the elders, in fact, she won't speak to anyone who doesn't call her Oh Great One. I'm sorry to tell you this, Windflower, but most people laugh behind her back and very few seek the wisdom of the well.'

Tall Oak, who had been listening to this, said, 'I think we would be wise to avoid her. I don't want Windflower to be upset.' He put his arm around her. 'Please, my love, I beg you, let's go home now before there's a scene.'

At that moment a boy came running to them and said between rasping breaths, 'There's—trouble—at—the—metal—maker's.' He bent over to ease a stitch.

'Trouble? What sort of trouble?'

The boy raised his head. 'Men wanting the metal—Degans I think.'

Tall Oak said he would go to see what was happening and refused to stop when Windflower protested. 'I must go,' he said and, placing his hand on their unborn child in her belly, added, 'Please keep the child safe. Stay here and wait for me.'

Windflower knew she could not detain him. The child within her kicked as if to remind her it must be kept safe and so, despite longing to go with Tall Oak, she sank down onto a fallen tree trunk and watched her man stride away with the old watchman following in his wake.

The rest of the villagers had already gone ahead, walking towards the processional way in readiness for the dawn, and so she sat alone, feeling sure the sight in the well had come to pass and trying to imagine what could be happening on the other side of The Great One.

A bird began singing, then another and another until the air was filled with their joyful, beautiful welcome to the new day. As the darkness slipped away she heard a shout from high on The Great One and knew the first ray of sunlight had kissed its heart. As the sun rose she heard the familiar sound of singing and laughter and visualised the women putting flowers in one another's hair and men wearing goat's horns or wooden replicas of them, inviting them to dance. She gave a wry smile, wondering how many babies would be born from this day and then, feeling her own child move, decided that now she could see the path in daylight, it would be safe to walk towards the other side of The Great One and find out what had happened at the metal maker's dwelling.

While walking through the trees she recalled the metal maker's arrival and how she had called him the shining man. It now seemed their lives had changed from that day. The quietude and tranquillity they had once known had been destroyed when the men were allowed to cut down the trees in order to make the fire that would create the metal. Now every man in the clan had a sharp blade in his belt and the old flints were no longer good enough for the women to scrape the animal skins or pare the roots. Even her mother, who admittedly had always been vain and controlling, had changed after the man's arrival, but she, it seemed, had fallen in love with the metal and not the man who made it. How and why her mother had then gone mad with her own power was a mystery to her and indeed to everyone else.

Her thoughts were interrupted when the old watchman came staggering towards her, calling feebly, 'Help! Help!' Then sank to his knees.

Windflower ran to him and put her arms around him.

The watchman whispered, 'They've killed …' then blood spurted from his mouth and he fell limply against her.

She lowered him to the ground and knelt down to close his staring eyes. 'I knew this would happen, I saw them,' she said.

Moments later one of the men who had worked with the shining man limped into view and leant against a tree trunk while saying, 'The Degans have killed all the other workers and taken everything; knives, spearheads and every scrap of metal they could find.' He gave a sob. 'I fell to the ground and when I woke up I saw them hacking everyone to death.' Tears rolled down his cheeks. 'I just lay there pretending to be dead.'

Windflower was still kneeling on the ground holding the dead watchman when several elders and the other two guardians arrived saying they had heard shouting and screaming and therefore had come down from the celebration to see what was wrong.

The metal worker repeated his story and it was agreed the elders should go to investigate what had happened while everyone else should go to the meeting place.

Once again, although longing to go with them, Windflower agreed. She could feel the child inside her was in turmoil, as though aware of the disturbing events in the world it would soon inhabit. She felt several pangs while walking along with the two guardians on either side of her and as they arrived at the meeting place, she admitted her baby would soon be born.

She of the Red said, 'We have to take you to your mother's dwelling.'

Windflower shook her head. 'No. That cannot be.'

She of the White said, 'Would you wish to give birth in front of the whole clan?'

Windflower looked at the people filing into the meeting place, all with anxious faces, evidently wondering what had happened, instead of the joyful expressions they would usually have on such a day and admitted she would not wish to have her baby in such a public place.

She then walked slowly with the two women to the well where her mother rushed past them carrying a bundle, followed by a woman carrying a spear.

Both she and the guardians called out in greeting, but there was no response from the guardian of the dark well.

They went into the dwelling and she knelt down on her mother's mattress in readiness for her labour. She heard one of the women comment on a hole in the earth floor and the other say it must be where the hoard was hidden. She heard them fetch water and heat it on the fire. She heard her own grunts and groans as she pushed and also her deep breathing in between the waves of pain.

In a dreamlike state she heard a man's voice and called to Tall Oak telling him not fight the men, to come back and see their child. And then, with one last huge effort, it was over and a tiny baby slid into the guardian of the red's arms. There was a long pause while all three women held their breath until a feeble cry announced she was alive.

A short while later Windflower sat up and, holding the sleeping infant in her arms, asked She of the Red how much time had passed since her arrival on the island before dawn.

'The sun is overhead, my dear. You had a shorter labour than I have ever known.' She of the Red went and knelt down next to her, adding, 'The child has come long before her time.'

Windflower agreed. 'That is the reason she is so small.'

She of the White looked up from putting wood on the fire and said quietly, 'A delicate flower, very delicate indeed.'

Knowing they were telling her the child was likely to die, Windflower whispered to the baby, 'I will do my best to keep you living.' Looking at the two women she thanked them for helping her and added, 'I must go and find out what has happened to...'

'No, no, you must rest,' they both cried.

Windflower explained her need to know if Tall Oak was safe and they both argued that he would want her to keep the baby warm and alive. Seeing her continued anxiety, She of the White said she would go to the meeting place and see if there was any news if Windflower would stay there and wait.

The older woman then left the hut with a promise to return very soon.

The wait seemed interminable. She of the Red, who was mother to Tall Oak, wept quietly as though sure he must be dead.

Windflower decided that if her man was alive he would have come to her by now and therefore he must have died in the fighting described by the metal worker she met in the woods. Holding the baby close she sang quietly to her, describing how brave and strong her father had been and how much she had loved him.

The door opened and a familiar figure, albeit leaning over sideways and holding onto the doorpost, but nevertheless unmistakeable, stood silhouetted for a moment before limping to kneel down with difficulty before her. 'I am honoured to hear such a beautiful song about all my virtues,' Tall Oak said, 'but it is too soon. I am not yet dead.'

'You are wounded ...' she could say no more amidst the tears streaming down her face.

'A scratch, that's all.' He held his side and leaned forward asking, 'Who is this in your arms?'

She introduced him to his daughter, saying, 'She has come too early and is, therefore, very small.'

He kissed both her and the baby and said, 'Small, perhaps, but beautiful like the tiny violets I saw while walking here. I was feeling dejected and sad after fighting with those ruffians. I have never killed a man before or seen many men lying dead. The metal maker was lying face down by the hearth where he worked his magic. It seemed he was struck down without knowing his attacker was there and all around his dwelling lay the bodies of men who worked with him, all taken by surprise I suspect. I thought all the murdering thieves had left when we arrived and was, therefore, horrified when I heard the watchman cry out and turned to find he was wounded. I could see a movement in the shadows and I picked up a rock and lunged for-ward—' he shook his head as though in disbelief '—I smashed his head with the rock, then I took his spear and followed the men's trail until I caught up with two of them who I recognised as the Degan chief's sons.'

He gulped and took a breath before continuing. 'I took them by surprise and killed them, but I was too late to catch any more. When I reached the shore I found their boats had already embarked and decided there was no more I could do.'

He took Windflower's hand. 'When I saw the flowers peeping through the grass beside the path, I was so astonished by their beauty, it was as though I had never seen them before.' He grimaced, gave a low groan and sank down lower to the floor. 'I would like to name her Violet.'

'Your wound is worse than you realise', she said. 'We must look at it.'

She of the Red, who had been hovering beside him, tried to pull away his clothes. She made little tut-tutting sounds while fetching a knife, then cut the cloth and eased it away from a gaping wound above his hip. 'I must stop the bleeding. I think you have already lost a lot of blood—' she gave a small scream '—oh, my Son, you have something lodged in there!'

'A spear head,' Tall Oak said quietly with a resigned, almost smiling expression on his exhausted face.

The door opened and a man with water dripping off his hair and beard entered the dwelling. 'There's been a terrible.... I have dire news—' he looked at Windflower '—your mother, She of the Dark Well... I don't know how to tell you...'

'For goodness sake, man!' She of the White grabbed his arm. 'What has happened to her?'

'She's dead, My Ladies. Drowned.'

She of the Red, who was kneeling beside Tall Oak, exclaimed without looking up from the metal spearhead lodged in his wound, 'Drowned! How could that be? She hated going in water.'

The man wrung his hands. 'A boy who saw her said she may have fallen from a boat. He ran to fetch us at the meeting place—' he looked down at Windflower 'I promise you I ran. We all ran as fast as we could, but she was dead.'

'I don't understand—' She of the White looked perplexed '—the water only comes up to my waist at that point.'

They were all silent until hearing the sound of men's voices, the man said, 'The others have brought her here.'

She of the Red told Windflower and Tall Oak to stay still and the two women went outside.

The voice of a man could be heard saying, 'My boy saw her running towards the landing point. Looking frantic she was. He offered to help when he saw her untying a boat, but she sent him away. He heard a scream so he looked back. and when he saw she wasn't there anymore he came and told me.'

Another voice said, 'She must've slipped and fallen into the water. It's not deep there, but she had this bundle tied to her—like a mother ties her baby to her front with her shawl and we think she couldn't get up.'

Tall Oak groaned.

Thinking he was reacting to this news, Windflower turned to him and saw the colour drain from his face. She called to the guardians, who immediately rushed to him and knelt down, one feeling his forehead and the other holding a small cup of water to his lips.

When both women sat back on their heels and shook their heads, Willow knew he had died. To her surprise, she not only felt calm and clear on realising this, but also she found her mind had floated up above her body and she was looking down on a man and a woman who had just died. They were young, which was sadder than if they were old, but she knew youth did not preclude death, only made it less likely. The man was he whom she had loved, Tall Oak; oh how she had loved him! And the woman with him, she calmly accepted without any regret or sorrow, was herself and surprisingly, was herself holding a baby. She recalled the labour so recently endured, then immediately remembered she had a child. Seeing the tiny face screwed up as though in pain or needing food she knew her newborn babe needed its mother's milk. With a tremendous effort Willow took the deepest possible breath and suddenly she was back down on the bed, alive and lying beside the corpse of her beloved.

She shed no tears; not while the guardians wrapped her man in his cloak and the men carried him outside in readiness for burial, nor when her mother was also prepared. When asked what should be done with the ornate headdress and the hoard of metal necklaces, bracelets and rings that had caused her mother's death, she asked that they be thrown into the heart of The Great One with the corpse.

The two guardians persuaded her to stay and mind the fragile baby in the hope it would live a little longer while the elders accompanied the men carrying the two corpses up to the heart of The Great One.

Shortly after the elders had returned and reported all had been done as she requested, there was a flash of light in the sky followed by torrential rain falling from dark black clouds. The terrifying storm went on until long after the sun had set. Then, shortly before dawn, a huge rumbling sound emanated from deep under the earth and the hut collapsed on top of Windflower.

She lay trapped by a beam lying across her legs until dawn when both the guardians came to make sure she was safe and after helping her out from under the debris of wood and thatch, they took her back to She of the Red's dwelling.

A day later Windflower wrapped little Violet inside her shawl and ignoring the advice of the two guardians that she was yet too weak, walked through deep mud to the meeting ground, with She of the Red on one side and She of the White on the other. There they found the watchmen, the elders and others who lived on the island, conferring about the recent events.

After greeting and commiserating with her and She of the Red on the loss of a husband and a son, the oldest elder asked them to turn around and look at The Great One.

The three women all gasped. The head and crown of stones on its top had disappeared and slid down the far side leaving the basic shape somewhat flattened. Everyone stood in silence until a young man ran to them saying he had climbed The Great One and found the opening at its heart that had been the access to the burial chamber was now filled with rocks and earth.

Windflower knew from the ensuing silence that no one wished to say anything to hurt her. It was clear that, had she not been with them, all these people would have voiced the opinion that her mother was the cause of this manifestation of The Great One's anger.

This was a moment of choice; she could return to the village and live as a widow among kindly people who would help her to survive, or, she could accept her destiny. Turning to face them, she said, 'If you will allow me, I will devote my life to serving you. If you will accept me I will take my mother's place and pledge to hold true to the ideals we all share.'

The most senior elder walked to her and took her hand. 'We accept you, as guardian of the dark well.'

Chapter Five

Louisa opened her eyes and stared down miserably at the muddy galoshes on her feet. The death of Tall Oak had left her saddened and deeply disappointed. Windflower's tragedy was unexpected and not at all like the happy endings she was used to in romantic novels.

Hearing the familiar polite cough, she turned to see the man in the floppy panama hat sitting on a step a short distance away. She waved at him in invitation to join her and smiled when he hurried to her side.

Lifting his hat he greeted her, 'Good afternoon, Mrs Wendon, I have brought a photograph to show you, but first I'd like to hear if you've seen any interesting visions today.'

'I have, indeed, Mr Francis. One with a disappointing ending, I'm afraid.' She then gave a brief description of the story and said, 'I think you take my meaning? '

Edward said, 'I too am sorry Tall Oak died, but at least Windflower had her baby and knew she would be the new guardian of the well.'

'I dare say you are right,' Louisa agreed. 'I fear I was expecting it all to come right as it might in a book, one in which her mother came to see the error of her ways and also was reconciled with Windflower, who could have lived happily ever after with Tall Oak—that would have been a satisfactory ending.'

He gave a sigh and said, 'Real life isn't always how we would like it to be, I'm afraid. I think *happy ever* after belongs at the end of stories that begin *once upon a time*.' He pulled an envelope from inside his coat and carefully withdrew a photograph from it. 'Here you are, Mrs Wendon, please accept this little gift from me.'

She took it from him and seeing herself sitting on the stone and framed by the arched gap between two mounds of brambles, she thanked him, adding, 'That is such a lovely composition. When I see a picture such as this I understand how one could find photography creative.'

Hearing the church clock striking, she said, 'I must go now to care for my aunt. I am sure this photograph will stimulate her determination to make an expedition here with me. I hope to obtain a Bath chair for that purpose.'

Edward lifted his hat and said he hoped to see her again on another of her free afternoons then walked away through the wet grass.

On her return she found Aunt Agnes awake and eager to hear of her experience in the abbey. Louisa placed the photograph on her aunt's lap. She fetched a magnifying glass and held it for her because the old lady's one good hand was too weak to keep it steady.

'It is—as though—painted in black—and white!' Aunt Agnes exclaimed, peering at the picture. 'Almost—chiaroscuro—do you agree?'

Louisa almost dropped the magnifying glass in surprise. 'Yes, Aunt, I do agree. The clever juxtaposition of light and shade could be described thus.'

The old lady gave a contented sigh as though pleased to have proved her brain was still working, despite her physical disabilities.

'Did you…' Louisa stopped and then started again. 'Do you enjoy art, Aunt?'

'I do, Louisa—that is the reason—there are too many—pictures on the walls.' The pale skin creased into well-worn lines on one side of the old lady's mouth as she smiled. 'Now pray—tell me of—your vision.'

When Louisa told the story of Windflower, her aunt listened attentively, making comments from time to time, especially about the guardian of the dark well. 'How could—she be—so foolish?' she asked. Also, 'How could—she be so—greedy for shiny—baubles?' Finally, on hearing of the drowning, saying resignedly and surprisingly clearly, 'There is nothing new—under God's sun. We humans are greedy—and weak. I know—there are some dazzled by gold—

and others who sell their souls—for diamonds.'

Louisa was surprised by this reaction. 'I was deeply upset by this vision, but I am almost reconciled to thinking that, although sad, good triumphed over evil, do you not agree, Aunt?'

'Oh yes, Louisa — but it cost Windflower and Tall Oak dear—as such triumphs often do—I could tell you …' she broke off and looked up at Louisa. 'Did you say—we would have salmon with—asparagus for dinner—this evening?'

A moment later there was a knock on the door and a maid brought an envelope to Louisa. 'There's a message for Mrs Govern, I explained she can't read nor nothin' nowadays, but the gentleman said as Mrs Wendon could read it to 'er, so I brought'n up. I hopes I done the right thing. The mistress is entertaining her friend ter tea and I didn't wish ter disturb 'er.'

'You did absolutely the right thing, Beth. I thank you—' Louisa gestured towards her aunt '—as would Mrs Govern were she able.' When the maid had left the room, Louisa gave a gently reproving look, while saying, 'You see how I am brought low into deceit on your behalf, Aunt Agnes?'

'I apologise—my dear Louisa. Now—what does the message say—and from whom does it come?'

Louisa opened the envelope and read aloud, 'Dear Mrs Govern, I trust you will forgive my intrusion into your affairs. Your niece spoke of the need for a Bath chair and it so happens that we have one at Great Yews, which needs a little refurbishment and could be made available for your use. I would be pleased to arrange for the delivery of it at your convenience. Yours sincerely, Edward Francis.'

Louisa was surprised to find he had evidently returned home and immediately written the letter then delivered it himself. She was more taken aback when her aunt's expression was anxious rather than pleased to hear of this news. With a frown she asked, 'Are you not pleased to know I can now take you out for a walk, Aunt?'

'To the abbey ruins?'

'That may be too ambitious, I don't know if we could manage the rough ground, but we could walk around the garden and possibly go further, we shall have to wait and see.'

The old lady sighed and said slowly, 'I—am—delighted—and—most—grateful—of course—but—I—must—wait—until—Edwina—has—gone—to—Brighton.'

Louisa knew there was no point in arguing that Edwina might be delighted to see her mother going out in the fresh air and was aware that her aunt's speech always deteriorated when distressed, she therefore said, 'Very well, I will write to Mr Francis accepting his kind offer and ask if we may arrange for delivery of the chair when you are feeling stronger. Will that be acceptable?'

'It will—my dear—it will be most—acceptable.' The old lady heard the maid bringing her tray of food and immediately closed her eyes as if asleep.

Louisa wrote a reply to Edward Francis thanking him and explaining that her aunt would like to accept the offer in a fortnight when she would be stronger and the weather more clement.

The following day, on receiving an invitation from her Aunt Rosemary to visit the following Monday afternoon, Louisa immediately replied that she would be delighted to accept. While looking forward to this meeting, she also regretted this would mean waiting until the following afternoon off to visit the abbey ruins again.

When Edwina announced at lunchtime on Monday that her commitment that afternoon had been cancelled and she would therefore be free to sit with her mother in Louisa's absence, the old lady was instantly reduced to a state of panic.

Louisa complied with her aunt's immediate wish that she should be helped back to bed, then stood looking anxiously at the pale face until the old lady muttered impatiently, 'Go!—Go with God—but go!'

Feeling deeply concerned for the old lady, Louisa silently kissed her forehead and left the room.

She walked hurriedly to the old stone house, remembered so fondly from childhood and felt the warmth of homecoming while standing before the heavy oak door. On reaching for the brightly polished knocker she was delighted when it immediately opened to reveal her aunt smiling and welcoming her.

'I heard you had come to visit the other side of the family. There's not much goes on that I don't know about,' the old lady said. Adding with a sigh, 'I was so sorry to hear Agnes has been unwell. I sent several messages saying I would like to visit her and received no response. I even called at the door and was told my friend was too ill to receive visitors. I shall go and see her when that silly daughter of hers goes to Brighton; I believe she will be going there soon to pack the house there in order to move here permanently.'

'You seem to be very well informed, Aunt Rosemary,' said Louisa with a smile.

They walked into the parlour and sat on familiar chairs, conversing so comfortably that, within minutes, Louisa had relaxed completely. She had been shocked at first to see the lines age had etched into her aunt's face, but had already accepted this change and saw it as the beauty time had bestowed upon her.

They talked for a while about earlier visits during childhood and how little had changed in the town since then. After a while Aunt Rosemary placed her hand on Louisa's and said, 'I am very sorry you have had to bear such tragedy and pain. So many losses you have had to endure, my dear—so many.'

'It has been a difficult time,' Louisa replied, feeling the familiar dull, cold ache in her heart.

They sat in silence for a while until, feeling more composed, Louisa said, 'I've longed to see you again. I used to dream of visiting you, but I was unable to leave the house for a long time.'

'I understood.'

'I appreciated all the birthday greetings and your letters of sympathy.'

Without planning to speak of the two sisters' row, Louisa blurted out, 'I've never understood the reason for the argument between you and my mother. You were always so fond of one another until that terrible …' she faltered, unable to find the words to describe their falling out, and wished she had not mentioned the subject.

Aunt Rosemary spread her hands in a hopeless gesture. 'Your mother was my beloved little sister. She was ten years my junior and I adored her. I would always give her everything she wanted, but on this occasion I could not agree to do as she wished.' She swallowed and shook her head. 'Your mother wanted me to sell this house and give her half the money. Your father was in some kind of trouble—I don't know exactly what it was about, but I think your father's brother had something to do with it.'

'Uncle Wilfred?'

'Yes, I never did understand why Agnes married him. He could charm the birds off the trees, I grant you—' Rosemary's mouth twitched '—he charmed the drawers off a few local ladies that's for sure! But he was a feckless young man and leopards don't change their spots, do they?'

Louisa was too astonished to speak and gave a nod.

'Your mother thought I refused to sell the house because of my jealousy when she married your father.'

Louise gasped with surprise.

Hearing the intake of breath her aunt leaned forward to pat her arm reassuringly. 'I assure you I was no longer jealous. I was over that silliness years before.'

Louise wondered if both sisters had liked her father and he had chosen her mother, but dared not ask if this was the case.

'I wanted to help,' the old lady continued, 'I really did, but I had already lent her most of my money two years earlier without any repayment. Our family has lived here for centuries and whether this is misplaced sentimentality or not, I don't know, but I feel a duty to keep this old place. Also, being practical, I knew it was of little value and I only have a small annuity to live on, therefore I could not have bought another house. The walls are damp and the windows rattle. The roof leaks when there's rain with an easterly wind and the water pipes freeze and ...' she rolled her eyes and waved her hands in the air. 'I must stop. You did not come here to listen to me going on and on about this old house.'

Louisa saw her saucer was badly stained and the cup was also dirty. Looking around the room she could see thick dust on the windowsills and several spiders' webs festooning the corners of the room, one in particular was so thick with dust it had evidently been there many years. 'Do you have servants to help you, Aunt Rosemary?'

'My dear friend, Alice, lives with me and has done for many years. She does all the chores except for the washing; we have a woman who comes in on Mondays for that. Neither of us is strong enough to boil the copper or deal with the wringer. I do the cooking and we work well together. She's an extraordinary person, much cleverer than I, but even poorer. Almost my age she is, and like me, she doesn't see very well, but we manage between us.'

They chatted for a while longer until Louisa explained that her other aunt would be in need of her and she must depart.

'I hope you will come and see me again.' Aunt Rosemary's eyes glittered as she added, 'Then we could look into the tea-leaves and see what the future holds for you.'

'I think it may be rather dull,' Louisa said with a sad smile.

'You are still young, my dear, thirty-one is no age.'

'I feel old, Aunt.'

'Remember my dear, your mother did not marry until she was past thirty and she had to wait another ten years for your arrival.' The old lady kissed her cheek. 'Don't forget; come and see me again soon. There is no need to write beforehand, you are family and may come unannounced.'

Louisa agreed and left the house. While hurrying along the lane and recalling her aunt's words, she realised the old lady was more than seventy years of age; forty years older than her and suddenly she felt younger. Perhaps there was a future for her after all?

Hurrying into her aunt's room, expecting to see Edwina there, she found the old lady alone, looking cheerful and was relieved to hear her ask what was on the menu for dinner.

〜 〜 〜

On the fourth Monday after her arrival, Louisa left Aunt Agnes sitting by the window and hurried down the stairs. On reaching the hall she saw her cousin emerge from the sitting room resplendent in an outfit of pale blue silk, topped by a very large hat.

'I shall not have time to say goodbye to Mama,' Edwina said, pulling on her long kid gloves. 'I have an appointment now and we shall leave for Brighton early in the morning. You have my address there if anything—' she paused, evidently searching for a word '—of great importance happens and you need to send a telegram.'

Knowing this implied she should only send word if her aunt had died, Louisa agreed she had the address, adding, 'You may rest assured, dear cousin, I will take the greatest possible care of Aunt Agnes in your absence.'

Edwina gave a stiff bow of her head in acknowledgement, which caused the ostrich feathers on her hat to flutter.

Louisa almost admired the hat, but remembered her lowly position and said, 'I trust you will have a safe journey and a very enjoyable visit.' She walked out of the house, down the wide steps and onto the gravel drive where four horses were standing in their traces waiting for Edwina and her husband to get into the coach.

Wishing the coachmen good day, Louisa hurried around to the back of the house, down the sunlit garden and through the gate in the wall.

She lifted her skirt while walking through grass that had grown longer in her absence and was still wet from earlier rain. Arriving at the seat by the wall she carefully avoided some narcissi shoots pushing through the grass and sat down hoping to see a vision.

After closing her eyes she was disappointed to see only the image of Edwina in her ornate hat. It was a beautiful hat, but it was probably out of fashion, as her cousin would find on arrival in Brighton; and besides, it was not worth thinking about!

In an attempt to bring other images to mind she listed the flowers about to come into bloom: periwinkle, violets, daffodils; again the image of the hat reappeared in her mind and in an effort to erase it she began breathing slowly and deeply. Deeper and slower she breathed, deeper and slower until a figure appeared in the distance, indistinct at first and slowly becoming clearer...

Chapter Six

The young priest was walking towards her. She thought he must hear her heart thumping loudly as he came closer. Looking around to see if her grandmother was watching and then remembering the old woman had gone to see the guardian of the red well who was ailing, she relaxed.

This man lived in her thoughts day and night—not that he or anyone else knew, or would ever know, of her feelings for him. He was her secret love and would remain so now that her grandmother had promised her to the priest, Hengar, who was highly respected by all and was now a widower looking for a new wife. Her secret love, as she named him, walked by the well almost every day and bowed his head politely when greeting her before commenting on the coldness of the wind, the wetness of the rain or the heat of the sun.

She liked his eyes, which were blue like the sky on a sunny day and sparkled like water from the white well when he smiled. She liked other things about him too; his strong square hands, his wide shoulders and the deep voice she could listen to all day.

On this occasion, knowing her grandmother was not within hearing distance, she responded to his greeting with a smile and they chatted for a few minutes before he politely said, 'Farewell, White Bird,' and walked away.

Having waited until he was out of sight, she went to the dark well, despite knowing her grandmother would not approve. With a fluttering heart she knelt on the stone beside it, hoping to see him standing on The Great One, holding her hands as they vowed to share their lives. An image began to form, but evaporated when she jumped on hearing a voice calling her name. 'White Bird, White Bird, are you at home?'

She hurried to the dwelling and found the portly figure of her future husband wrapped in the white woven cloak that marked him out as the most important of the priests.

She politely acknowledged his greeting, agreed it was indeed a fine day and then said she had been sent by her grandmother to fetch a healing plant for the ailing keeper of the red well. 'It's urgently needed,' she added, hoping the old woman did not arrive before he left.

'I heard She of the Red was very ill. Wish her well for me,' he said then bade her good bye and walked away.

She ran quickly back to the dark well and looked down into it again in the hope of seeing her secret love taking her hand. She desperately willed the vision to appear, but nothing happened. Just when she was about to give up, the picture of a man appeared, striding towards her. He was strangely dressed with leather skirts swaying above his knees and sandals tied with thongs criss-crossed up his strong bare shins. Behind him were others similarly dressed and pulling carts loaded with stone and rocks.

When the vision disappeared she stared at the water for a long time, thinking it seemed blacker than usual with a strange dense look. She felt sure the sighting had been portentous and something bad would come from those men. Although knowing people should be warned of this danger, she now had a dilemma: if she told her grandmother about the vision, the old lady, who insisted on being present if White Bird looked in the well, would be enraged by this flagrant disobedience, but if she did not tell her then the outcome could be disastrous for the clan. She returned to the dwelling and felt deeply disturbed while skinning the hare she had trapped early that morning.

When the old woman returned, White Bird asked how the sick woman fared and then said she needed to fetch the pungent leaves of garlic from the woods to flavour the hare. She ran out along the path to the dwelling beside the red well and knocked on the door.

On being told to enter, she found the ailing woman lying on her sleeping shelf wrapped in a thick blanket and huddled beside her was the guardian of the white. 'You've just missed your grandmother, dear,' said She of the White, who gestured towards She of the Red and added, 'Not long now, I fear. She's been sleeping for days. No, dear, she won't be long.'

White Bird tiptoed to the bed and touched the papery skin on the hand of the sleeping woman. 'I was hoping for advice from her,' she said.

'In love are you, dear?' asked She of the White.

Knowing that the old lady thought of little else but love made White Bird smile despite her anxiety and she said, 'It's another kind of problem, my lady. I have seen a worrying sight in the well and I daren't tell my grandmother.' She described the men with leather skirts, adding, 'They're dangerous, I know they are. We should warn everyone on the island, including the priests.'

The old lady closed her eyes, wrinkled her large nose and then shook her head. 'I think you saw some of the foreigners that have been seen working on the marshland beyond the island. They're powerful people who build with stone. Very clever they are, dear. Worship strange gods so I'm told. There's a lot of them over the other side of the wetlands—' she giggled like a young girl '—lots of *them* I mean, not the gods they worship.' She patted White Bird's hand. 'I've heard there's no harm in them if you keep out of their way. And besides, your grandmother won't take kindly to you looking in the well, will she, dear?'

White Bird nodded.

'Nor would she like you to warn everyone without her consent, would she?'

White Bird nodded again. 'I know that's true, but I feel sure there's danger ahead from those men.'

They sat in silence for a while until the old lady lying on the bed stirred and gave a whimper, whereupon the guardian of the white well knelt down with difficulty and soothed her friend as one would a child.

White Bird crept away and sat beside the red well nearby, wondering what she should do next now that her warning to the guardian had come to nought. She leaned over the rocks stained with the bright red sediment from the water and looked down into the depths where the spring bubbled up from beneath the surface, wondering why it was so different from the magical black stillness of the dark well. She cupped her hand and dipped it into the water, then, leaning to drink, slipped and spilt it, so she took some more and drank it. While standing up to leave, she looked down at the rock on which she had splashed the water and seeing a picture in the shiny wet surface, she gazed in awe at a boat with a full moon reflected on the water in its wake.

The image vanished when the water dried and she was left staring in astonishment at the rock. The realisation that she had seen a vision without looking into the dark well was a great shock and it was not until walking back close to the yew trees that she paused to wonder what the sighting could mean.

She had never been on a boat except to fish in the shallow waters close by, for, like her mother and her grandmother before her and the ancestors going back she knew not how long, she had never left the island since her birth. This, so she had been told since very young, was where she and they had always belonged and always would. It was their destiny to live here and guard the well. She would one day have a girl child who would replace her and so on and on without end.

The thought of having a child reminded her of Hengar and caused her to shudder at the idea of being embraced by him after they were pledged. In an attempt to think of something less disgusting she wondered again what the picture on the wet rock could mean, until, seeing the sun was low in the sky, she hurried away, across the meeting place and down the short path to the dwelling beside the dark well.

Her grandmother was sitting waiting for her with the black look in her eyes that White Bird recognised of old. She took a deep breath, knowing she had done something wrong and was about to suffer the consequences.

'I'm told you insulted your chosen one this day.' Her grandmother pointed to the ground at her feet indicating that White Bird should kneel there and waited until she had complied, then went on, 'I am displeased, Granddaughter. I have told you many times that you are promised to him. I know he's older than you, but this means he's also wiser. He is a highly respected elder of the priests and will take good care of you while I live and then will watch over you when your time comes to replace me.'

'He's old and repulsive and I don't....'

'Enough!' Her grandmother held up her hand and swiped the air in front of White Bird's face. 'I will not listen to your silliness. When I met him and he asked if the plant I had needed you to fetch so urgently had been of benefit to She of the Red, I knew you had lied to him—' she glowered angrily at her '—and I suspect he knew also. I was so embarrassed that, in order to reassure him of your acceptance, I promised him you will take hands with him at the next spring celebration, and that's the end of it.' The guardian of the dark well pushed her face close to her granddaughter's. 'The end of it, do you hear me?'

White Bird was swallowing tears as she nodded, knowing she would now hear the story of how the priests had allowed the women to guard the wells when they took over The Great One.

'We have made peace with these *usurpers*, as my mother's mother called the priests who make their ceremonies upon the top of The Great One and bury the dead at its foot. Your mother's father was one and my father also, now you must do the same as we did. This way we keep our line, keep our sacred well safe.' Her grandmother's tone was softer as she leaned forward and took her hand. 'Time was, so my grandmother's mother said, when the three guardians of the wells, the red, the white and the black, led the way through the yew trees along the processional way, then around and around the path and into the heart of The Great One to give thanks for a harvest, or to plead for the crops to grow. In those days we buried our dead in the heart of The Great One—long, long ago, before the priests came and made their avenue of oaks and worked their magic with mistletoe.' She pulled White Bird to her and kissed her forehead. 'I know you will see sense, dear child, for the good of our line. Since I lost my dear daughter at your birth, you have been my only consolation and my dearest love. You will be a good girl for my sake and for the future of our kind, won't you?'

White Bird reluctantly agreed and fetched the hare then stuffed it with the bright green leaves she had collected on her way back from the red well. While putting the meat on a stake and placing it over the fire she ached inside, knowing she had only the short days of winter to enjoy her freedom before the spring ceremony when she must obey her grandmother and succumb to the old man.

As the days grew longer so her dread of what was to come increased and by the time of the celebration of spring she was thin and pale.

'He'll think I've been starving you,' her grandmother said while preparing for bed on the night before the ceremony.

White Bird, who was already curled up under her blanket, pretended to be asleep.

Her grandmother gave a great sigh as she lay on her mattress and wished her a good night before falling asleep immediately.

Finding she was still awake long after going to her bed, White Bird crept out of the dwelling and went to kneel before the dark well. When a tear ran down her cheek and dropped into the water she feared it might be contaminated and was then greatly relieved to see distant figures moving towards her, until she felt their anger and malevolence. They were the same men she had seen before, but this time they were holding round shields and wielding big knives. The whole picture suddenly was the colour of blood before disappearing and the water was once more dark and blank.

She sat up the remainder of the night wondering what terrible violence was going to be done and to whom, until her grandmother stirred. They walked out in the moonlight to the processional way where they were soon joined by a group of giggling girls and boys who were also on their way to celebrate the coming of spring.

When they arrived on top of The Great One they found Hengar flanked by his three sons and many others who had already gathered for the ceremony. White Bird still had the image of the strange men in her mind and had difficulty in focussing on anyone around her. All she could think of was the blood that would be shed and therefore she only vaguely heard the words of the priest who was joining her hands with Hengar's.

As though in a dream she made her responses when required and felt numb as she walked down the hill with her new husband. Throughout the feasting and dancing around the fire that followed she gave the appearance of being alive whilst feeling dead inside.

When the time came for her to be led to her new home, she dutifully went and greeted the wives of her husband's sons who lived in dwellings all around Hengar's and then went into his house with him.

Soon after they lay down on their bed he pulled her to him and quickly joined his body with hers. To her surprise she felt nothing. She had expected to feel revulsion, or distaste at the very least, but she kept her mind on the memory of a beautiful bird she had seen swooping to catch a fish in the water that morning and then flown off with large wings effortlessly lifting it up towards the bright blue sky and therefore what he did was purely to her body and made no impact on her heart and soul.

The following day she ignored the giggles and stares of his sons and their wives and children and quietly and calmly began her new life. She kept her eyes averted from everyone the whole time and soon the family assumed she was somewhat simple-minded and ignored her.

For three seasons she lived in a trancelike state. She dreamed of the young priest by night and lived with him in her mind by day, imagining how they would laugh together and love one another, maybe even weep together in times of tragedy. She saw their children born and then grow up into adults and pictured herself ageing contentedly with her beloved man.

And all the time, while living a story in her head, she carried out the general duties of a wife, fetching water from the spring nearby, making the fire and cooking on it and also spinning, weaving and sewing. To her relief the old man rarely wished for fulfilment of her most intimate obligation and once she was with child he stopped altogether.

Although longing to have a baby to care for and make sense of her miserable life she still could not be contented with her lot. Her husband's family treated her with little or no respect and Hengar rarely spoke other than to demand food or water.

Despite feeling nothing for her husband, she was sure that she would love his child and assumed all would be well until it ceased to move. Fearing the worst she went to visit her grandmother and saw the old woman's eyes flicker while looking down at her swollen belly; it was only for an instant, but it was enough for her to know the baby was doomed. There was no need to ask if the old woman had consulted the well; neither of them spoke a word, but their eyes met in a deeper communication of womanly understanding and compassion.

Her son was born very soon after this, when day and night were of equal length. On leaving her body he drew no breath nor made a sound. Despite having known this would be his fate, she grieved for many days and walked alone in the woods where the quiet grace and beauty of the trees gave her comfort and also acceptance of humanity's transience. Placing her hand on the trunk of a great oak she wondered how many generations before her had touched it and seeing small saplings grown from acorns she tried to imagine the future people yet to be born who would walk in their shade.

Her husband's family now shunned her. The sons made plain they thought she had betrayed their father; and their wives hugged their babies closer whenever she went near them. One of the most outspoken of the women often muttered darkly about the number of things that had gone wrong since Hengar had married White Bird and said she had brought bad luck to them.

One wet day she was standing alone under the branches of a majestic oak tree when the young priest came walking along the path towards her.

Seeing her he stopped, hesitated for a moment and then joined her, saying, 'I greet you, wife of Hengar. I'm sorry to hear of your tragic loss.'

She thanked him and explained that the trees gave comfort and helped her to accept the pain of grief.

'Some of my best friends are trees,' he said with a smile.

She laughed for the first time in many months and replied, 'They're good listeners I find and, above all, they can't answer back!'

'We revere all nature,' he said seriously. 'We believe all plants and every living thing is sacred and we also believe that we are born many times into many different forms.' He reached out and touched her hand with the tip of his forefinger, adding, 'I believe your baby has been reborn in another life…'

'You think he's someone else's child?'

'Maybe, or perhaps he's an animal or plant—who knows?'

'I like that idea,' she said, knowing she would take comfort in the thought that the spirit of her dead son might be reborn in another life.

'I thank you, Priest.'

'My name is Damon the Bard,' he said.

'You tell stories?'

'I have learned the ancient tales handed down through my family and I tell them at our gatherings.' He smiled. 'I've seen you attend with your husband and—' he raised an eyebrow '—I think you usually slip away before my turn.'

'I'll make sure to stay and hear you next time,' she said.

He bowed his head and then walked away through the avenue of oaks.

During the darkest, coldest days of the winter following her baby's death, White Bird's grandmother began to cough. White Bird went to visit her every day and made hot drinks with the plant that usually soothed such afflictions, but to no avail. The cough persisted and her grandmother grew weaker day by day. She asked for advice from the guardian of the white well who was very knowledgeable about the healing properties of plants and also consulted the new guardian of the red well, but both women suggested all the remedies she had already used.

'There is little to be done if her time has come,' She of the White said with a shrug. 'No healing water whether red or white, no plant, no prayers to any god or goddess will save us from our destiny.'

'But she can't die!' White Bird exclaimed. 'I can't let her die.' She felt hot panic rise within her. 'If she dies, that would mean...' she broke off, staring into the guardian's pale grey eyes.

'You would be the guardian of the dark well, my dear.' The old lady put a thin arm around her shoulders. 'I know you can do it. You have the gift just like your mother and grandmother. Remember what you told me that day about strangers coming. You saw that clear enough, didn't you?'

White Bird agreed sadly and returned to the dwelling where she lay down beside her grandmother and stayed awake all night listening her rasping breath.

Shortly before dawn, when the first bird began to sing, she went outside to fetch wood for the fire and stood watching the sky lighten while other birds joined in and sang their own sweet songs. The days were already getting longer, but there was hard frost on the grass and icicles hung from the thatch roof. Sniffing the air and sensing snow would soon be falling she longed for the warm sun to ease her grandmother's suffering.

She collected some wood and carried it into the dwelling. The stillness of the silent room told her the old lady was dead. She ran to the shrunken corpse and cradled it in her arms. For a long while she crooned lullabies from childhood to her grandmother, until, feeling sure the spirit had left the frail physical remains, she wept, both for her loss and with fear of the future.

In a ceremony at the foot of The Great One, where some graves had been dug before the frosty weather, in readiness for the inevitable winter deaths, her grandmother's body was buried with two other corpses, both of whom had been too old and frail to withstand the severe cold.

She stayed in the dwelling close to the well for many days, aching for the loss of the woman whom she had loved and missed with all her heart.

One day Hengar came to see her and said in an aggrieved tone, 'I feel you are neglecting your wifely duties. You have abandoned me completely since your grandmother died. If this is how you intend to continue, then I believe I have the right to take another wife, one who will do as I wish.'

The relief made her laugh inside as she solemnly replied, 'I agree you have the right to replace me. I now have to...'

'No—' he held up his hand authoritatively '—you misunderstand me. You will still be my wife, but since you are not behaving satisfactorily, I have the right to take a second woman into my home.' He narrowed his eyes. 'I am giving you the freedom to perform your duties at the dark well, that is all.'

She shrugged and wished him well, knowing there was no point in disputing with one of the priests who made the rules governing the community.

From time to time she saw Damon the Bard, of whom she still dreamed most nights. When greeting him politely she kept her eyes downcast for fear of showing any sign of her continued feeling for him. She knew Hengar would never set her free to join hands with a younger priest and therefore she must never encourage him or show her feelings for him.

The local residents of the island and the clans in the area all accepted her as the new guardian of the dark well and came to her for guidance. It was from people living in the wetland villages that she learned of the work being done by foreign soldiers who were draining the marshes far away towards the sea. Most people seemed to accept these strangers were benign and carried on their lives as before, but when Hengar came to speak with her one day she knew something serious was on his mind and when he looked anxiously towards the marshland she guessed what it was.

'Good day, Wife, Guardian of the Dark Well,' he said.

'I wish you well, Husband, Priest of the Sacred Island,' she replied.

'I've come to warn you that the clans will come together soon at the meeting place across the water.' He shook his head sadly, before adding, 'I fear there may be bloodshed if the young men have their way.'

'You would have them let the foreigners take the land?' she asked.

'I would have them live. Our way is to live in peace and I do not wish for my sons to die in a hopeless battle with those invaders.'

She thought of the young priest with sky blue eyes and nodded. 'I agree. I would have them live and wait until the foreigners leave.'

His eyes glittered with hope. 'They will go back to their homeland?'

Although having seen nothing in the well to make her think this would be the case, White Bird felt certain they would go. 'I don't know when they will go, but I feel sure they will one day, perhaps after many, many seasons; perhaps in the time of our children's children and beyond.'

'Our children?'

She swallowed her revulsion and said, 'I'm sorry I could not give you a living son. I hope you will soon father a son with your second wife and also your sons will live to father many children.'

'I thank you.' He avoided her eyes. 'I wish there could have been a different conclusion. Your grandmother promised you would be a dutiful wife to me. I took you on in good faith and you have made a fool of me.'

'I had no intention of making you look foolish. I regret I could not stay with you. I cannot change my destiny.'

He gave a sigh. 'I will tell the clans you think the foreigners will leave.'

'But not, as I said before, not for a long, long time.'

He narrowed his eyes. 'I suspect you know more than you're telling me.'

She looked at the ground, thinking that to speak of bloodshed would serve no purpose. 'I can only say I think the foreigners will stay for more than one generation of our people.'

'I see.' Hengar bade her good day and walked away.

She sank to her knees and looked down into the dark water. And there it was again; the image of a boat with a full moon reflected on the water in its wake and this time she could discern the dark shape of a man silhouetted against the sky. Perhaps, she thought, the foreigners would come by night—that would make sense if they wished to surprise everyone on the island. She wished her grandmother were still alive to give her help. She might know exactly what the vision meant and therefore whether or not the people should be warned of the danger.

❖　❖　❖

The foreigners arrived soon after the next full moon. They came striding towards her with leather skirts swaying above strong bare legs, exactly like the image in the pool. Watching them approach, White Bird wished She of the White had taken her warning more seriously and that word could have been spread around the area. For a moment she wondered if it was possible to hide the well with branches from the yew nearby and then realised there was no time for this.

The men were talking in a strange tongue as they stood on the path looking down at her. Wondering desperately how to save the sacred water from desecration, she sank to her knees and bowed her head. A shiver of fear ran through her. What if these men brought their animals to drink here and allowed them to trample the earth and foul the water?

One of the strangers said, 'We come in peace, lady.'

She was astonished. He spoke with a strange lilt, making the words form an unusual pattern, but they were understandable nevertheless. She was swallowing in order to speak when she heard the sound of shouting followed by a roar and a piercing scream.

'We come in peace.' His eyes flickered towards the sounds and he gave a wry smile. 'If we are met in peace.' Without waiting for her to reply, he explained that his men were going to work on an area of marshland towards the coast and would be using this and other islands to make camp from time to time.

She guessed they would be taking over the meeting place for this purpose and the scream had been from someone who tried to stop them. Knowing how hot blooded some of the young men were, especially Hengar's sons, she wondered if one of them had suffered a humiliating defeat in order to be made an example of and to prove that resistance was futile.

As though reading her thoughts the man said, 'If you work with us and not against us, no harm will come to you.' He turned to leave, then, looking back at her small dwelling, he asked, 'Why do you live so close to the water?'

111

She gulped and explained, 'I am the keeper of the well, sir.'

'Are you a priestess and, if so, which god or goddess do you serve?'

Although longing to say she merely saw guidance in the well that she then passed on to others, she hesitated. Unlike the members of her clan who would need no explanation, these newcomers apparently did not understand the purpose of a dark well such as this. 'I am the guardian of the spirit of the well,' she said.

'I understand. In my homeland you would be called a priestess. We are very respectful of your kind. Tell me please, what is the name of this spirit?'

No one had ever suggested it should be called anything other than that of the dark, or sometimes, the black, well, but now, having heard he would respect her as a priestess, she guessed the spirit should have a name that he would understand. Sweat trickled down her body as she frantically wondered what to call it, then without consciously making the decision, heard her voice say, 'She is the goddess of shadows and very sacred to my people.'

'Very interesting,' he said rubbing his chin with a long forefinger. 'I can see her water is very dark.'

'And mysterious,' she said, wondering if that was going too far.

'Indeed,' he said thoughtfully. 'I see it is completely still, unlike the other wells I have seen where the gushing spring is constantly running into it.'

She heard shouting and screaming in the distance and felt a cold shudder of fear run through her body. She looked into the pale blue eyes of the stranger and knew him to be ruthless. He was not like Hengar's ancestors who had, over many generations, gradually taken control of The Great One; this man had no time to waste patiently waiting for local people to accept him. In contrast with the priests, who had allowed the traditional guardians of the wells to live in peace by the sacred waters of the red, the white and the black: the stranger would, she felt sure, kill her without a second thought if she was not submissive in her manner.

He bent down and dipped his finger into the water, causing circles of light to ripple outwards towards the stone around the edge of the pool.

She gasped, but said nothing. There was no point in telling him that she would be unable to see into it that day because he had disturbed the surface and like as not it would show nothing until after the next full moon had shone upon it.

He stood up and asked, 'Do you drink this water?'

'No, sir.'

'Why not?'

'It belongs to the goddess of shadows and is too sacred to drink.' She gestured around her. 'There is plenty of water to drink from many small springs all around the island and also—' she looked towards The Great One '—both the red and the white wells are renowned for their healing and the priestesses who guard them are greatly respected in our community.'

'I see.' He nodded and strode away followed by his cohort.

Watching him walk back towards the meeting ground, she hoped he would also treat the guardians of the red and white wells with similar respect now that she had called them priestesses. She was tempted to run to see them and explain the situation until realising she would have to pass all the foreign men on the meeting ground and the man she had spoken with would guess she was going to warn them.

There was also the possibility that if she left the well unguarded it might be defiled in her absence. Furthermore, while away from it she would be vulnerable, whereas here, beside the well, as the respected priestess of the goddess of shadows she could perhaps avoid violation.

The day seemed very long. From time to time she heard men shouting and the occasional scream. When the guardian of the white well appeared, staggering slowly along the path towards her, she ran to hold her and help the frail old woman into the dwelling.

'They have killed She of the Red,' the old woman gasped.

White Bird groaned, guessing that the new young guardian, who was sharp of tongue, had argued vociferously. 'Oh no. I thought they would respect you both as priestesses.'

'No, there was no respect, my dear. When she told them in that harsh way of hers to go back where they came from, they …' the old woman's voice had grown faint. She paused to raise a limp hand to wipe tears from her eyes and then whispered, 'They violated her and killed her, then hung her naked body on the big yew beside the well for all to see.'

'As a warning I suppose,' White Bird said, utterly appalled and knowing there would either be little resistance now or, very possibly, a suicidal fight to the death by the local young men.

The old woman gave a feeble response and then slumped down, silently staring at the fire.

White Bird looked into the blank eyes of death and gave a small cry of shock. Then, knowing her life would never be the same again, she wept helplessly and hopelessly.

That evening, when the sun was almost below the horizon, she heard footsteps approaching and went with trepidation to see who was visiting so late in the day. To her surprise she found a man wrapped in a brown woollen cloak and with his face covered.

'I come in friendship, My Lady, Guardian of the Dark Well, ' the man said, holding out his hands to show he held no weapon.

She recognised his voice, and felt her heart quicken its beat. 'I know you, Damon the Bard. You are welcome, sir.'

He looked behind him, as if thinking he might have been followed, then said, 'My life is in danger and therefore I must go very soon. I was determined to tell you something before I left.'

Seeing him look furtively around while talking, she suggested he could enter her dwelling and speak without fear of being overheard.

He accepted and went inside, where he sat by the fire and said, 'One of my friends told me that a stone carver has been instructed to make the figure of a goddess with long wavy hair.' He looked at her and smiled. 'Maybe like you, my lady.'

She blushed and averted her eyes to avoid his admiring gaze.

'My friend also told me that blocks of stone have already been quarried from the local rock in readiness to put into the dark well.'

She gasped. 'You mean they plan to fill in the....'

'No, no—' he held up his hand '—they will line the hole with stone and the place the figure of the goddess beside it.'

'Why would they do that?'

He shrugged. 'I don't know. Maybe they think it better to drink from water that is kept in stone, or perhaps they want to make it easier to clean it. Whatever the reason, it's what these strangers do.'

She shook her head sadly. 'The well will lose its power. I suppose I could try to explain...'

'I beg you, White Bird—I mean, Lady of the Dark Well, please don't try to reason with these people. They are determined to do what they believe is right. They will build a shrine to their deity, no matter what you say. ' He shrugged. 'They have their belief, we have ours and you have yours; and we all feel sure our belief is the truth.'

She slumped disconsolately for a while and then sat up, saying, 'If I can't stop them then I must leave here.'

'I think that would be wise. These foreigners will kill anyone who resists them. They have already proved this with the guardian of the red well and many of my fellow priests have been slaughtered for trying to defend the stones on the sacred mound below The Great One. One of our most venerable men, Hengar, your husband, is dead.'

White Bird was horrified. 'How could that be? He told me he wished to avoid bloodshed.'

'His sons, I fear, were intent on fighting and were no match for the foreigners. I heard that Hengar intervened and was pleading with them to make peace when he was struck down.'

'And his three sons?'

'All dead.' Damon held his head in his hands and sighed. 'The foreigners' blood is up now and they are killing anyone who they think might rise up against them in future and what's even more worrying, I heard that any prisoners they take are made slaves.'

She understood his fear. 'You'd be a suspect wouldn't you?'

'I would indeed. Not only am I a young man, I'm also a priest of The Great One. That's the reason I have decided to leave. I've hidden a boat under some willows close to the landing stage and will go tonight when the moon is high.' He cleared his throat. 'I would be glad to take you with me.'

'But I have nowhere to go. I have neither kith nor kin since my grandmother died. She used to say we once came from the Berhanii clan over towards the horizon, but I don't know for sure.'

'I have kinfolk in a village out in the wetlands where we could start a new life.' He swallowed and then added, 'Together.'

Her heart sang as she remembered her vision of the boat in the moonlight. 'Together,' she echoed. 'You can keep the stories alive and hand them down to—' she hesitated, then threw caution to the wind '—to our children. And I can continue to give guidance as is my destiny, because I now know I don't need the dark well to have visions, all I need is water from a spring and a stone!'

Chapter Seven

Louisa sat smiling to herself after the picture had faded. Not only was the happy ending a relief; she realised also, with great joy, that her occasional sights on windows must be similar to White Bird's experience with water on stone.

'I hope I'm not interrupting,' Edward Francis said as he approached. 'I was looking out for you in the hope of telling you the Bath chair is almost ready for Mrs Govern.'

'That is so kind. I will only take her out in it when the weather is clement. I fear she is still quite frail and also she will be unable to descend the stairs.'

Edward gave an understanding nod. 'I used to carry my grandmother up and down when she lost the use of her legs and I'm sure I could do the same for your aunt, if she would allow me.'

'I will tell her of your generous offer.' Louisa leaned forward in readiness to stand up.

'I was wondering if you have had any further interesting visions?' Edward enquired with a smile.

'Indeed I have.' Louisa sank back onto the bench and waited while he joined her, then gave a brief summary of White Bird's story.

Edward sat for a few moments before saying, 'You must meet my Aunt Rosemary; she will be fascinated to hear about this.'

Louisa stared at him and then laughingly said, 'I, too, have an aunt by that name. Does your Aunt Rosemary live in a stone house by the abbey wall?'

He nodded.

'My aunt is Miss Rosemary Govern.'

'So is mine, although, I confess, she is an aunt by marriage and probably more of a second or third cousin at that. She has always been an important member of our family and is much loved by us all. I'm sure none of my sisters would have married without consulting the tea-leaves and my brother too, if truth be known.'

Louisa remembered her Aunt Agnes speaking of his wedding and opened her mouth to ask if he also had looked in the teacup before proposing to his bride: however, seeing his expression change to one of sadness, she remained silent and waited for him to continue.

'Aunt Rosemary was a good support to me when I came home from South Africa and found my brother James had died and she has also been of great comfort to me since then.'

'I'm so sorry,' Louisa said, 'I know the pain of losing someone you love deeply. I'm afraid there is no cure for grief. I've found one has to learn to accept it and live with it.'

'I know you are right, but I feel guilty, as though I don't deserve to be happy.' He gave a helpless shrug. 'Although not poor, we are also not rich gentry. While my brother was always expected to take on the management of my father's property, I was the younger son and needed to earn a living. I became a soldier, which I hated, because I was neither clever enough nor suited for the cloth. Now I have the enjoyable task of helping my ailing father and every day I wish it could still be James in my place.' He frowned, added, 'Also…' shook his head as though changing his mind and said, 'I hope we meet again, I do so enjoy hearing of your visions.'

'I thank you for your interest.' Louisa heard the church clock chime four times and stood up. 'I must get back to my aunt.'

'And I must continue my dowsing.' Edward raised his hat, bade her goodbye and walked away.

On her return she found her aunt eager to hear of any vision she might have experienced and once again told the story of White Bird.

'That—is—so—romantic!' the old lady said dreamily. 'I'm so glad—she went off—with Damon the Bard.' She paused to take a few breaths then continued, 'It makes me—think—of my—elopement—

with Wilfred—such a handsome fellow—your uncle—and so charming! All the girls—were in love—with him—I was so proud when—he proposed—to me.' She turned and looked out of the window.

Louisa sat quietly watching her aunt gazing at the sky as though seeing the past in the distance. Recalling Aunt Rosemary's opinion of Uncle Wilfred during her recent visit, she felt sure the expression on the old lady's face reflected unhappy memories from her married life. Seeing the gnarled fingers of the old lady's good hand agitatedly clasping the blanket over her knees, while the thin lips of her lopsided mouth seemed to be silently echoing words from long ago, she wondered what pain from the past was being relived within the frail heart.

Later, lying in bed and looking at the moon through the window, Louisa thought of the vision experienced earlier that day. Remembering White Bird giving birth to her dead baby, she knew this would have happened time and time again for thousands of years. All women would have known there was a risk that their child, especially if it were a boy, would not survive; also, there was always the possibility of their own death, either in childbirth or from puerperal fever after the birth.

The discovery of antiseptics had greatly reduced the risk of mortality from giving birth, but, as she knew to her cost, serious diseases such as scarlet fever still lay in wait for the babies while they grew up.

Suddenly all rational thought about childbirth and other women's babies receded. The pain of losing her own child overwhelmed her and, at last, she wept the tears that had been locked inside her for the six years since little Charlie died.

The following Saturday, having sent a note of warning to Louisa, Edward walked to the house pushing the Bath chair and left it before the steps to the front door while he called upon Mrs Govern.

When the old lady saw him walk into the room she immediately blossomed with a beguiling, albeit lopsided, smile and the young woman she had once been could be seen shining through the aged shell. She held up her good hand for Edward to gently shake in greeting and although moving her lips slightly, she did not speak.

Knowing the old lady was keeping up the pretence of dumbness Louisa felt a flicker of irritation, then said, 'The sun is shining. We should go now and take a walk in the garden; don't you agree, Aunt?'

When the old lady looked agitated, Edward said, 'I will carry you downstairs, Mrs Govern and we will see if you like the chair. Then, if we all agree—' he gave Louisa a boyish grin '—we can take a short walk around the garden.'

Louisa fetched blankets and scarves while Edward carefully lifted the old lady and carried her down the stairs then out to the front drive.

Looking dubiously at the wicker chair with two main large wheels either side and two smaller ones at the front, Aunt Agnes remained silent while her good hand plucked nervously at the blanket.

'My father had it made especially in the lightweight material in order that my sisters and I could take our grandmother out for walks.' Edward grinned. 'We also used to give each other rides, but not, I hasten to say, when Grandmama was with us.'

He carefully placed the old lady in the chair. Louisa wrapped the blankets around her then asked if this was comfortable and was relieved when she nodded happily.

They walked along the gravelled paths to the back of the garden. While admiring the shoots on shrubs and roses, Louisa delighted in her aunt's enjoyment of this adventure, but her own pleasure was short-lived. She soon realised that this chair, while very safe on flat surfaces, would be impossible to manoeuvre on the uneven grass in the abbey grounds.

'You are looking anxious, Mrs Wendon,' Edward said, while standing back to allow the old lady to see the sunken rose garden below her.

'It is a wonderful gift and I am very grateful, but I fear it would be dangerous on rough ground. I regret I won't be able to take it to the abbey, Mr Francis.'

'That's true. We will have to think of some other expedition.' He ruffled his moustache thoughtfully.

Louisa gazed towards the abbey and then, seeing the church tower in the High Street, suggested, 'I'm sure I could push it along the lane into town.'

Following her eyes, Edward nodded enthusiastically. 'My grand-mother loved going to church in this very chair.'

When they explained the situation to her, the old lady showed her silent disappointment, but soon agreed that church on Sunday morning would be acceptable.

Louisa admitted to being worried about who would carry her downstairs.

'It would be a pleasure for me to do this,' Edward said.

Louisa shook her head. 'No, this is too much of an imposition. Your family and ...' she was about to say that his wife would not approve of their Sunday being disrupted when Edward interrupted her. 'I will be at the house on Sunday morning soon after ten o'clock, unless it is cold or raining.' His tone allowed no argument and seeing her aunt was already looking forward to this outing, Louisa accepted the decision, albeit with some concern. While placing her foot on the back of the chair she had been aware of his glance at her ankle and having heard about the roving eye of her uncle, despite being married to Aunt Agnes, she was wary of encouraging similar attention.

The housekeeper and two maids were hovering in the hall when they returned and watched with interest as the old lady was carried into the house.

'I am delighted to see the mistress looking so well,' the house-keeper said to Louisa. 'We all are so fond of her, you know and very grateful to you and Mr Francis. Our gardener, Walker, is a strong young man and would be very willing to carry Mrs Govern up and down the stairs in future.'

'That would be perfect,' Louisa said with a sigh of relief.

The old lady remained silent as usual when in the company of anyone other than Louisa.

Edward looked impassive while accepting the decision and avoided Louisa's eyes when she politely thanked him for his kindness and wished him goodbye.

The following morning the gardener carried the old lady down the stairs and Louisa pushed her in the Bath chair to the parish church in the High Street and sat in a pew at the back with her aunt. The service was similar to those she was used to in the London church and the vicar's sermon was a deeply felt and rather lengthy tirade against the sins of modern life and the need for women to know their place as helpmeets to their husbands and good mothers to their children.

After the final hymn, All Things Bright and Beautiful, Louisa knelt to pray. Her first request was for women to get the vote and immediately wondered if God would choose to listen to her or to the vicar, who obviously disagreed with this request. She prayed earnestly for harmony between Edwina and Aunt Agnes and for her own understanding of the reason the old lady wished to keep her recovery secret from her daughter. She gave thanks for the strange gift that enabled her to see the visions. And finally, as usual when in a church, she asked God to care for the souls of her dead loved ones.

Having positioned the chair just inside the church a few moments before the service began, Louisa was able to get out before most of the congregation stood up to leave. She had thought this was a good idea until later when her aunt listed some of the people she had seen in the church and expressed disappointment at having made no contact with them.

'I shall make sure we are seated further forward in future, Aunt,' she said, thinking that pretending to be unable to speak to these people would surely make life more difficult and again wondering if the old lady was senile, but having decided to make no comment on the situation she regarded as ridiculous, she made no further comment.

On Monday afternoon, having settled her aunt beside the window and promised she would wave to her from the garden, Louisa left the house.

Arriving at the bench beside the wall, she took out her sketchbook and began drawing a view of the land as she remembered it from her visions. From time to time she stopped to watch birds fly overhead or listen to them singing in the bushes nearby. Spring was in the air and she was glad to be alive.

She had drawn the outline of a small thatched dwelling and was wondering where to place the well when the birdsong changed and became a harsher tuneless sound. Almost metallic, she thought, as the familiar feeling overwhelmed her....

Chapter Eight

She could hear the steady clink of metal being hammered reverberating around the valley and put both hands over her ears. Her mother had warned her that the blacksmith would be making new neck irons for the men and wrist irons for the women in readiness for the departure. When she had asked the reason for this her mother said, 'So we can't run away, of course.'

'Why would we do that?'

Her mother had given a hollow mirthless laugh and replied, 'Being a slave here is bad enough, but no one knows what it will be like there.'

There was the foreign land that her father must return to—not that she was supposed to know he was her father, but everyone accepted that she and her brothers were his offspring. His wife pretended she didn't know, but sometimes, when caught unawares, her eyes were frighteningly black with spite and Luna knew that one day there would be trouble for her mother and the children born to her. The more she thought about this place far away where her father and his wife had been born, the more she was sure it would be bad for her and the more determined she became to avoid going there.

She could hear her older brother calling her name, 'Luna, Luna, where are you?'

She snuggled further down into the small cave formed in the cliff overlooking the villa and rubbed the metal bracelet on her wrist while remembering three slaves chained together after they had been caught trying to run away and guessing the steady clink, clink, clink of metal was to make sure all the neck rings were in good order and ready for chains to be fitted if necessary.

When her brother's voice had faded away she crept out of the little cave. After waiting a moment to be sure no one was near, she walked carefully along a narrow ledge then climbed down a hole and into a passageway in the rock that led her down into a large cavern with a fire burning at one end.

The old woman sitting by the fire looked up and greeted her with a friendly smile. 'I hear they're packing up to go, little one.'

'I know and I'm frightened of what will happen to me. The slaves are all being given new neck rings and bracelets. My brother's neck is badly burned from his. He says I'll be sold as soon as we get back to my father's home and men will do horrible things to me. He says he's heard the others talking and they're sure the mistress will take her revenge on the master's children when she gets there. They say she's been waiting for this moment and she'll punish us all, especially me. I don't know why she hates me so much. My brother says it's 'cos I'm my father's favourite. What do you think, dear lady?'

'I think you're wise to be frightened, little one. Many a man would pay a good price for a young virgin with eyes so blue and hair so golden.'

'But how can I stay?'

The old woman looked thoughtful while stirring the contents of an iron pot hanging over the fire and then said, 'If you were to slip away when there's a distraction.'

'A distraction?'

'Maybe the mistress might lose a special necklace or some bauble or other. Is there something small she prizes greatly?'

'She has a beautiful amulet she always wears around her neck. She's frightened to go anywhere without it. I might be able to conceal it somewhere, I suppose, and then while they're all searching for it I could come here and hide.'

'That sounds about right—' the old woman grinned '—you'd best not come here though, your brother knows you come to visit me and he's found you here more than once.' She looked up and listened, then, hearing no warning sounds of a boy approaching, added, 'I think he knows you're here now, if truth be told, but you can't always rely on him pretending he can't find you, not when there's a punishment on the end of it.'

'But where else can I go?'

They both sat in silence for a considerable time until the old woman said, 'I'd have preferred you to be older, little one. But maybe we have no choice in the circumstances.' She pointed out through the entrance of the cave and went on, 'There's where you must go, child.'

Luna looked across the shining water to the hill that dominated all the others in the landscape. 'You think I should go to the island?'

'I have two sisters living there. One is the keeper of the white well and the other is the keeper of the red well. They know the where-abouts of the third, most sacred of the three wells, of the sacred is-land. It has been hidden for many, many moons since the foreigners came and took over this land and now—' she beamed beatifically at Luna '—the time has come for it to be found and brought back to life. And you, my dear little friend, are the one destined to do this.'

Luna stared at her in astonishment. 'How can you know this, my lady?'

The old woman reached into a leather pouch hanging from her belt and pulled out a calcite ball. 'From this, my dear.' She held the ball in both hands and rubbed it lovingly for a long while before looking into Luna's eyes. 'Yes, little Luna, your time has come.'

Staring into the milky green depths within the old woman's eyes, Luna felt the grey walls of the cave spin around her for a moment and then, when all was still, she said firmly, 'I shall go to the island and find these sisters.' She swallowed and added with less conviction, 'I'm not sure...'

'Yes, you can do this, Luna. Although still a child, you are brave and strong. Soon you will be a woman and your life will be long, very long. There will be many after you, many descendants will come to carry on until…' she broke off and shook her head sadly.

'It will end, my lady?'

'It will stop for many moons, when the water is contaminated with blood.'

'And then?'

'One day, I know not how far into the future, but one day, it will be found again.' The old woman replaced the ball into the pouch, saying, 'There, that's enough of that! Now you must go and prepare to leave. I'll not see you again, my dear…'

'Can't I come and say farewell?'

'No, we must part now. Go with my love, child.' She kissed Luna's forehead.

Tears blinded her as she hugged the old woman, then, wiping her eyes with her hands, unable to say a word, she turned and walked out of the cave.

All the way to the slave's quarters behind the villa she wondered how to get hold of the mistress's amulet. The task seemed impossible, but in the event, it was simple. On arrival she found her mother in great distress because the blacksmith had burned her arm when fixing a new metal wristband and, not only was she in pain, but the mistress had summoned her to assist with her daily bath and she was desperate to avoid displeasing her.

'I've heard the mistress's father is an important man in her home country and I fear she'll use him to get rid of me when we are there,' her mother said, nursing her swollen arm. 'She uses every little excuse to scold me and I'm so…' tears streamed down her beautiful face.

'Don't worry, I'll go in your place, Mother,' Luna reassured her.

'But you should go for the wrist…'

'I'll get that fixed after the bath,' Luna said and then ran to the bathhouse at the back of the villa.

She knew the routine, having watched her mother light the fire to heat the tank of water and then run it through the lead pipes into the beautifully tiled bath. Once it was ready she went and informed the mistress who looked for a moment as if she would refuse, but then, with an imperious nod at Luna, she summoned her favourite slave and led the way into the bathhouse.

When the slave assisted the mistress to disrobe and unhook the thong on which the precious amulet hung around the woman's large neck, Luna hovered in the background watching for her opportunity. While bending to ensure the water was the right temperature, she saw the amulet had been placed on a ledge beside a small sculpture of the mistress's favourite deity. Peering beneath the figurine she could see a gap between a few pieces of the mosaic floor and guessed the heat from the pipes underneath had caused the mortar to crumble. She waited until the other slave had joined the mistress in the bath to scrub her back and then, while stooping to pick up a pair of sandals, quickly grabbed the amulet and pushed it down the crack before placing the sandals ready for the mistress on her emergence from the water.

At that moment the slave told her the water needed more heat and so she hurried out to the furnace and added more wood to it. Then, seeing there was no one nearby, she decided to take her chance and ran out from behind the bathhouse, past the huts where the slaves lived, around the lines of vines on the slopes and on and on, weaving through trees and keeping in the shadows, until she reached the river. Without stopping to think, she climbed into the water and waded along beside the bank in the shadow of the willows. Soon she found the water getting deeper and, as the river widened, she saw the stretch of water reflecting the sky all the way to the island with the sacred hill silhouetted above it.

'Do you need a ride, maiden?'

Luna turned to find the prow of a boat edging out from a deep clump of willows and said, 'I have no payment, ferryman.'

'None is asked, maiden,' the man said as he pushed the boat towards her.

He was wearing a woollen cloak and trousers and tunic woven in the grey and green of the local tribe, but his voice had the accent of her father's people and she hesitated. Such a man might take her back to the villa where she would be severely beaten at best, or killed at worst, for hiding the amulet and running away.

'You will be safe with me, maiden,' he said, holding out his large square hand. When she made no move, he added, 'I have deserted my unit and chosen to stay here.' He looked at the metal band on her wrist. 'I know of several villages where you could hide if you so wish.'

She decided to take a risk and said, 'I would prefer to go to the sacred island, sir, if that is possible.'

'It is. In fact that's where I was heading when I saw you.'

She took his hand and climbed into the shallow craft.

He removed his cloak and handed it to her. 'Put this on and pull up the hood.' When she had done so, he added, 'If you sit hunched up like an old woman no one is likely to mistake you for a missing slave girl—' he grinned '—just supposing anyone might be looking for one.'

As they travelled through the silvery water she heard voices shouting in the distance and wondered if people from the villa were calling her name. Her brothers might be anxious for her safety of course, while other slaves would be wishing to gain praise for catching her.

Her mother would be desperately worried; the poor woman was already in pain with her burnt arm and frightened what would happen to her when she arrived in the foreign land. And her father too, until this moment she had not thought of him and suddenly she felt tearful; he had always shown kindness to her, especially in his wife's absence, and now, how would he feel about her? Might he worry for the safety of a daughter who had disappeared, or would he be angry with the slave girl who had run away? He liked her to sing to him in the evening when he returned from the mines on the hills behind the villa.

'Come, little Luna, let me hear your songs while I eat,' he would say and often, when she paused for breath, he would give her a tasty morsel from his bowl. She smiled at the memory and wished she could have kissed him farewell.

'Are you thinking of a sweetheart left behind?' the man asked dipping his pole into the water.

'No, I was thinking of my father whom I loved dearly.'

The man looked surprised. 'I wonder why you run from him if you loved him so?'

'He has to return to … to,' she hesitated then said, 'to your land and I am afraid to go with him.'

'He is Roman?'

Luna explained her parentage and how she feared his wife would deal with her mother and the children once she was on her home ground.

'I think you were wise to leave, Luna,' the man said.

'You know my name?'

'We have a mutual friend who warned me you might have need of my services.'

She knew he referred to the old lady in the cave and said, 'She has proved to be a very good friend indeed!'

'And a wise one,' he said with a smile.

'What is your name, boatman?'

'Darius,' he replied and added, 'Perhaps you would like to sing for me?'

She sang all the way to the island and as he helped her onto the wooden landing stage he said, 'That was the best payment I've ever received.'

When she asked if he knew the whereabouts of the red and white wells he offered to show her the way, and so they walked together along a path through woodland until they reached two huge old yew trees.

'There,' he said, pointing to a thatched hut, 'that is where the keeper of the red well lives and further up the hill is where her sister tends the white well.'

When he turned to leave she asked, 'Shall I see you again, Darius?'

'I will always be at your service, Luna.' He bowed his head and then walked away back towards the landing stage.

Luna was nervous when approaching the red well and knocked tentatively on the door. Hearing a booming voice shout, 'Is that a fairy I hear tapping or little mouse nibbling the thatch?'

Luna knocked again more forcefully.

'Come in, come in and state your name.'

She pushed the door open. 'I am Luna and was told to come here by your sister in the cave across the water. She said I shall look into the black well and know something—I'm not quite sure what.'

To her amazement the woman sitting by the fire did not look in the least surprised on hearing this. 'Did she indeed? Well I've been waiting many moons for you.' She pushed long grey hair back from her thin face and beckoned with her forefinger. 'Come here, child.' And when Luna had gone to stand before her, she added with a frown, 'You're not quite what I had in mind, but if my old sister says you're the one then I'll not argue with her.'

Another woman, also with long grey hair and a thin face, soon joined them and she too scrutinized Luna with a doubtful expression. 'Well, I suppose our old sister knows what she's talking about.'

'Won't know until we've put her to the test,' said She of the Red.

'Hmm—' her sister of the white looked quizzically at Luna '—did she consult anything when she told you this?'

Wondering what she meant, Luna shrugged. 'She looked at a kind of marble ball.'

'How big was this?' the old woman asked.

'Sort of—' Luna cupped her right hand and looked down at it '—big enough to fit in one hand like that.' She raised her head and saw both women beaming at her.

'You must be the one,' said She of the Red.

'Definitely,' agreed She of the White. Seeing Luna yawning she fetched a bowl of fish and vegetables for her to eat while her sister made a bed of dried sweet grass in a corner of the dwelling.

They both fussed over her, insisting she must sleep before seeing the other well. 'Or, rather, we should say, the place where it is buried,' said She of the Red.

Luna fell asleep wondering if she would need to dig into the earth and dreamed she was down in a deep hole in the ground, scrabbling frantically at the loose earth and rocks that were falling down every time she tried to get out.

The following morning the three of them left the small hut and walked through some trees to a clearing in which was a circle of stones. From there they went around a large yew tree and stood before a pile of rocks.

'It's been buried under there since the foreigners left last winter,' She of the White said, scuffing some dead leaves with the toe of her shoe. 'Local boys have been making a mess of it ever since. I'm afraid that's what boys do, destructive young so-and-sos.'

Luna said, 'I shall need some strong men to lift those rocks and—' she bent to look closer '—that looks like a statue of Minerva who's seen better days.'

A chuckle from behind made her look round to find Darius with a thick rope hanging over one shoulder. 'I've come to offer my services,' he said.

'Do you know this man, Luna?' She of the White asked with a frown.

'He is the boatman who brought me here. Your sister is his friend.'

'Is she indeed?' She of the White looked Darius up and down.

'The wise lady in the cave has been good to me and I have tried to do favours for her in return.' Darius smiled reassuringly, then added, 'Your sister asked me to be ready with my boat to bring Luna to the island and to assist her in any way she needs once here.' He glanced down at the rope. 'I guessed this would be useful if you wish to clear the rubble from the well.'

The two old women exchanged meaningful looks and nodded in unison.

Luna said she would be grateful for his help.

The work took several days to complete. First some large rocks had to be removed and then the statue was pulled upright. After that a large slab of stone was lifted slowly and carefully to reveal what appeared to be a circle of shiny black stone, surrounded by lighter stone.

The sight of it took Luna by surprise, despite having been told it was the black well. She knelt down on the edge and, looking at the round hole of darkness, saw a figure walking towards her. 'I see a man holding what appears to be two pieces of wood tied together to form a cross.'

Darius, who was standing behind her, said, 'He sounds like a follower of the new religion I've heard about. Many people are converting to it.'

'The most important thing,' said She of the White, gesturing towards Luna, 'is that we have a keeper of the dark well again.'

Darius helped Luna build a small thatched dwelling that also covered the well so she could keep guard of it by night and day. He stayed nearby in a small shelter at night, keeping guard and spreading the word of her arrival by day while ferrying passengers to and from the island.

Sitting by her fire one evening, after they had eaten a fish he had caught and brought to her, she admitted how much she missed her family. 'It's not just my mother and brothers,' she explained, 'I miss my father's joyful greeting whenever he saw me. Such a big handsome man you know and so—' she searched for the right word to describe him '—so exuberant, you could tell where he was in the villa or the vineyard, or anywhere within earshot, because he would be laughing and talking so loudly.'

'And his wife?' Darius asked.

'Oh very different, yes, very different indeed!' Luna shook her head, remembering the whippings she had suffered for any petty misdemeanour such as being too slow to fetch something, or for laughing with her brothers within earshot of the mistress when she was taking her rest in the afternoon.

Darius looked pensively into the fire for a few moments then said, 'I know how hard it is to be a slave.'

With a surprised look for the telltale scar from a ring on his neck, she asked, 'Were you a slave too?'

He gave a mirthless laugh. 'Oh no, not me. I fell in love with a maid who worked at the villa a long way over there.' He pointed across the water to the north. 'It was a beautiful place owned by an important General of the Roman army. Like many another lowly soldier I was employed as a glorified watchman to guard his hearth and home from pilfering locals who stole the occasional bunch of grapes, or something equally valueless.'

Although desperate to know more, Luna waited while he stared into the fire again.

'We ran away together,' he eventually said, with a sigh. 'We travelled down this way and lived on a small island for—' he shrugged '—quite a while. We caught fish and ate plants in the summers, and we managed quite well in the winters too, although food was scarce as you know.' He swallowed. 'Then in the third winter, she gave birth to a boy.' He wiped a tear from the side of his long straight nose. 'All blue he was. Never took breath. My dear one cried and cried. I thought she'd never stop.' He spread his hands helplessly. 'I didn't know what to do. Then her legs swelled and she was red hot and ranting wildly. I went to the nearest village for help and a woman came with me to see her, but it was too late.' He shrugged. 'Birthing fever, she said. Happens all the time, she said. Nothing you can do she said…' his words trailed into sobs and he wept.

After a while Luna moved closer and put her hand on his shaking shoulder until he was calm again and then she said, 'I have been so grateful to you for staying nearby at night to guard me while I settle in. I wonder if we could make it a more permanent arrangement? We could build you a better dwelling next to this one and we could help each other. We could be family for each other, if you see what I mean.' Then, thinking he might get the wrong idea about her proposal and guess her secret love for him, added, 'You never know, one day you might find another woman you like and then you could leave here and go to live with her.'

'I should like to be your family.' He smiled and took her hand. 'I won't offer to be your father, or your brother, but I could be your uncle I suppose. I would be very happy living next to you; so long as you will allow me to be your protector and provider of fish as well as ferryman to the people.'

'That's settled then, Uncle Darius!' Luna exclaimed happily.

During the next few days he built a small dwelling with a thatched roof and bed of dried sweet grasses inside it. When the house was finished she stood surveying it and said, 'I shall feel much safer knowing my new uncle will be close at hand if any of my father's men come looking for me.'

Actually, the fear she might be found and taken to a foreign land lingered on, as did the knowledge that her father's wife would not only whip her severely, but also make sure she was sold for men's sexual pleasure and she continued to be nervous of all people other than Darius. She was especially nervous whenever he went off to the landing point to see if anyone needed to be ferried to one of the villages in the wetland.

The two keepers of the other wells were the first she came to trust and it was to them that she went when overwhelmed with anxiety about her mother and brothers. The two older women reassured her that her family would be pleased she had escaped. They also made up a story regarding her background, telling local people that the girl who had recently arrived was their niece whose mother had died.

There was one man, named Thorus, who frequently asked questions about her. He stared at her with narrowed eyes, asking from which clan and which waterside village she had come and also made plain his disapproval of the resurrection of the dark well.

One day, after Thorus had been snooping around her house, she knelt by the well and, looking into the flat dark surface, saw it was he who had covered it with rocks, accidentally knocking down the statue in the process. She also saw him destroying the stone building dedicated to Minerva on top of the sacred mound and knew he wished to be the high priest of the sacred island and hold sway over it now the foreigners had gone.

When Luna told the keepers of the red and white wells what she had seen, they both shook their heads sadly. 'We know he wishes to take power,' said She of the White.

'But we are helpless to stop him,' said She of the Red.

Luna was perplexed and asked, 'Why does he want to have power over the island?'

She of the Red shrugged. 'To be important among our people I suppose; and if he has control of our most sacred place, then he will be so.'

She of the White gave a great sigh and said, 'He won't succeed for long. Others before him have tried and after they die or leave, the land remains unsullied by their arrogance and is just as strong as it ever was.' The old woman leaned forward excitedly, 'Take the mound for example, my old grandmother's grandmother told her that long, long ago it was called The Great One and was sacred to our people before the foreigners came with their temples, before the priests came with oak trees—so long ago that no one remembers when it was. But at that time the people saw the mound was made in the shape of a woman one side and a man on the other.'

Luna exclaimed in amazement at this, 'Really! Is that true?'

'It is indeed. Earthquakes have since changed its shape, as have the hands of invaders—' She of the White sighed '—who always want to put a temple or shrine to their gods on top of it, but you can still see the figures, albeit not so clearly. And above all, the power is still there.'

'And what's more,' She of the Red straightened her back and said proudly, 'our forebears buried their dead in a cave within the heart of The Great One, where the female and male met.'

'So remember— ' She of the White pointed her forefinger warningly at Luna '—be careful what promise you make on that mound, for you are swearing on the sacred burial ground of your ancestors.'

Feeling honoured to be part of this extraordinary place Luna thanked them for their kindness and returned to the dwelling by the dark well.

Sitting by the fire that evening she told Darius all she had learned from the sisters at the red and white wells and he agreed she would be wise to avoid antagonising Thorus and should attempt to live in peace with him. 'I spent my early years learning to kill,' he said. 'Believe me, fighting and making war is a waste of the precious gift of life. Live and let live, respect others as you would have them respect you.'

'That's very wise, Uncle Darius,' she said.

When the season had changed and become colder, with no sign of anyone arriving in search of her, she began to relax her guard with the people who came for guidance from the well and soon found she enjoyed telling them what she saw in the dark surface of the water.

Gradually more and more visitors came for guidance and by the time two more winter seasons had passed, it was generally accepted by everyone that she was the keeper of the dark well. One evening when sharing food with Darius, she said, 'I know I'm safe now, old Thorus greeted me respectfully as Lady of the Dark Well.'

'That's not respectful!' He replied with a frown. 'Maiden is what he should call you.'

She felt a hot blush colouring her face. 'I think many people assume…

' her words trailed into silence.

'Assume what?'

She shrugged. 'You know …' she swallowed and looked into the fire. ' They assume we're sort of…'

'Sort of … Oh, I see what you mean! Well, I realise you're no longer a child, in fact you … you're a beautiful woman now.' He was now the one to blush and look into the fire. 'I'm sure you would wish for a younger man than I, would you not?'

She saw his shaking hand and reddened neck and wondered if perhaps he might return the feelings of love she had harboured in her heart since their first meeting.

'I have no desire for anyone younger than you,' she said.

He turned to look at her with love shining in his eyes and took her hand. 'I suppose we could prove old Thorus right, if that would please you, Maiden of the Dark Well.'

She felt the happiness welling up in her heart and laughed as she pulled him to her.

The following day they walked to see the keepers of the other wells and asked if they would climb the mound with them and witness their joining of hands. Both sisters were overjoyed and agreed enthusiastically. She of the White said, 'We would love to witness you make your pledge to one another on The Great One—as we like to call the sacred mound. Unfortunately Thorus and his men are busy on the top, they've almost demolished the Roman temple up there.'

She of the Red said, 'We can keep out of their way if we go to the spot that was once the entrance to the tomb of the ancestors—the most sacred place of all.'

The next day the two sisters led them, rather slowly and breathlessly, to some large rocks protruding from the earth and there they promised to share their lives, their joys and troubles for as long as they both lived. She of the White tied their hands together with trails of ivy, while She of the Red placed wreaths of greenery and flowers on their heads they all laughed and cried with joy.

On their return to the dwelling they celebrated with a small feast and Luna entertained them with all the songs she knew, while Darius surprised them with the beauty of his voice as he sang with her.

During the following days it was evident that word of their coupling had spread and local people brought gifts of food, firewood and other useful things. When Thorus came one morning to give them a blanket made by his wife they thanked him with genuine gratitude and expressed the hope they would all live in harmony on the sacred island.

'I too wish to live without strife,' Thorus said. Adding with a gesture towards the blanket, 'My wife has long wished to be a good neighbour, but felt shy of approaching you.'

Luna guessed the woman would like to consult the dark well and feared her husband would not approve. 'I would be honoured to receive a visit from your wife,' she said solemnly. 'I believe good neighbours make for a peaceful life.'

He agreed and went on his way towards the hill.

When his wife appeared a few days later, Luna greeted her cordially and agreed to her request for a consultation with the well. The vision that appeared was disconcerting. First Luna saw the woman embracing a man of shorter stature than Thorus with darker hair and beard and then she saw the woman holding a baby and laughing with joy.

'I see you with a child,' Luna said.

The woman gasped and asked, 'Are you sure this will be so?'

'I can only tell you what I see?' Luna replied.

'I am barren ... I mean I had thought ...' the woman swallowed and bit her lip. She was silent for a while and then asked, 'Do you keep these sights to yourself?'

'I tell only the person who asks me to look into the well for them.'

'And no one else?'

Luna placed both hands over her heart. 'I promise you that no one will ever hear this from me.'

'I thank you, Lady of the Dark Well. My husband was not pleased when you came. He feared you would undermine his position of authority.'

'I wish your husband no harm. I seek no power over others. I must fulfil my destiny to offer guidance of the well to all those who need it, that is all. While doing this I ask only to live in peace with my man and my two dear friends, the keepers of the other wells, She of the White and She of the Red.'

'I too wish to live in peace. I will do my best to reassure Thorus he has nothing to fear from you.'

Luna said, 'You could say I told you that a miracle might happen if you stand beneath the full moon and wish for a child.'

The woman brightened. 'I thank you, Lady of the Dark Well.'
While watching the woman walk away Luna wondered how soon her own baby would come to live within her. She looked again in the well, but as it sometimes did, it stayed a flat black pool of water and gave her no answer.

❖   ❖   ❖

Life on the sacred island was peaceful thereafter. The keepers of the three sacred wells lived their lives with no interference from Thorus and his followers. Each group tolerated the other and respected their beliefs.

As for Luna and Darius, their life together was a wonder to them both and each would frequently exclaim to other how happy they were and how surprised to find themselves the beloved of such a wonderful person.

When their first child was expected Darius was very anxious for Luna's safety and fussed over her, insisting she should not carry heavy logs or bunches of firewood and must not tax herself with too many hours looking into the well each day.

She knew the reason for his anxiety and was also fearful, knowing how many women died giving birth and also how frequently the babies, especially the boys, died either at birth or soon after. She longed for their child to be born, but at the same time, just in case death would bring this happy life to an end, she also dreaded it.

When the time came she survived the travail with the sisters from the other wells in attendance, one holding her from behind while she leant against her and the other kneeling between her legs to help the baby into the world.

Darius, who had been in such a state of turmoil and fear before the event, was a perfect example of calmness and encouragement until, on seeing his newborn son, he burst into tears.

When Luna had recovered sufficiently, they carried their son to the rocks on the sacred mound and gave thanks, both for his arrival and for Luna's survival. She understood that while Thorus and his people held ceremonies nearby, or even on the same spot, the power on the mound was strong enough to sustain them both. Holding her son aloft, Luna said, 'We present our son to the ancestors who walked this earth before us. We hope he will follow their path with a true heart and good spirit. His name is Aven. Long may he live!'

'Long may he live!' the sisters of the red and white shouted in unison.

❖   ❖   ❖

The seasons changed, sometimes one winter was harsher than another and one summer hotter and drier than another, but time passed as it always had. Their son had grown into a sturdy little boy when a fine strong daughter was born one bright spring morning just as the sunlight beamed through the doorway. They named this girl Dawn and were delighted with her.

Everyone admired Dawn's cleverness, her beauty and her bright spirit. She was quick to learn words and entertained everyone with her winning ways. She learned to walk early and was running about unaided, chattering gaily when another daughter was born two winters later.

This little girl came earlier than Luna had predicted and she was deeply troubled when the pains began. The travail was much shorter than the others and when a tiny creature slid into life she gasped in surprise to hear a feeble cry. Although sure the little girl could not survive long, she held her close to her own heart, hoping it would give her strength to live.

Luna could see from their sad expressions that both sisters of the red and white wells thought the baby had little chance of survival. She also saw them peer at the purple birthmark in the centre of her baby's forehead and shake their heads.

She was moved when Darius wept on seeing his new daughter and agreed when he said, 'I fear, my love, she has left the womb too soon and is not destined to stay with us for long. '

Although not wishing to share his opinion, she had to agree, until, having tied the baby close to her chest and wrapped a warm cloak around them both she went to consult the well. There in the black water she was surprised to see the old woman in the cave who had told her long ago that she must come the sacred island. Wondering what this meant, she saw a small figure kneeling by the well, waving her arms and almost falling in with excitement. When the child turned to smile at her, she saw a purple mark in exactly the same place as that on her new daughter's forehead. She called Darius and told him, 'She will live and take her place after me as keeper of the well.'

Darius was overjoyed, 'I should like her called after my mother, Flora,' he said, 'she was tall and strong both in body and spirit.'

With a smile down at the tiny child asleep on her chest, she said, 'I fear she may not follow her grandmother in body, but I have hope for her spirit.'

She of the Red and She of the White were extremely happy and joined in the celebration of Flora's arrival with singing and feasting around a big fire on the meeting ground. When Luna looked around for Dawn and having failed to find her by the fire with the other children, she handed the baby to Darius and went in search of her other daughter.

Eventually, after a long while, Luna found Dawn hiding behind their house. Seeing how miserable the girl was she tried to explain that this new sister was not more important than her and also attempted to put her arms around her, but the little girl pulled away and would not be cuddled.

As time went by the only sadness in Luna's otherwise happy life was Dawn's continued rejection of her sister. Little Flora was a delightful child who adored her older sister despite being ignored by her most of the time. Aven, who was a quiet thoughtful boy, was a great comfort to his parents and much loved by both his sisters.

The keeper of the white well died in the darkest days of the coldest winter in living memory and her sister, who had seemed in robust health shortly before, did not waken one morning a few days later.

After they had been buried at the foot of sacred mound, two of their nieces arrived from their village in the wetlands and were soon ensconced in the abodes at the red and white wells. Both women, one of similar age to Luna and the other much younger, soon became good friends with her. Neither of the new keepers of the wells had born children, having chosen to remain virgins after seeing their mother die in childbirth, but they loved Luna's children and were immediately considered as aunts by them.

❖   ❖   ❖

Life continued without serious incident for many seasons. Luna was much respected throughout the area, as was Darius, who had been elected an elder of the clan and was relied upon for a balanced view in the disputes that came before the council moots.

Luna was very grateful for this happy, peaceful and uneventful life. She had already given thanks for her good fortune one day when her son Aven came running to her. Too breathless to speak, he pointed back along the path and soon she saw two men carrying a bier made of birch branches tied together. She knew without being told that it was Darius they carried.

She heard the voices of the men who had brought him to her, but not their words or the meaning of them. When they left she sat holding his cold hand and sang for him.

Later, when Aven explained tearfully how the two fishermen had found Darius dead in the water, she listened impassively.

'There was no sign of the boat.' Aven paused to wipe his eyes. 'No one knows what happened. Most people think the boat hit one of those trees that have been floating in the water since the last storm. Some of the big ones are lying on the mud submerged and ...' he broke down into sobs.

Luna held her son close and laid her head on his shoulder. Although wanting to weep with him, she could not shed any tears and sat with dry eyes, aching for her son, her daughters and for herself.

The whole clan grieved for the man they had respected and had accepted as one of their own, despite knowing he had been born one of the invaders from Rome. They buried him with honour at the foot of the sacred mound and celebrated his life with song and feasting around a fire on the meeting ground.

Luna now questioned her own gift of the sight. She, who had looked into the still black water so often and seen the tragic loss in the future of others, had not seen this most terrible of disasters coming to her. How could she ever look in the well again in the hope of giving guidance when she had so evidently failed for herself? She covered the well with two large flat pieces of wood and sank into such an agony of grief for the man she had loved that she fully expected to die from the pain.

After three seasons, realising she had not died of grief and had learned to live for the sake of her children, she helped local people

144

with her knowledge of healing plants, but refused to look in the well for them, explaining, 'The pain of the present prevents me from seeing the future.'

She was a good mother to Aven and encouraged him to take over as ferryman. She tried to be a good mother to her daughters, both of whom were distraught on losing their father. While the grief brought her closer to Flora, it seemed to open up an even greater chasm between Dawn and herself.

One day, when the earth had warmed enough for the plants to grow and the birds were collecting twigs and moss to make their nests, a young stranger, with red hair and his beard not yet formed, came on Aven's ferry from the land where Luna once lived. The young man had nothing with him other than two pieces of wood tied together in a cross and looked so exhausted that Aven brought him to Luna, saying, 'I fear he will die soon without nourishment, My Mother.'

Luna took him into her dwelling and gave him food and drink. When she asked his name, he said, 'Please call me Brother, my lady.'

After a while, having eaten and regained some strength, his eyes glittered as he said, 'My God came to me in a dream. It was a wondrous experience. He told me I must come here to this most sacred island. He said I must carry a cross, such as the one on which his son was crucified and I must build a place wherein he could be worshipped.'

Her heart sank at the thought of a new god with new priests and new ceremonies. She knew there would be trouble if he built anything on the sacred mound. The priests, who had long ago replaced the Roman temple with large stones that lit up at sunrise of midsummer's day, would not take kindly to the newcomer's arrival and would fight to stop any new construction. This pale young man, whose green eyes burned with such passionate conviction, could inadvertently cause great disruption and destroy the peaceful life of her people.

For the first time since Darius died Luna wondered if she should look in the well. She gazed at the far end of the room where the wooden planks were laid on top of the rocks surrounding the dark circle of water and was tempted.

As she rose from sitting beside the fire to walk to the well, the words Darius spoke many years earlier came to her, *'Believe me, fighting and making war is a waste of the precious gift of life. Live and let live, respect others as you would have them respect you.'*

She knew Darius would have been kind to this young man and respected his certainty that his god had directed him here, just as he had understood her own belief that her destiny was here with the dark well. Deciding she had received a message from her dear man and therefore did not need the well, she pointed through the open doorway and said, 'I suggest you could make your god's building near here. Make it far enough away for us to each have space of our own and then we must each agree to live alongside in tolerance and peace.'

He jumped up excitedly and walked outside. Looking at the clearing in the trees nearby, he said, 'I'm sure anywhere here would be acceptable.'

'You agree that others have the right to celebrate their beliefs on the great hill over there?'

He shaded his eyes from the sun while peering up at the circle of huge stones on the top of the sacred mound and paused to think, then said, 'My dearest wish is to tell people the good news of my god and his son who was made man to save us all from sin. I would wish everyone to know the truth, but, yes, I agree others have the right to celebrate their beliefs wherever they choose.

She relaxed, feeling sure they could live in harmony. 'I'm not familiar with the word sin, but I do know evil when I see it and also, even if my truth is not your truth, I respect your right to believe it. If you can be tolerant of me, then I can be tolerant of you. '

He agreed to her terms and thanked her for her kindness. Within days he began building his chapel a short walk from her dwelling. Soon several people joined him and together they made a building with the trunks of trees and mud, topped with thatch on the roof.

Luna heard the man called Brother telling anyone who would listen about this god and the son called Jesus He sent down to live on earth. She enjoyed the stories of miracles that Jesus performed and watched with interest as more and more people went to hear about them.

The priests who made ceremonies on the sacred mound were not pleased with the arrival of this newcomer, but they too agreed to be tolerant in the interests of harmony on the island.

Dawn, her older daughter was intrigued by this new arrival and went often to see Brother and listen to his preaching. When asked by Luna why she did this, she raised one side of her upper lip in the usual insolent sneer and replied, 'I'm obviously not good enough to take over from you as keeper of the well, so I'll see who does want me.'

Luna tried in vain to explain that Flora, despite being the younger girl, had inherited the ability to see in the well and therefore must fulfil her destiny. Nothing would persuade Dawn to accept this and she stayed away until one day she arrived at the dwelling carrying a small wooden cross.

'I have been baptised with a new name.' Dawn announced defiantly. ' My name is Mary and I am a Christian now.'

Luna felt sure this was a statement of defiance rather than deeply felt belief, but did not express this opinion. 'I am pleased you have found your truth.' She also wanted to say that she hoped Dawn would be more content now that she had a new name and a new religion, instead, she said, 'I only wish you to be happy, My Daughter.'

When Dawn left the dwelling to go and pray with Brother, Luna knew she must now consult the well. She removed the wooden planks and laid them to one side, then, with a deep sigh, she knelt on the familiar stone.

Any hope of seeing the situation between her daughters resolved amicably in the future was quickly dashed. It was clear that Dawn would continue to resent Flora and cause trouble for her in the future.

147

She saw Dawn emerging from the chapel with a young man and was pleased until she saw time had passed and her daughter was cowering away from him and weeping.

A short while later Flora, who had detected signs of movement around the well, asked Luna to look in the well for her. 'There is a young man from the clan across the wetlands,' Flora said, with attempted indifference.

'I would have thought you knew your own heart,' Luna said, while eagerly pulling the cover off the well.

Looking into the dark water she said, 'I see you holding the hand of a broad shouldered man with golden hair and beard. You have flowers in your hair,' she paused to look at her daughter who was smiling joyfully. Returning her attention to the well, she went on, 'Now I see you laughing with two young children.'

When the picture had faded, Luna beckoned to her daughter. 'Now, Flora, tell me what you see.'

'I see you looking very happy, My Mother. You are looking into this well and giving guidance to many people.'

'How strange!' Luna exclaimed. 'I can see you and you can see me.' She hugged her daughter. 'I knew you would be the one to follow me.'

When word spread that the lady of the dark well was giving guidance once more, many people came to see her. Although never happy again, as she had been with Darius sharing her life, she found contentment living with the dark well beside her.

She watched Dawn, now Mary, marry her young man in the Christian chapel, then sang and danced with Aven and his beloved, and finally celebrated on the sacred mound with Flora and her golden haired young man.

Luna delighted in Flora's happiness with her beloved man and in due course, adored their noisy, laughing children, playing with them and teaching them songs from her childhood during their many visits with her.

Mary was a great source of worry. Every baby she carried was either born dead or died after birth and her unhappiness was clear for all to see. Luna was careful to keep the peace with her, no matter how difficult and critical her older daughter could sometimes be with her. While never criticising the man she knew was beating her older daughter, she made ointment made with the large leaves from the plant that eased bruises and gave it to her regularly.

Time passed and one by one the people of her own time died. When each of her cousins were buried at night in the secret cave under the sacred mound, Luna accompanied the corpses and witnessed their successors pledge their lives to guarding and keeping the sacred well. Each time she looked around her at the bones and skulls of her predecessors she thought her own body would soon be laid to rest among them.

In fact the wait to join them was longer than expected. For many seasons Luna lived on and by the time that kneeling to look into the well became very painful she was renowned and highly respected for her great age. When, eventually, she admitted her difficulties to Flora, they agreed Flora and her family would move into the dwelling that housed the dark well while Luna would live in the smaller home attached to it on one side.

This decision caused a ripple of anger from Dawn, now known as Mary, who accused Luna of always preferring her younger daughter. Knowing her older daughter's deep unhappiness while also tied to a cruel husband, Luna showed no reaction, despite her distress, and the matter was soon forgotten.

Several seasons passed in which Flora was accepted as the keeper of the dark well and proved herself to be a gifted seer. Luna meanwhile, spent her days looking back at her life, sometimes sitting near the great yews, if the weather was kind and sitting by the fire when it was not.

On a sunny morning, soon after the celebration of spring, Luna felt sure her time would soon be over. For a while she sat in a warm spot close to the dwelling, enjoying some of her happiest memories. Thinking of her family in the Roman villa, she wondered what became of them. Her father would have enjoyed a good life back in his own country, but what of her mother and brothers? Once again, as on countless times before, she longed to know what had befallen them after she ran away in fear of being punished and of being sent far away to a cruel fate in a foreign land.

On impulse, in what she thought would be a vain attempt at one last vision; she hobbled with a stick into the dwelling that was now her daughter's home. Seeing only her young granddaughter playing with a rag doll, she greeted her and then went to the well and bent over it as far as she dared.

The little girl cried out, 'Take care, Grandma!'

'Fear not, child,' Luna reassured her. Ignoring the searing pain in her knees, she knelt on the stone and peered into the darkness.

The sight came immediately and so shocked her it caused her weary heart to falter. She said, 'Tell your mother to come quickly, child! Tell her they will cover the well with a great stone building... .' She stopped, hearing a familiar voice calling her name, 'Luna! Luna!'

'I'm coming, Darius,' she said, 'I'm coming.'

Chapter Nine

Louisa was feeling overwhelmed with emotion. She sat staring at the sky, wondering if it was possible for spirits to be reunited after death, as Luna and Darius appeared to have been. She thought Luna might have been dreaming while dying, but on the other hand… And so her mind went back and forth, first believing the couple had met again beyond the grave, and then deciding it was not possible.

Looking around her and seeing no one, she felt disappointed, before realising to her horror that she had been hoping to see Edward Francis. In a firm voice she told herself this behaviour was unacceptable! He was a married man and she should not be harbouring expectations of seeing him whenever she came to the abbey ruins. He had been friendly to her once or twice and had very kindly lent the Bath chair to her aunt; now she could forget him.

While walking back to the house she heard children laughing in a garden on the other side of the wall. This sound always caused a deep ache within her and yet she felt able to listen to it for hours.

Memories of those few golden years with her son flooded her mind and she was still thinking of him on arrival in her aunt's room.

'Did you see a vision, Louisa?'

'I did, Aunt. It was a lovely experience, although sad when she died at the end.'

'We each—must have a—sad ending to—our story. We are mortal—after all—are we not?'

'We are, dear Aunt Agnes.' She wondered if the possibility of spirits being reunited should be mentioned and decided it might not be appropriate: Aunt Rosemary, on the other hand, might be very interested in the subject; and, now she came to think of it, would also enjoy coming with her to the abbey.

'I thought you were—going to tell me—about the vision.'

'This time it was about a girl who was half Roman.'

'Half gypsy—did you say?'

'No, Aunt, her father was a Roman general during the time they occupied England.'

'Good heavens! Did he—wear a—toga?'

'I don't know. I expect he did.' Louisa was wishing she had not embarked on the story, but felt compelled to continue. 'He had been recalled. The army was leaving and the girl wanted to stay here. She was afraid of what might happen when she reached Rome.'

'Such a beautiful place—I have seen—pictures of the Vatican—and a big building—I forget—what it is called.'

'The coliseum?'

'Yes, that's it.'

Louisa was wondering if she should continue when her aunt said, 'Well! What happened—to the girl?'

'Her name was Luna and she was destined to become the guardian of the dark well.' Louisa told the story up until the final moments.

The old lady sat looking thoughtful then said, 'So she knew—the abbey would be built.'

'Yes, I felt a little sad about that.'

'But she allowed—the young man—to build his little—church there—in the first—place, Louisa. Without her—generous—gesture we would not—have had the abbey there.' The old lady waved her good hand in the air while adding, 'Well, we don't have it —we only have—the ruins now.'

Listening to this slow but lucid speech Louisa wondered again why her aunt feigned dumbness and unable to bear it any longer, said, 'I'm so sorry, my dear Aunt, I really wish you would explain why we have to pretend you can't hear or speak.'

The colour drained from the old woman's face. Her mobile hand clasped the paralysed one. 'Very well —I will tell you—my reason.'

She paused to take a breath. 'I heard—when first ill—they thought I would—die—shocking—' her chest wheezed alarmingly '—so—shocking—wanted—die—quickly,' her mouth was distorted as she struggled to breath. After a moment she continued breathlessly, 'Will…' she gave a strangulated gasp and then was suddenly still.

Louisa thought for a terrible moment that her aunt had suffered another stroke and had gone to meet her husband Wilfred. On feeling the feeble pulse in the thin wrist she fetched a glass of water and helped her to sip it.

They sat in silence for a while, until, thinking her aunt had recovered from almost dying, asked, 'Did you see your Wilfred?'

This question was evidently perplexing. 'George, it was—George.'

'Did George say something to upset you?'

The old lady nodded.

'But surely that does not prevent us from telling Edwina of your recovery…'

'No. No!' The old lady became very agitated and Louisa stroked the papery skin on her hand while reassuring her there was no need to tell her daughter if that was her wish.

'She—tell—him—you—see.' The old lady's chest wheezed as she struggled for breath. 'She does not—know—he wants—me—to—change it.'

Louisa wondered if George had wanted her to change her will and started to say, 'Surely Edwina wouldn't go against your wishes,' but seeing the agitation her words engendered, she stopped and said, 'Very well. I won't let anyone know.'

The old lady's distorted face was ashen white and her good hand grabbed Louisa's as she wheezed, 'Promise—me!'

'Very well, Aunt, I promise this will be our secret. No one will know you can understand what is being said and can talk perfectly well yourself.'

The faded eyes shone with emotion and one side of the old lady's mouth trembled. 'Thank—you… Better—this—way. Leave—things be.'

Both were silent for a long while. At first Louisa watched for signs of a stroke and blamed herself for asking such evidently distressing questions. On hearing the breathing settle into the regular, albeit slightly wheezy, pattern of sleep, she relaxed a little, hoping she had not caused the old lady's condition to deteriorate and all would be well.

While sitting beside her sleeping aunt, Louisa wondered what reason George could have for wanting his mother-in-law to change her will. She assumed the estate would be divided equally between Emily and Edwina. Perhaps he wanted to change the division, property to Edwina and money to Emily or vice versa? Could he want her to cut out Emily altogether? It seemed a strange situation and difficult to fathom. Whatever the reason was, it was upsetting for her aunt and therefore she would support her.

Although the old lady showed no ill effects from the incident, in fact she seemed more alive than ever, Louisa watched over her with even more care than usual during the following days. On the Sunday, when her aunt insisted on going to church, Louisa attempted to dissuade her, but soon admitted defeat.

They arrived early for the service and were, therefore, able to take up a position whereby Louisa could sit on the end of a pew with the wheel chair next to her, in a place where it would not obstruct the passage of other worshippers.

'Perfect!' the old lady whispered conspiratorially, when Louisa bent to rearrange a blanket over her aunt's knees. 'I can see—everyone—coming and going.'

Many local people waved to the old lady and several spoke to Louisa in a hushed voice before taking their places on the pews.

When a woman entered with three children, Louisa was thinking what an attractive family it was when a man walked in and sat beside them. Although carrying a felt hat, not the usual battered panama, there was no doubt this was Edward Francis wearing his Sunday best and her heart missed a beat. She kept her eyes averted from that moment, hoping he would not see her.

The service seemed interminable. The vicar's sermon was the longest and dreariest she had ever heard. When the final hymn had been sung and the congregation was dispersing, Edward Francis appeared next to them. 'Good morning, Mrs Govern, I'm so pleased to see you here.' He bent over the old lady and clasped her hand, then turned to Louisa, 'Good morning, Mrs Wendon, I trust you are enjoying the spring weather.'

'I am, I thank you, Mr Francis.'

'I hope we may meet again in the abbey grounds.'

Louisa smiled politely. 'Indeed, I hope so.' She turned to an elderly lady who wished to speak to her aunt and explained, 'Mrs Govern has lost her speech. She has been unwell, but is much improved and we are so grateful to Mr Francis who has lent us this chair.'

Several other people came to speak to them and when leaving the church they met the vicar, who was bidding his parishioners goodbye as he usually did after the service.

On their return to the house; upstairs where no one could hear her, the old lady said, 'You have been—very quiet—Louisa. Are you unwell?'

'No, Aunt Agnes, I am quite well, thank you.'

'In love?'

Louisa looked into the surprisingly alive blue eyes and replied firmly, 'Certainly not!'

A maid brought in the trays of luncheon for them and they were silent until she had left the room.

'Chicken!' the old lady exclaimed delightedly.

While cutting up the food Louisa was thankful for the interruption and hoped the subject of love, no matter how flippantly, would not be broached again. She had now seen Edward Francis with his wife and children and she would no longer allow herself any feeling of

155

attraction to him. He was simply a kind gentleman who happened to be dowsing in the abbey grounds when she was there and whilst interested in her visions, he was not at all interested in her. Henceforth there would be no difficulty if she met him by the ruins.

When her aunt had eaten her meal, she asked, 'Has Rosemary read—the tea-leaves—for you yet?'

'No, aunt, not yet.' Louisa chuckled, knowing the old lady's mind was set on romance.

The following day was Monday. While watching Louisa put her sketching book and pencils into a bag, the old lady said, 'I hope you see—Luna's daughter today —I would so love—to know her story.'

'I may not see anything, Aunt dear, and if I do there is no way of knowing whose story it will be.' Louisa looked at her aunt whose eyes shone within her pink face and wondered which of them was more excited. She went and kissed the old lady's forehead. 'The housekeeper has said she will come if you ring the bell.'

'I shall do perfectly well on my own,' the old lady insisted. Peering up at her she frowned. 'Do you not think—it time you softened—your mourning attire?'

With a sigh, Louisa said, 'I am used to black, Aunt. I have worn it now almost continuously for six years.'

'For so long—too long.'

'First for my little Charlie, then three years later for my dear husband and now for my father.'

'I know it is only—a few months—since your dear—father's death but I do feel —you could wear —a prettier hat—and perhaps some—nice lace around your—neck. Go to the—wardrobe there—and bring me—the hat box—please.'

Louisa did as she was bid and soon a wide brimmed hat with a pale lilac chiffon drape around the crown was declared suitable. 'Not too frivolous—but charming—nevertheless,' the old lady said. She pointed to a dressing table drawer and Louisa found there several lace collars, one of which was decided upon.

'So much better!' the old lady declared. She reached up with her good hand and touched the silver locket now nestling against exquisite cream Italian lace. 'It looks perfect. Now go and—have an adventure!'

Louisa thought her aunt's speech was less laboured and said, 'You are definitely much better too, Aunt Agnes, I am so pleased,' then kissed her cheek and departed.

She made her way to the abbey ruins and sat in her usual place, which was bathed in sunshine. Raising her face to feel the warm rays she wondered if it was possible to control the vision and choose its subject. Like her aunt, she would like to know what happened to Flora and her family. Luna told her granddaughter about the stone church that would be built. Maybe she could....

Chapter Ten

She could hear her mother calling from the dwelling and sank lower onto her knees. She wanted to look secretly into the dark well, to know if Tamas loved her as she loved him. Tomorrow would be the celebration of spring and maybe he would declare himself to her.

Peering down into the black water she saw monks walking towards a beautiful array of bright colours under an arch. She had never seen such a wonderful sight. This, she thought, must be a vision of the heaven that the monks on the Tor believed in. No wonder they lived so piously if they thought their celibacy and devotion would be rewarded with such beauty after death! The picture became clearer and she could see the building was enormous with a vast vaulted ceiling supported by giant pillars, all adorned with an array of intricate carvings.

'Raven! What are you doing?'

The picture vanished and was replaced by the reflection of her mother's face distorted with fury.

'Well! Answer me, girl.'

Struck dumb with fear, Raven looked down at the stone slab on which she was kneeling.

'Might it have anything to do with the celebration tomorrow?'

Raven nodded.

'And the boy with red hair I've seen hanging about morning, noon and night?'

Raven mumbled that this was the case and waited for the next eruption of anger, but was surprised when her mother said, 'I suppose you'll make your own mistakes, just as I made mine. We each have our destined paths to follow.'

With a sigh of relief, Raven asked, 'You forgive me for looking in the well without your permission?'

'I'd have preferred to be with you to see what the image was.' Her mother took Raven's hand and led her to sit on a log near the dwelling, then went on, 'I've never let you look into the well without me at your side for a reason. Sometimes we see strange and frightening sights that cannot be explained.'

'I saw many monks in a huge, enormous building and they were looking at a vision of bright colours; it was very beautiful.'

Her mother was thoughtful for a moment then asked, 'Do you think it was a church—' she pointed to the stone building in the middle of the meeting place '—like that one?'

'It was not like that one, Mother, not at all. It was much, much bigger and very tall. I don't think anyone could build such a place as that. I think it must be the heaven I've heard people speak of.'

'You saw heaven! That is extraordinary!' Her mother sat in silence for a long time. Eventually, giving a shiver and pulling her woollen shawl around her shoulders, she said, 'I don't know what you saw, Daughter. I wish I had seen it too, but we can't always choose to see what we wish.' She smiled and touched her arm. 'There is one good thing to come out of this, my dear Raven. No matter what befalls tomorrow, I now know that you are gifted with the sight and when I die you will be able to take my place as keeper of the dark well.'

That night Raven lay awake for hours thinking about the sight in the well. When, eventually, she slept, her dreams were of the magnificent arches and carvings adorning the approach to a brightly coloured heaven.

In the early hours of morning, while the birds still slept, she crept out into the darkness and walked to meet her cousins close to the dwelling of their mother, the keeper of the red well.

The three girls each took a drink from the gushing spring known as the red well. After wiping her face because she feared the water might colour her skin, Raven asked, 'Do you know which of you will follow your mother as keeper here?'

Both girls shook their heads. The older one looked sheepish. 'I hope it's not me. I don't want to stay here for the rest of my days, keeping the place tidy and being nice to people all the time.'

'Well, nor do I!' Her young sister declared. 'I don't want to stay here day after day, offering pilgrims a drink before they climb The Sacred Mound and then giving them another one after they've done it.'

The older one made a face. 'And I'm tired of being treated by the monks as though we're some sort of silly country folk hanging on to the old ways of celebrating the end of winter and beginning of spring like we are today. And—' she pointed down at the gushing flow of water '—they look down their noses at us for believing in the sacred waters running from The Sacred Mound.' She shrugged. 'Maybe they're right. I don't know.'

'And yet,' Raven said, 'the monks have built their monastery on The Sacred Mound and, what's more, they drink the waters of both the red and white wells.'

'Everyone drinks the waters.' The younger cousin pointed out. 'I believe the flows from both springs meet and mingle on their way to other wells.'

At that moment a group of young people came walking up the path, whispering and giggling. Seeing them, Raven suggested they should follow or they would miss the celebrations.

The three girls left the well and walked up the path to the mound, taking care to avoid stones or roots hidden from sight in the darkness. On the way they passed the dwellings of monks and put their fingers to their lips, shushing one another and giggling. Then, keeping below the church on the top, they walked to some large boulders where a group of people were standing quietly in a circle.

When the first bird began chirruping there was an intake of breath and as the sky lightened and more birds joined in, so the people began singing, very quietly at first, but getting louder as the light increased, until dawn had broken and the sound of their voices filled the air.

Suddenly with a joyful whoop, a man, wrapped around with trails of ivy and a mask with horns on his head, jumped into the circle. He skipped around, bowing to all the girls until he reached Raven and then, grabbing hold of her hands, he pulled her in to dance with him.

She knew this was Tamas, whom she liked, and thought her heart would burst with joy and pride. They danced on and on while other men drew girls to join them, then they skipped and jigged down the path towards the meeting place. On reaching a clump of trees, Raven found herself pulled away from the crowd and made no resistance as she was led along a narrow trail through dense undergrowth to a sheltered place beneath overhanging rocks.

She saw the bright red of his hair hanging under the mask, she saw his deep golden eyes, felt his hands pulling her down onto a soft bed of sweet grasses and with a glad heart she joined with him in making love, until they fell asleep. On awakening they went to drink from the nearby stream and ate some nuts he had in the pouch at his waist. Soon they began kissing again, and loving again, then slept and drank from the stream and so on and so on, until the following morning.

At dawn, after saying he must keep an agreement to meet someone, he walked with her to the path leading to her dwelling and said, 'I bid you farewell, dear girl. I shall never forget this wonderful time we spent together.' To her astonishment, he turned and walked away.

Overwhelmed with hurt and disappointment, Raven stared after him, wondering if this was the usual way of men. After a few moments she sank down and sat with her back to the trunk of an ancient yew to weep and think about his words.

He had called her 'dear girl' and said he would never forget their wonderful time together, which was good, but there had been no mention of joining hands in celebration of their union, or even when they would meet again. Eventually, having decided he could not possibly have behaved as he did unless he wished to join hands with her, she felt calmer and washed her face in a small stream before following the path home.

On opening the door she was horrified to find her aunt and two cousins sitting with her mother. Seeing the anxious expressions on their faces replaced by relief as she walked in, she realised for the first time that they had been worried and stammered an apology.

Her mother burst into tears.

Her aunt screamed, 'How could you do this, you wicked girl? Your poor mother was convinced you had run away with that ginger headed, good-for-nothing boy. We have none of us slept for the worry. You have brought shame on my family and....'

Raven stopped listening. She heard her younger cousin give an embarrassed giggle and saw the older one roll her eyes and smirk. She clearly remembered seeing the latter embracing a boy just before being led off the path. She guessed, from the look on her cousin's face, that she too had made love that day, but had had the sense to go home at a reasonable time.

'I'm sorry I caused you so much worry,' Raven said, knowing there was little conviction in her voice. 'I lost track of time.'

'For a day and a night!' her aunt exclaimed incredulously.

Raven spread her hands in the air, unable to explain that she had been lost in a wonderful wood with a perfect lover who would soon come to claim her. She wanted to tell them that he and she would join hands before long and they would make a perfect match. She wanted to say that this was the beginning of the rest of her life and she was so happy it hurt, but she dared say none of these things to her aunt who was glowering ferociously at her.

When, after another diatribe about her wickedness, thoughtlessness and downright irresponsibility, her aunt swept out followed by the two cousins and Raven was left standing before her mother, who gave her a mournful look and then walked out to kneel before the well.

Days passed and the young man did not come to claim her. She waited patiently, feeling sure he would come. When no blood flowed at the next full moon, she began to wonder if a child had begun to grow inside her and by the following one she felt sure, but dared not tell her mother.

Shortly before the third full moon after the celebration of spring her cousins came to see her looking excited and eager to speak with her alone. When they were safely away from the dwelling, the younger girl said, 'We saw your young man today.'

Raven's heart leapt with joy. 'Did he speak to you?'

'No—' the girl gave one of her nervous giggles '—he doesn't speak to anyone now.'

Raven stared uncomprehendingly at her. 'What d'you mean? Surely he's not lost his voice. Has he been ill? Is this the reason I've not seen him?'

'No, dear Raven,' the older girl said. 'He has joined the monks on The Sacred Mound and will speak to no one until he takes his vows.'

'I don't believe you. He would have told me if he had any thought of doing that.'

'I promise you, Raven, I met his brother and he told me Tamas left home two days after the spring celebration. He said he'd been meditating in the woods and...'

Raven heard a giggle and more words, but could make no sense of them. She walked away to the landing stage where a ferryman was helping a woman and children onto his boat. She waited until they had left and were travelling towards the village in the distance and then stood looking down into the murky water. She could swim and therefore would need to put heavy stones in her bodice to weigh her down ...

'I love you, Daughter. Please come home.'

She turned to her mother and said, 'I'm with child.'

'I know.'

A wave of cold like an icy wind blew through her as she forced the words from her tight throat, 'Tamas is a monk.'

'I know, my dear, I know.' Her mother held out her hand. 'Shall we walk home now?'

The baby was born at dawn, shortly after the time when day and night are of equal length. When her mother had delivered the tiny girl and exclaimed at her beauty, she carried her to the door of the dwelling, saying, 'Listen to the bird singing of your arrival. Listen, little one, hear all the other birds joining in and singing for you. What joy! They are saying to one another, here is new life, new love and new hope!'

She turned to go back inside when she heard a scrabble on the roof followed by a flutter of wings and saw a white bird land on a nearby tree where it sat for a moment before flying away. Although fearing this was a portent of the child's departure, she held her close and whispered, 'Don't leave us yet, little one. Stay a while with us and warm out hearts.'

She carried the baby to Raven and after placing the small bundle in her arms, she said, 'The most beautiful white dove was here with you for the birth.'

'Then that is her name—' Raven kissed her daughter '—welcome White Dove.'

White Dove was exquisitely beautiful and a joy to both mother and grandmother, who doted on her and pandered to her every whim throughout the years of her growing up to womanhood. If there was little food in the dark days, then the larger portion was given to White Dove, likewise, if a beautiful new cloak or piece of cloth was given in gratitude to her grandmother for guidance from the dark well, then it was White Dove who wore it.

One person who did not care for the child was the younger of Raven's two cousins, who made plain her feelings about the way White Dove controlled her mother and grandmother and also berated them for their foolishness in allowing her to do so.

The older sister, who had given birth to several babies, none of whom survived beyond a few days, was more understanding of their love for White Dove. She frequently pointed out that her sister had kept her vow to remain a virgin and neither approved of the sexual experience enjoyed by Raven and herself, nor understood the love of the child resulting from it.

Each celebration of spring White Dove was the most beautiful of all the maidens who danced with the young men wearing stag masks and draped in leaves. She always returned early, with no sign of interest in any of them: until, inevitably, so Raven believed, the time she stayed out until the next morning. On this occasion she returned hand in hand with the son of a chief from a village in the wetlands out towards the horizon.

Raven had been watching over her ailing mother all night and was therefore exhausted from lack of sleep and the worry of what might have happened to White Dove. She saw the joy of love in her daughter's eyes and said none of the things she had been practising in her head, saying only, 'Your grandmother is close to leaving us, my dear. Go in and bid her farewell.'

White Dove kissed the young man and watched him walk away to the landing stage where his father and brothers could be heard shouting impatiently to him. She smiled her sweet smile at Raven and said, 'He will return soon and take me to live in his village.'

'Of course he will, dear daughter,' Raven replied. When the girl had gone into the dwelling and was sitting beside the dying old woman, she went quickly into the hut nearby and knelt to look down into the dark well. Soon she saw a snowy white bird sitting on a nest high up in a huge great oak tree. The bird was stretching its neck to see over the edge of the nest. Its bright eyes looked out over the land towards the silvery water beyond. And far away, getting smaller and smaller, was a little boat sailing towards the horizon. Raven closed her eyes, but could still see the image of the bird's arched neck as it watched the boat disappearing from view. She knew history was about to repeat itself and wept for her daughter.

Her aunt and two cousins came that night to keep vigil while her mother quietly slipped out of life. The cousins came back the following night and helped carry her mother's body to the secret cave below The Sacred Mound. Once inside, surrounded by the bones of her ancestors and with her cousins holding lighted torches on either side of her, Raven said, 'I promise to devote my life to the most sacred well of the most sacred island.'

The older cousin wiped tears from her eyes as she declared, 'Men may come and men may go. Men may deface this sacred mound with wood or stone but The Great One lives on, guarding the ancestors.'

Raven and her younger cousin said, 'So it shall be.'

'And the wells shall flow while sun and moon both shine,' the older cousin continued. 'The red, the white and, most sacred of all, the black.'

'All three shall flow while sun and moon both shine,' Raven and her younger cousin repeated.

The three of them placed one hand on their hearts and said in unison, 'So shall it be for all eternity.'

❖   ❖   ❖

Raven took on the mantle of keeper of the dark well with great joy, knowing this was her destiny. She awoke each morning wondering who might come seeking guidance and fell asleep each night feeling grateful for a fulfilling day.

She tried hard to be sympathetic with White Dove who, for the first time in her life, had been thwarted and deeply hurt. She sat by the fire night after night listening patiently while her daughter complained of her discomfort, expressed her wish that *the thing*, as she called the baby, would die before birth, or be stillborn, and constantly berated the young man for his fickleness.

Raven knew the herbs that would cause a baby to leave the womb in the early days of its conception and had told others who had been forced by violence to conceive, but she did not let her daughter know this, despite many requests and much emotional pleading. She felt deep in her heart that this child was meant to live and decided that if its mother would not care for it then she would do so.

When the baby was born before the expected time, Raven took the tiny baby girl and cradled her in her arms all night while her daughter slept.

On awakening, White Dove asked, 'Is it dead?'

'No, my dear, your beautiful daughter lives.' Offering the baby to her, she asked, 'Will you suckle her now?'

White Dove whined. 'I can't, my teats hurt.'

Raven swallowed her anger and said, 'I have made a soothing ointment with the marigold flowers I dried last summer for exactly this purpose.' She fetched the ointment and applied it, then, looking at White Dove's swollen breasts, went on, 'You will find suckling will ease the discomfort—' she placed the baby in the crook of her arm '—just try it for my sake, I beg you, Daughter.'

Raven turned away and went to fetch wood for the fire. On her return she was relieved to find the baby suckling and felt tears of joy filling her eyes. She knew White Dove would never love the child as a mother should, but at least, all being well, the little girl might live to give her grandmother joy.

'Have you thought of a name for her?' Raven asked several days later.

White Dove shook her head.

Looking down at the sleeping child on her lap, Raven suggested, 'Golden Bird might suit her if she has your coloured hair.'

When her daughter did not respond she tried again, 'Or Snow Flower perhaps.'

White Dove shrugged. 'I don't care what she's called.' She picked up the small leather pouch containing the ointment and after dipping a forefinger into it applied it to her nipples. Looking down at the orange ointment, she said, 'You can name her Marigold, for all I care.'

Raven kissed the baby and sang, 'Sweet Marigold, the sun shines when you smile. Dear Marigold, make the sun shine for me.'

White Dove snorted with disgust and turned over to look at the wall.

❖   ❖   ❖

Many old people died during the following winter, which was a much colder and seemingly much longer season than usual. The two keepers of the other wells both died within days of one another. Raven's older cousin immediately took the place of her mother at the red well, while the younger cousin persuaded the elders that she was the ideal candidate to take over from her distant relative at the white.

For a while Raven thought her life was now on a safe straight path. All the three wells had able guardians, her granddaughter was thriving and all that could go wrong had done so.

Although worried about her unhappy daughter, who seemed indifferent to her baby and often left her in a crib while she went out, Raven nevertheless believed that time would heal the broken heart and love for the child would blossom. In the meantime, while waiting for this affection to grow, she often picked up the Marigold when White Dove was absent and tied her close with a shawl and carried her while collecting healing plants or seeking guidance from the dark well.

Despite knowing there would never be a strong bond between the infant and her mother, Raven was surprised to find that White Dove had left the baby behind when she ran away the following summer.

It happened one beautiful sunny day when Raven took some healing plants to the Cousin of the Red, in the hope of easing the pain she had been suffering in her knees. While waiting for the leaves to boil in a pot on the fire, the two close friends were reminiscing about the times of their youth when the Cousin of the White arrived, changing the atmosphere, as she always did.

After sniffing the smell emanating from the pot and wrinkling her nose with distaste the younger cousin looked pointedly at her sister's knees and said, 'I don't know why you waste your time. There is no remedy for increasing age.'

When neither of the women responded, she pursed her lips, turned to Raven and said, 'I assume you've heard the rumours?'

'About what?' Raven asked, wondering what malicious gossip she was about to hear.

'About your daughter and the young carver in the church—not that I believe everything I hear, of course.' The Cousin of the White gave a mirthless laugh and added, 'Although I have to admit that figure in the church does rather give it away!'

This news came as a shock to Raven. She looked to the Cousin of the Red, hoping for a rebuttal of the story but, seeing the sympathy in her expression, knew there was some truth in this tale.

She also knew the carver, having seen him many times as he walked past her dwelling carrying a bag of tools. She had liked his open friendly smile when he responded to her greeting, but thought no more about him, until now.

Turning to her Cousin of the White, she gave a stiff nod and a polite smile. 'I know you meant well when telling me this and I thank you for your kind concern.' She heard her Cousin of the Red sigh and resisted the desire to exchange glances with her, then continued, 'I will visit the church on my way home and will speak to White Dove. My daughter may not always meet with your approval, Cousin, but one thing I know; if I ask her for the truth, she will give it to me.'

After making some inconsequential chat in order to hide her urgent desire to see the young man and the carving he had made, she departed and hurried along the path to the church.

On entering the small stone building she saw a monk kneeling on the ground before a painted carving of a man hanging on a large wooden cross and wondered if she should retreat. A moment later she saw the stone figure of a woman standing to one side of the crucified man and decided to venture forth.

Not wishing to disturb the monk, she tiptoed to the female figure and stared in amazement at the carved image of her daughter.

'Do you like Our Lady?' a deep voice asked.

Without turning around, she replied, 'I'm sorry to disturb your prayer. Yes, I do indeed. I like her very much.' Aware that the monk had moved to stand behind her, she looked round to face the man in a brown habit. For a moment she thought he might be Tamas, the boy she had once loved, but dismissed the idea as preposterous and said, 'In fact I think she has the most beautiful face I've ever seen.'

'I agree, our Lady Mary is indeed beautiful.' He stretched out his hand and touched the carved folds of the figure's gown. 'Such exquisite work! It is as though the young carver was inspired.' He gave a slight bow of the head while adding, 'He finished her yesterday. You are the first to see her completed.'

She thanked him and walked away to the door. As she stepped out into the sunlight she heard him say quietly, 'Farewell, my love.' Remembering these were his last words to her, she knew it was Tamas and hesitated momentarily before making her way home without looking back.

Arriving back in the dwelling she found baby Marigold crying and no sign of White Dove. This absence of her daughter was not unusual, but the dwelling felt empty. She saw there was no fine woollen blanket on the bed, no garments strewn around, no shoes or shawls and, as she realised with a cold knot in her chest, not one of her daughter's most precious possessions. It was clear to her that White Dove would not return.

She picked up the baby and soothed her. Knowing she must find milk of some kind, she tied her shawl around Marigold and walked to see an old woman who had three goats on the far side of the island. By the end of the day she had negotiated the purchase of a nanny goat in milk and the skin of a kid.

On her return she made a small bag from the skin and milked the goat. After putting some milk into the bag in which she had made a small hole, she offered it to the child who suckled immediately. Once the baby had drunk her fill, she laid her down to sleep and went to the door intending to visit the dark well in the hut close by. Hearing the baby whimper she went and fetched her. The child instantly closed her eyes and so, with Marigold asleep in her arms, she went to the well and looked down into the black water in the hope seeing what had become of White Dove.

The image was very clear, as though she was looking through a gap in a hedge or into an open doorway. A figure wearing a brown garment with a hood exactly like the monks wore and holding a cross, just as they did, was standing in a small building. She could hear the sound of women's voices singing a very beautiful song and as the figure turned to face a group of others she could see they were not monks, as she thought, but women in similar garb. The way the standing figure stood erect and then moved gracefully to lead the others in procession from the building was so familiar she felt a stab of pain in her heart. White Dove had never shown any inclination towards the monks and their beliefs, but perhaps at some time in the future she would join their church.

Sitting by her fire that night she pictured the strange sighting in the well and wondered when the meaning of this would become clear. After a while, remembering the monk in the church, she smiled to herself at the thought that, while he had been the one and only love she had ever known, so had she been the only one for him. But, she decided, although she had known great heartache and pain because of his abandonment, his loss was greater than hers; for while he was unwittingly revering a stone replica of the child he had fathered, she had their daughter's daughter to love and cherish.

Raven heard no word of White Dove's whereabouts, nor did she expect to receive any. She did not visit the church again for fear of seeing Tamas, knowing they had taken their different paths and must stay on them, as was their destiny. Her life continued contentedly as the keeper of the dark well and grandmother to the grandchild she adored.

Marigold grew straight and strong with a lovely disposition that won people's hearts, even including the Cousin of the White Well, who, to the surprise of her sister and Raven, doted on the child. The Cousin of the Red noted with amusement more than once that, 'It does not occur to Marigold that anyone might bear any ill will towards her and consequently, no one, not even my Sister of the White, does so!'

The girl had the gift of sight and also was quick to learn which plants had healing power for the ailments suffered by the local people. She was, as Raven often thought, golden by name and golden in spirit,

Time passed. Raven was reminded of her own mortality from time to time when friends and acquaintances died. One spring day a woman who came for guidance reported that her nephew, the monk who had once been known as Tamas, had been found dead on The Sacred Mound and Raven calmly expressed her sympathy while screaming with pain inside her head. This grief remained in her heart from that day on.

Despite sadness and the fact that time was taking its toll on Raven, she felt blessed and secure in the knowledge that her dear gifted Marigold would take over the dark well after her demise.

One day, while kneeling by the dark well, after giving guidance to a woman who had not been pleased with what she had seen, Raven felt weary and low in spirit. Her back ached as did her head and knowing it would ease her pain, she went to find the plant that

Marigold had collected the day before and left hanging to dry by the door. While steeping it in hot water, she wondered why Marigold no longer wished to look into the well and often seemed distracted and withdrawn. Also she was often absent from the dwelling for long periods of time and was evasive if questioned on her return. Twice, when walking past the church, she had seen her entering the building and once had caught sight of her talking with a monk in the shadows beside it.

While drinking the potion she thought of the changes afoot at the church and felt discomfited and disturbed. She knew the monks were planning something because they stood together in huddled groups and occasionally one or other of them would look her way as if they were talking about her. Once or twice she caught a word blowing on the breeze, 'stone,' was one, 'scaffold,' another. She had wondered if someone was to be hanged for some misdemeanour or other, but decided they would do that in the usual place, not here by their church.

Thinking the keepers of the other sacred wells, especially Cousin of the Red, might have heard what was planned for the church, Raven walked to the dwelling beside the red well and drank some of the healing water then sat with her beside the fire.

The Cousin of the White soon came to join them and greeted her with usual forthrightness, 'Cousin of the Dark, I'm pleased to see you, but sorry to see you looking so anxious, are you worried or ill?'

'I am indeed worried,' she replied. 'I fear there are big changes afoot and I wondered if you'd heard any talk about the building of a new church.'

'I have heard. And it's going to be very big,' Cousin of the White said, evidently pleased to be knowledgeable on the subject. 'I heard they've been looking at more than one quarry hereabouts. And much of the forest will be cleared too—I know that because when I asked the men why they were cutting some down trees they said a lot of scaffold poles would be needed for them to climb on when they're making such a huge building, as well as the wooden beams and suchlike.' She stopped and looked at Raven with a satisfied smirk.

'Actually, I didn't like to say before,' Cousin of the Red said apologetically, wringing her hands. 'I've heard there's stonemasons and carvers already arrived looking for work. The word has gone out far and wide—' she sighed '—that means they'll need dwellings when they get here and ...' she paused to look agitatedly at Raven before adding, 'The old ferryman, the one with the bald head, says he's heard they'll cover the whole meeting ground with their buildings of one sort or another.'

Raven said, 'But they can't do that...'

'Oh yes they can, Cousin of the Dark, they can do whatever they please and no one can stop them. We have no say in the matter. The days when we had any clout have long gone.' Cousin of the White frowned. 'Look at what they've done on The Sacred Mound. Once upon a time it was hallowed ground, but no longer; now there's dwellings for monks on the slopes and a church on the top where the priests' stones used to be.'

Cousin of the Red said, 'There's no respect for the old ways.' She shook her head sadly. 'We have to accept that everything is changing— they're not even content with altering the look of The Sacred Mound and making it look like any old hill, they're calling it the Tor now.'

All three of them sighed and sat in silence for a while.

Eventually Raven said, 'Here we are, all three of us old—too old to keep up with the times and unable to understand the changes taking place. I wonder what's to become of us and, more importantly, what's to become of the ones who will follow us?'

Cousin of the Red said, 'We have nieces waiting to take our places, eager in fact to do so and you have your granddaughter, do you not?'

'I fear Marigold is not as dedicated to the dark well as I would wish.'

'We had heard rumours,' Cousin of the Red said tentatively.

Raven had not spoken of her fears until this moment and found her mouth quivering with emotion as she said, 'I've not wanted to burden you with my worries, dear cousins, but I must confess to you, I have very grave concerns—' she paused to swallow and dab at the tears in her eyes '—I think she meets with one of the monks.'

'You think she might run away with him?' Cousin of the Red asked.

'Worse than that, my friend, I think she may join his church.'

Cousin of the White giggled. 'That's a new way of putting it.'

Cousin of the Red snorted in an attempt to swallow her mirth and Raven found she too could not contain her amusement and suddenly all three were laughing.

Wiping away tears from her eyes, Cousin of the White, said haltingly, 'Do you remember our first spring celebration and we couldn't find you, Raven.'

'And you said—' Cousin of the Red struggled to keep her face straight '—you'd got lost in the beauty of the moon.'

Raven grinned. 'That was true.'

'What you meant was you got lost in the beauty of that boy who fathered your child!'

Raven conceded this was true, adding, 'He made me laugh.'

'Made you cry an' all,' Cousin of the Red said with a shake of her head.

Raven nodded, remembering the pain when he went to join the monks on the Tor.

'Is he still up there?' Cousin of the White asked.

'I don't know,' Raven replied. Then, regretting the lie, added with a tremor of emotion in her voice, 'I heard he died the spring before last.' She heard them both give a slight gasp and knew they now understood she had never stopped loving him, despite pretending to the contrary. In an attempt to cover her own embarrassment, she looked at the Cousin of Red and said teasingly, 'I don't think I was the only one to lose her virginity that night.'

'I'm afraid that's true, Cousin of the Dark. We neither of us have the right to criticise the young ones for their folly after the foolishness of our own youth. The baby I bore from that night died at birth, poor little lad.' Cousin of the Red shook her head sadly. 'None of my boys lived and I never did have a girl, whereas you had only one girl—' she looked quizzically at her '—have you ever heard tell of White Dove?'

'No, not a word since she ran off with that young stone carver.'

'I think of her every time I see the statue in the church,' said Cousin of the White.

'Me too,' Cousin of the Red agreed, 'it's a very good likeness. I often pop in to look at her.' She chuckled, adding with a shake of her head, 'I don't suppose the monks would be too pleased if they realised the mother of their god was the spitting image of her creator's lover.'

Raven smiled and dabbed at the tears rising in her eyes, 'I knew when I first saw my White Dove and looked down into her newborn face that she would be a beauty.'

'She broke a few hearts hereabouts,' said Cousin of the Red.

'And mine when she left,' Raven replied.

'At least she left her child with you,' Cousin of the White said wistfully.

'That's true,' Raven agreed, wondering if her cousin now regretted her youthful pledge to remain a virgin. After sitting a while in companionable quiet, she took her leave and walked slowly home in the twilight across the meeting place and past the church to her dwelling.

The following morning she looked at her granddaughter, who was singing while mending a tear in her cloak and said, 'I don't trust those men, Marigold.'

'They won't do you any harm, Grandmother. They're just going to build a new church that's all. Anyway, there's not much you can do to stop them doing whatever they want to do.' Marigold stood up and smoothed her skirt. 'I'm going for a walk, I won't be long.'

'Long enough to meet with that monk?'

Marigold looked askance while replying, 'He wishes to save my soul.'

'Go and save your soul, granddaughter.' Her laughter was an old woman's dry cackle without the ironic note she had intended. 'But don't bring any wailing infant to me as your mother did.'

The girl stood for a moment, evidently lost for words and looking so like the lovely young woman who had borne her.

'Go! Go with your new God, but go from me and leave me in peace.' She watched her granddaughter walk away towards the church and felt tears rising in her eyes and then running down her cheeks. She tasted the salt and wiped it away with her hand and remembered doing the same thing as a little girl after falling over and hurting her knee. In those days she always ran to her grandmother for comfort and the old lady would hold her tight while telling her tales of long ago when invaders came to the sacred island with their new gods and goddesses. 'But we survived, Raven. Oh yes, we're still here.' She always gave a self satisfied smile at this point, adding, 'Like I always say; the wise willow bends with the wind and survives the gale.'

Remembering her grandmother and her sayings, she wondered if perhaps the girl was right to go with these men in their church. Perhaps Marigold would survive by working with them and not against them?

She knelt with difficulty by the well and looked into the darkness. When many figures in hooded cloaks walked into a huge archway and then stood before a brightly coloured vision she felt a sharp pain in her chest and gave a groan before the picture faded away.

Marigold did not return for several days. When at last she appeared with a wooden cross hanging on a thin rope around her neck, she said, 'I've been baptised, mother. I am now a Christian and my name is Maria.'

The pain in her chest was like searing fire, but she was determined to show no sign of this. 'Welcome, Maria, my granddaughter,' she said.

She saw the surprise in the girl's lovely face and knew that a different response had been expected. 'You are still my beloved granddaughter, no matter by what name you are called and regardless of what god you choose to worship.'

'You accept the faith?'

'I accept it is your faith, that is good enough, isn't it, Mari ... I mean Maria?'

Without a word they embraced and clung to one another for a long while, until Raven said, 'I hope you will still collect the plants for me. I find I'm so stiff these days.'

Maria agreed she would gladly do so and they sat by the fire looking into the flickering flames in companionable silence until it was time to sleep.

Although she had accepted her granddaughter's faith, she was still worried about the new building. The men seemed to be forever walking around her dwelling and looking at the shelter covering the well beside it.

She knew the numbers of people who came for guidance from the well had diminished over recent seasons and those who did come seemed nervous on arrival and apprehensive when leaving, but enough had kept coming to reassure her that she could continue to serve the community as her forbears had done. Many said that while they were going to the church they still wanted to keep up some of the old ways, such as seeking guidance from the well and asking for advice about their ailments which, to her, made good sense, but seeing the men looking more and more frequently at her, she felt a chill wind of fear.

One night, after an anxious day watching large quantities of stone being brought on carts and piled high on the meeting ground, she lay awake worrying and wondering what the men with their hammers and chisels were going to build when she remembered the sight in the well soon after White Dove had left. At the time she had assumed the figure holding the cross in front of other women had been her daughter, but now she realised that it was Marigold. She longed to tell the girl of this, but knew that since she no longer believed in the power of the well, there was little point in doing so.

The following morning, having thought long and hard what she should say, Raven waited for her granddaughter to return from her early morning devotions in the church, and after greeting her, asked, 'Is there a place where women can be monks?'

Marigold, now known as Maria, looked thoughtful and after eating the food Raven had prepared for her to break her fast, she left the dwelling and walked away towards The Sacred Mound, or Tor, as it was now known.

The sun was low in the sky when the girl returned and Raven kept her head down over the food she was cooking lest the anxiety in her face might show.

'I have been walking and thinking,' Maria said.

Raven silently waited for what was to come and stirred the pot without looking up.

'I walked to a place I love, it's below the Tor on the other side from here, where the ground rises above the wetlands and I stayed there a long time praying for guidance.' She sat down close to Raven and touched her arm. 'I have been called to give my life to God.'

Raven reached out and squeezed her hand. 'Tell me how you will do this, my dear.'

Maria straightened her back and replied, 'I shall build a place for women to serve God and also—' she brushed a tear from her eye '— to use the knowledge of healing plants I learned from you to serve the sick people—as you know there are many poor people who suffer from serious ailments.'

Raven thought her heart would burst with joy. While feeling unable to tell the girl that she had seen this destiny in the well long ago, she nevertheless wanted her to know she was pleased and put an arm around her shoulders.

Maria gave a sob and said, 'I thought you would be so disappointed in me. After all you have taught me and also—' tears streamed down her face '—you thought I would be keeper of the dark well one day, didn't you?'

'I'm proud of you for finding your own destiny.' Raven dabbed at the girl's face to dry her tears. 'I did hope you might follow me, it's true, but I have no right to stop you following your heart and I give you my blessing providing—' she hugged her again '—you will promise to pray for me from time to time, will you do that?'

Mary agreed and then they laughed and cried at the same time before eating their meal, during which they frequently smiled lovingly at one another.

Shortly after this, when her granddaughter had left to live in a small shelter on the spot where she intended to build her sanctuary, Raven found two local men digging a trench close to the hut housing the dark well. When she asked what they were doing, their only response was, 'Just doing what we're told, lady.' Then they averted their eyes and continued digging.

Standing looking at the line they were following it was clear to her that whatever they were doing would run between the well and her dwelling. Also, two other men were digging a similar trench opposite them. She then realised that, not only was this new building going to be very big, it would encompass the sacred dark well. Furthermore, seeing two men arrive and start hacking at the ancient yew tree close to her dwelling, she experienced panic such as never before known to her. With a burning pain in her chest, she went out onto the meeting place intending to seek help from her cousins.

While weaving in and out of piles of stone and heaps of tree trunks, she came face to face with a man who seemed familiar. When he wished her good day she greeted him and was about to continue when he put his hand on her arm, saying, 'I heard there was a new church to be built and came to find employment, but also I came in the hope of making amends to you.' He swallowed before adding, 'I'm Dekan the man who ran away with your daughter.'

Her heart thumped loudly as she looked into his clear blue eyes and asked, 'Is she here with you?'

'I fear not,' he replied with a shake of his head. 'She left me four summers ago when I was working on a rich man's house a long way from here, but—' he smiled '—she did not take our child and for that I shall always be grateful.'

'A child!' Raven exclaimed.

'She is the delight of my life and I would like to bring her to see you.'

'I long to see her. Oh, how I long to see her!' Raven thought she was going to pass out with excitement and he evidently thought so too because he led her to a lump of stone and helped her to sit down on it.

A few moments later, when her heart had settled into a normal rhythm, she watched with interest when two men appeared and began talking to Dekan about the stone. While listening to the conversation she could tell they were planning the building and they respected Dekan, who had recently arrived to oversee the stonework. She knew all these men were used to giving orders and having them obeyed, therefore she waited patiently for the right moment to simper sweetly, in what she hoped was the right manner for a subservient old lady, and say, 'I live close by and would be most grateful, kind gentlemen if you could show me the extent of your building.'

Dekan said he too would like to see the bounds of the walls and when the men grudgingly agreed, they all walked around the edges marked with rope on pegs in the ground and men digging a trench for the foundations. After they reached the shelter over the well and her dwelling, Raven stood still, determined to keep calm as she waited for them to speak.

One of the men gave a cough then said, 'I thought it had been made plain to you, lady—' he coughed again '—I thought you understood that...' his voice trailed off into silence.

She was resolved to keep her nerve. 'Understood what?' she asked.

The other man said, 'I think it was assumed that you would leave, Lady.'

Dekan said, 'I believe this lady's family have lived here for many generations— ' he pointed to her dwelling and then to the hut close by '—and they have kept guard of the ancient well in there.'

The first man looked uncomfortable and shifted from one foot to the other while the second coughed and said, 'We've been told to build around it...'

'What!' Raven exclaimed shrilly, all thought of remaining calm forgotten.

Dekan put a hand on her arm and said, 'Let's hear him out, Lady Raven.'

She nodded, unable to speak.

'My instructions,' the man continued, 'are to include the well within the walls.' He walked to the line of the ditch and looked along it then nodded and returned to them. 'Yes, it will be within the wall, so it would be under cover just as you have it and as you see, we need to remove that great yew tree to make way for the building.' He gestured with his head to the other man and they walked a few paces away then had a discussion during which they kept looking around them.

When the men returned, the first one said, 'In order to show our good will to local people, we have decided to make you a generous offer, lady. We could build you a small stone dwelling somewhere else.'

Her whole body shook and her head felt as though it would burst. For a moment she thought death might release her from this nightmare, but, feeling Dekan's hand holding hers, she gained strength and grasping both him and life, she asked, 'Somewhere nearby, sir?'

The man went and looked around the area then pointed to an oak across the meeting ground. 'That would be the best I can offer.'

She had no means of bargaining with him and was powerless. Remembering her grandmother's wisdom about the wise willow in a gale, she decided to bend with the wind. 'Yes, I thank you, sir, that will do very well.'

She bade them good day and waited until they had left before going to the dark well and weeping. 'I have betrayed all that my forbears worked for, but I have no way of stopping them,' she said, unable to see into the water while so distressed.

After a while she walked to see her Cousin of the Red and told her of this shocking event. Soon, after drinking from the red well while sitting by the fire and hearing comforting expressions of support, she felt calmer. Hearing a knock on the door Raven opened it, expecting to find Cousin of the White. To her amazement she saw Dekan holding the hand of a child as beautiful as White Dove. Knowing this was her grand-daughter she was overwhelmed with joy and immediate, undying love.

'This is your namesake, Lady Raven,' Deklan said, adding with a smile, 'I suggest we call her Little Raven to avoid confusion.'

In the days following her arrival Little Raven and Raven became inseparable. The child soon decided she wished to stay with her grandmother and rarely left her side. Few people dared to come to the dark well now the building had commenced and Raven was free to enjoy the child's company while preparing to move to the dwelling that Dekan soon arranged to be built for her.

Although knowing the dark well would soon be hidden, she never-theless showed it to Little Raven who peered down at the black water and said, 'There's a man in there and oh dear, a sad lady! And oh, how funny!' She giggled and pointed down at the well. 'There's a really funny lady in there.'

Raven leaned over and saw a woman wearing a wide hat draped with pale mauve cloth and delicate cream cloth at her throat, with what looked like a shiny pebble hanging from a thin chain around her neck. Although wishing she had also seen the man and the sad lady described by Little Raven, she felt relieved to know that at some time in the future, no matter how far ahead, a strangely attired woman would somehow find the well and look into it.

When Dekan asked if the little girl could live with her while he was working on the building, Raven was overjoyed. She now had a purpose in life and when the little stone dwelling had been built close to the oak tree she moved into it with more excitement than she could possibly have imagined before Dekan's arrival.

❖   ❖   ❖

Raven lived the last of her years watching the huge abbey church and other buildings for the monastery being constructed on the meeting ground.

She expressed her admiration to others of the beautiful building with a tall roof that replaced the yew tree and her dwelling, but secretly she pined for her old home.

When the wall was built to enclose the monastery she was not distressed to find it butting up against her new home; it was only her separation from the dark well that saddened her. Dekan heard of her unhappiness from his daughter and built a window in her dwelling that overlooked the abbey. Thereafter she was content to sit for hours gazing out at the great stones of the wall that enclosed the well while holding the image of its still darkness safe in her heart.

In later years she often walked with Little Raven to visit Dekan and his new wife in their cottage near the entrance to the abbey. From time to time she would see him watching his daughter playing with his new family and knew from the faraway look in his blue eyes that his thoughts were of White Dove.

Their visits to the cousins at the wells below the Tor were also frequent. Invariably, as they turned left outside their stone dwelling, Little Raven would say, 'Please tell me about when you were little like me, Grandma.'

Raven would then look up at the Tor ahead of her while walking on the path beside the new wall and reminisce about her life. Little Raven always listened with wrapt attention and in this way many happy memories were shared on the way to the red and white wells. But, although explaining how the Tor had once been called The Sacred Mound on which she and her cousins had danced on May Day morning, Raven made no mention to Little Raven of the day and night she spent making love with Tamas.

When her cousins died she shared her knowledge of plants with their nieces. Neither of them was known as keeper of the wells at this time, but they lived nearby, discreetly giving advice to local people and caring for the wells: dressing them with flowers to welcome the spring and keeping them clean.

After Little Raven married a charming young carpenter she and her husband went to live in the house by the abbey wall with Raven and cared for her until she died two years later.

A few moments before her death she held her newborn great-grandson, who had been named Tamas at her request, and said, 'What a handsome fellow! And a ginger lad like your grandfather!'

Chapter Eleven

Louisa touched the lace at her throat then held the silver locket containing a picture of her husband and a lock of her son's hair and remembered both Little Raven and Raven looking into the well. The fact that she had seen herself through their eyes seemed magical and altogether too impossible to accept, and yet, she knew it had been so. With a shiver of excitement she looked at the locket in her hand. Yes, there it was, shining in the sunlight, just as it had when Raven and her granddaughter saw it in the dark well.

Knowing they had seen her in the future made her wonder if she too could see more than the past and might see her own future if the well could be found. There were many wells around the Tor. Could the dark well still exist hidden away somewhere? How wonderful it would be to find the most sacred of all wells, the one that was mysteriously still and black enough to act as a scrying mirror for one with the sight. It had, she admitted, probably been lost: a watercourse may have been redirected by farmers wanting a place for their animals to drink; or an inlet filled in deliberately by human hand while building houses; and nature, as was its wont, would have then filled in the resulting void, choking it with roots of trees and covering it with ivy.

She prepared to leave and while reaching for her sketching bag saw a group of four people walking towards her. Hearing their voices increasing in volume as they drew nearer, she lowered her head and pretended to be drawing in order to hear and see them.

They were all flamboyantly and richly attired; this fact and the extravagant gestures added to the cultured London accents with which they destroyed the tranquillity of their surroundings gave the impression they wished to flaunt their difference from the rest of mundane society.

Louisa was fascinated. She had seen Bohemian artists on occasional visits to art galleries, but had never mixed socially with them. These people were evidently artistic in some way, painters perhaps or poets. The two men wore wide brimmed felt hats and flowing cravats around their necks and the women wore exotic, richly embroidered shawls with long fringes hanging over their brightly coloured dresses; one emerald green and one scarlet.

As the women walked past Louisa, the taller of the two women was holding her hands out as though sleepwalking with long green sleeves hanging elegantly before her while saying, 'I can feel the energy is very strong here.' This beautiful, colourful creature with loose flowing hair exuded such confidence in every word and every gesture that Louisa was deeply envious of her.

Hearing one of the two men walking behind the women say to his companion, 'The bones were found in eleven ninety-one and the monks made a new tomb in ...' Louisa knew they were discussing the possibility of King Arthur having been buried nearby.

After they had walked away Louisa stood up and followed the path back to the house, with the sound of their voices, but not the meaning of their words, still carried on the breeze.

Once in her room and having removed her plain black cape, she laid it on the bed. Running her fingers over the woollen fabric and then fingering her black skirt, she thought of the two confident women and wondered if she could ever have the courage to wear brightly coloured shawls and silk dresses like them.

A moment later, hearing her aunt giving a cough designed to get her attention, she went into the old lady's room and told her the story of Raven.

When she reached the point where Little Raven saw her in the future, the old lady became very excited. 'That is so—wonderful! And—you were—wearing my hat too!'

All thoughts of colourful clothes were dismissed from her mind as

Louisa touched the lace at her throat. 'I could not have chosen anything more lovely than this to wear for such an occasion.'

The weather was warm enough on most afternoons for the old lady to venture out into the garden. Each day Louisa could see an improvement in her aunt, both in her speech and also in her general demeanour. Several times the old lady reminisced about the times when her children were young and always there was a tinge of sadness when she spoke of Emily.

On the Saturday, when, with a faraway look in her eyes, the old lady said, 'I loved her—but she was—always difficult—to love.'

Recalling Emily's words when speaking of her mother after the funeral in London,' Louisa said, 'I am certain she loves you.'

'I hope—so. We never—got on. Very sad.' The old lady shook her head. 'Very strong willed and—awkward child—not dainty—like Edwina.'

The sisters were completely different in every way, as Louisa knew, but she also thought that, despite having directed all her efforts into her work instead of following convention and taking a husband like Edwina, Emily was a far more loving person than her older sister.

They went to church on Sunday and while the old lady was delighted to be greeted by many people, Louisa was very relieved to find Edward Francis was not among them. Although having determined not to think of him, she was nevertheless glad to avoid the possibility of being attracted to him.

On Monday Louisa waited patiently for the morning to pass and gave her aunt some luncheon before preparing to leave. Seeing the yearning expression on the old lady's face, she said, 'I am so sorry I cannot take you with me. I wish it could be possible, but the ground is not suitable for the Bath chair.' Then she hurried out of the house and through the garden as usual to the bench beside the wall of the abbey ruins.

While drawing her impression of the well as it had been in her last vision she became gradually aware of the scent of a bonfire and wondered if a gardener was burning rubbish somewhere nearby.

The familiar feeling washed over her and she allowed her eyes to go out of focus....

Chapter Twelve

'Look over there, My Lady. The woods must be on fire.'

The young woman pushed Annie out of the way, put her face close to the narrow pane of glass and screwed up her eyes. It was evident she could not see the smoke, but would never admit to having poorer sight than the English maidservant and therefore said, 'I wonder what could cause such *feu*. Is it usual for the people here to burn their trees?'

Annie waited for her mistress to stand back and allow her to look again through the window. Then, seeing the pall of smoke rising above the trees and realising the location of it, she exclaimed, 'That must be the woods near the monastery!'

'*Mais*, that's where my fiancé has gone, is it not?'

'It is, My Lady.' Annie was careful to be respectful with this young ward of her master, who had arrived three days earlier to await her arranged marriage with a friend of his. She had worked for most of her life in this house and was proud when the mistress had chosen her to serve the young visitor whose maid had been too ill to travel.

''Is Lordship has gone to visit the Abbot and zen ze men will go hunting—' Leonie made a face '—zat is what men do is it not?'

'It is, My Lady,' Annie replied while wondering if this situation could lead to employment as maidservant in a grand mansion near Bath.

Leonie simpered. 'I am used to speaking French at court, you know. But when I am married next Sunday I shall be a real English lady, shall I not?'

'You will indeed, My Lady,' Annie replied sweetly, knowing that Leonie was rumoured to be the bastard child of the King and had been brought up by commoners outside London.

Annie sidled to the casement and peered through a small pane of glass. Seeing the huge plume of smoke rising high above the woods and realising where it emanated from, she exclaimed, 'Dear God! That's not the trees, it's the monastery!' Her heart raced as she thought of her brother within the walls and her mother living outside them.

Suppressing a feeling of rising panic, she said in a stilted, but calm, voice, 'I could make enquiries about the fire, if you are worried about His Lordship, My Lady.'

Leonie shrugged her narrow shoulders. 'I suppose that would be a good idea, if you think he's in danger.'

'I'm sure His Lordship is quite safe, but it would be good to be reassured, perhaps, My Lady?'

Leonie pouted and looked towards the window. '*Oui*, go and ask what is 'appenning.'

Annie curtsied and walked stiffly and slowly as possible from the room. Once on the landing she ran across it, past the wide wooden staircase and then down the narrow servants' stairs. Arriving in the kitchen she asked the cook if there had been any word of fire at the monastery.

'I've not heard, my lover, but then I'm always the last to know anything.'

Annie grinned, knowing this was far from the truth. Then, hearing voices outside, she ran to the cobbled yard where a groom was saddling a horse. 'Have you...'

'Can't stop to gossip, Annie,' he said. 'I must go seek the master. He went with his friend to see the Abbott and it looks to me like the Abbey church is on fire.' He licked his finger and held it up. 'I don't like the way the wind's blowing.'

Annie imagined her young brother fighting the flames and then thought of her mother in the little cottage by the wall. What if the wind carried sparks that landed on the thatch and set it on fire? 'I need to go there too. Would you take me there?'

'You can't do that, you silly wench.' He mounted the horse and looked down at her while adding, 'You'd never be able to come back to work here if you went without permission.'

'I don't care. I must go to my mother.' She reached up to him. 'I beg you, Michael, give me a ride to the monastery wall.'

He grabbed her arm and pulled her up, then, with her sitting in front of him holding onto the horse's neck, he rode out of the yard.

She heard a voice shouting her name, but did not look back to see who was calling her. Nothing else mattered, only the fire and its consequences. The time in the grand house was over. She was going back to the old life, no matter how bad or hard, she could not leave her mother alone, not when there was a threat of fire. The poor woman would be terrified and in an agony of worry about her beloved son who was soon to take his vows.

When they arrived at the main gate to the monastery she could see thick smoke billowing over the wall. She thanked the groom and dropped to the ground then ran around the outside wall, bumping into people as they crowded round to watch the fire.

On arrival at the tiny cottage she found her mother standing in the doorway. 'I had to come, Mother,' she said.

'I knew you would, Annie, I knew you would.' Her mother wrung her hands. 'What of my boy, what will happen to him?' And she burst into terrible sobs.

Holding the frail body in her arms, Annie crooned gently to her, saying that he might be safe and they must wait for news of him before thinking the worst. But in her heart she felt sure he was in danger. Closing her eyes she called his name and in a flash she heard him say, 'I'm guarding the well, Annie.'

They stayed outside the little dwelling all night while the fire lit up the sky. In the early hours of the morning a light fall of rain helped to dampen the already dying flames and by dawn only a terrible smell of burning hung over the devastated remains of the church and all other buildings of the monastery.

Leaving her mother huddled in a blanket, Annie went to the main gate to get news of her brother. She joined a queue of other relatives all seeking the same information and waited while one after another was either reunited with a novice, or assured their son or brother was safe, until eventually it was her turn.

'He's alive,' the monk said. 'He's lying by the wall with the rest of the wounded.'

Without stopping to think she blurted out, 'He was guarding the well.'

The monk looked surprised and then frowned. 'We found him in the well house. He's badly hurt I'm afraid.'

'May I see him?'

The monk said this would not normally be allowed, but in the circumstances he would ask for special permission, adding, 'He's still a novice and, therefore, I think your request might be granted.'

She waited for a long time and then a young novice came forward and led her around the inside of the wall only a short distance from the smouldering ruins of the church

A monk with kindly eyes came to her and whispered, 'He may not stay with us long. I fear his legs are too badly broken for him to walk again and his spirit is very low.' He led her to a figure lying on the ground wrapped in a blanket and made the sign of the cross over it. 'We found him this morning lying with his upper body over the well and a roof beam on his legs.' The monk shook his head. 'I can only think he wished to get water to put out the flames.'

Kneeling beside her brother she could smell smoke and blood. 'Don't leave me, dear Graeme,' she whispered. Taking his limp hand in hers she prayed for him to recover and come back to live with her and their mother. 'We'll make a life somehow,' she said then sank down beside him and fell into an exhausted sleep.

She awoke in the darkness to the creaking of wheels and saw two monks picking up the monk next to them and putting him on a cart. Realising they were collecting the dead and taking them for burial, she grabbed her brother's hand and tried to find a pulse in his wrist. In her panic she was unable to find the right spot and as the cart creaked towards her she bent close to her brother's chest and heard he was still breathing.

'He lives!' she cried, seeing them coming towards her.

The two men looked at one another. One bent over and took Graeme's wrist. 'I can't feel a beat,' he said.

'Please, I beg you, leave him be a little longer.'

They looked doubtfully at one another. One said, 'I suppose we could leave it 'til the next watch after Matins.'

The other shrugged and agreed.

When they had picked up another corpse and were about to pull the cart away, she ran to them and asked, 'Could I borrow the cart while you are saying your prayers in...' she broke off and looked around at the still smoking devastation, wondering where they could go to pray.

The older monk looked up to the starry sky and said, 'I'm sure God will forgive us for worshipping in full view of the heavens until we have a new church.' He looked over at her brother and evidently understanding her intention, added, 'I expect we will be too busy with our devotions to notice if you happen to follow us and borrow the cart for a short while. In fact, now I come to think of it, this would be a good place to leave it in readiness for—' he gestured towards two other monks wrapped in blankets '—other possible fatalities.'

'I will take my brother to my mother's house just a short distance away outside the wall and return the cart by daybreak.' She curtsied and thanked him, adding, 'My mother would be greatly comforted to be with him when he passes.'

Both monks nodded and walked away pulling the cart. Returning only a short while later with it, the older monk said, 'God bless you child and give you strength to bear the loss of your dear brother whom we all loved. I pray you will meet in heaven.' He then bent down on one side of the recumbent figure while she took the other side and they lifted him up and put him on the cart.

Annie waited until he had disappeared and she could hear men singing on the other side of the ruins before pulling the cart to the gate and out into the lane.

After a few paces a young man emerged from the shadows and asked if he could see who was in the cart. Thinking he was searching for a lost relative, she pulled back the cloak to reveal her brother's pale face and heard a gasp that could have been either relief or shock, she did not know which. When he offered to help pull the cart she agreed and so they soon arrived at her mother's house.

The young man insisted on carrying Graeme inside and laid him gently on the bed beside the fire where his mother could sit close to him.

Annie knelt beside her brother and kissed him then stood up and thanked the young man.

'We were friends when young,' he replied, looking down with a tender smile.

'I must go and return the …'

'No. I shall take the cart back and give the monks thanks.' He was gone before she could argue and so she began gently unwrapping the blanket to see what damage had been done to Graeme's legs.

Her mother's calm demeanour when surveying the dreadful sight of the misshapen legs was surprising. While Annie could only gasp in horror, the old woman said, 'We must put splints on these before he awakens from the blessed sleep of this affliction.' When Annie stood in dumb shock, unable to lift her feet, her mother snapped, 'Go quickly! Fetch me pieces of stick from the wood pile, while I tear this old shirt of your father's into strips.'

Annie obeyed and then helped to straighten Graeme's legs and tie the sticks to them. From time to time he made moaning sounds and she held her breath fearing he would awaken from his deep sleep and then, on each occasion, was relieved to see him sink back again into unconsciousness.

When the deed was done and he lay wrapped in the blanket, his mother said, 'Now we have to wait and see if he comes back to us.' And she sat down beside him with a bundle of wool and began spinning.

Annie almost laughed with relief. She had expected the old woman to be overwrought and unable to cope with this terrible event, but in fact she was completely in control of the situation. Hearing a knock on the door she opened it to find the young man who had helped her.

'I bring a small gift,' he said, handing her a length of blue woollen cloth.

'But it is I who should give a gift of thanks to you!' she exclaimed.

'Well, a cup of water would be welcome,' he replied with a grin.

She went to the leather bucket outside the door and filled a cup from it. While handing it to him she said, 'I don't know your name, sir.'

'Geoffrey,' he said with a bow.

She ushered him inside and introduced him to her mother who said, 'I remember your family. They went to work far away didn't they?'

He nodded. 'My mother died last Michaelmass and my father soon after. My sister married a shepherd and I brought the cloth I made to...'

'You made this!' Annie exclaimed.

'Aye.' His eyes sparkled with pride. 'But I shall make no more. The lord of the manor has taken back the cottage we lived in now my father no longer works for him.'

Annie looked at her mother's reel of spun wool and then into Geoffrey's eyes. 'We have nothing but this small cottage. My brother, if he lives, will be a cripple and my mother and I can only....'

'I will build a loom—' Geoffrey stood up and walked the few paces to the end of the dwelling '—here.' He pointed to the amount of floor space it would take up and then looking above her head, said, 'I will build a platform, what some folk call a talfat, over there for you, or, if he can climb a ladder, for your brother to sleep in.'

'And in return?' she asked.

'In return I will sleep under the loom at night and weave on it by day.'

The old woman said, 'You thought of all that very quickly, Master Geoffrey.'

He looked shamefaced. 'I confess I thought of it while taking the cart to the monastery. I will go now if you wish and …'

'No, I didn't say t'was a bad thought, now did I?'

'No, mistress, you did not.' He looked at the floor as though studying it very carefully until the old woman chuckled.

'I say we try it for a full twelve month. Annie, you've been unusually quiet. What say you?'

'I agree with you mother…' she broke off on hearing a voice whisper her name and dived down to kneel beside her brother.

The following days were filled with much activity. Wood was cut and smoothed outside and hammered into place inside. Annie fetched water from the nearby well, kept the fire alight, made gruel for them all to eat and also helped Geoffrey with building the loom, while the old woman sat by her son, spinning all the while. Graeme did groan from time to time, but mostly bore the great pain he suffered with fortitude.

On the day that the loom was finished Annie was sweeping the floor when she noticed her brother smiling. 'Are you pleased with it?' she asked.

'I am,' he replied. 'I'm also delighted to tell you that, though it pains me greatly, I can move my right leg.'

The old woman who was as usual sitting beside him, said, 'That's wonderful!' and burst into tears. Annie started weeping also and Geoffrey, hearing them and fearing the worst, came in and soon had tears running down his cheeks.

Graeme's recovery was slow. It was clear he would never walk normally again, but with the aid of crutches he learned to move inside and around the outside of the dwelling. He had learned to sing in the monastery and once he felt well enough he sang to entertain them and their neighbours.

One evening as they sat by the fire and he had sung for them as usual, Geoffrey said he had looked over the wall and seen the monastery was being rebuilt.

Annie said she had seen the stonemasons at work and asked Graeme if he wished to go back. 'No,' he replied with a sad shake of his head. 'I no longer feel I have the vocation. It's almost as though my duty was to keep the sacred well safe and having done that I no longer need to be there and can keep my faith in God outside the wall.'

Geoffrey looked puzzled. 'I thought the two sacred wells were the red and the white at the foot of the Tor.'

'We might as well tell you, now you've heard Graeme say what he did—' the old woman gave her son a withering look '—but you must promise to keep it secret.'

Geoffrey swore he would do so.

The old woman said, 'A long time ago there was another sacred well and the guardianship of it was handed down from one generation of our family to the next. My mother's mother told me that when the big church was built in the monastery this sacred well was simply taken over and there was nothing could be done about it.'

Geoffrey looked admiringly at Graeme, 'You were very brave. You could have been killed!'

'Silly fool!' the old woman exclaimed. 'It's not sacred any more after all these years.'

'Yes it is, mother. That's how I knew there would be a fire.'

'You mean you saw it would happen?' Annie asked excitedly.

'I did.' Graeme looked smugly at his mother. 'I also knew that this good friend—' he reached out and held Geoffrey's hand '—would come back to me.'

Annie suddenly understood. She had assumed for a short while that the young man had designs on her and when he showed no interest she had been somewhat perplexed, until this moment. Being aware that her mother would be shocked to hear of the two young men's affection for one another, she said nothing. Looking up and seeing Graeme's eyes fixed on her, she smiled and saw relief flood his face.

The following day when their mother had gone to visit an old friend, Graeme said, 'We need to talk to you, Annie.'

Geoffrey left the loom and joined them beside the fire, saying, 'I've been longing to speak the truth since I first arrived. Now Graeme tells me you understand, is that right?'

She had seen two young grooms beaten unmercifully by the master then dismissed from his service and replied, 'I understand your feelings for each other, but I nevertheless fear for you. If the people here get any idea of …'

'They won't get the chance,' Graeme said. 'We plan to leave very soon and…'

'Leave! You'll break our mother's heart!' she cried angrily.

'Not so badly as it would be broken if we stayed and she saw us attacked and even possibly murdered.' Graeme reached out towards his friend while adding, 'I've heard of terrible punishments given to our kind. A monk told me that in other countries men who love one another are burned to death.'

She felt a cold fear clutch at her heart as she imagined him dying at the stake. 'Was your friendship with Geoffrey known to the monks?'

'No, not my friendship, but that of two other novices who were discovered together—they were excommunicated from the church and sent from the monastery in disgrace.'

Geoffrey said, 'We realise that soon the neighbours will spread gossip about us and …'

'Could we not pretend I am your wife?' she asked desperately.

'No, dear Annie—' Geoffrey smiled sadly at her '—much as I love you for your good heart, it would not be honest and also, we could not prevent you from finding a man to share your life in the same way as we have found each other.'

She guessed from this response that they had considered this possibility and discarded it for her sake.

Graeme said, 'We have come to the conclusion, Sister dear, that if we wish to be together we must accept that we are regarded as sinners by the Church and most of the people in this land and therefore must find a place of safety where we are not known.'

She watched as they clasped hands and both looked plaintively at her. Feeling only love for them both, she said, 'Where can you go and be safe from attack?'

'We will go to London and say we are brothers.' Geoffrey smiled conspiratorially at Graeme.

'Surely people there will attack you just as they would here.' She looked down at her linen skirt and then at her brother's young and beardless face. 'You would look no different from me in women's clothes.'

Suddenly the three of them were smiling.

'Of course! That's the answer!' Geoffrey exclaimed.

'The answer to what?' The old woman asked as she came in.

Annie jumped up guiltily and said, 'We've been wondering what to do, Mother. Since Geoffrey hurt his hand and cannot weave at present.' She gulped and placed a hand on his shoulder. 'And the answer is that he will teach me how to use the loom.'

'Yes, that is so,' Geoffrey, who has already withdrawn his hand from Graeme's, held it cradled in the other as though in pain. 'Also, dear friend, I have thought that Annie should have a tall stool to sit on because she is shorter than I and will have difficulty reaching to push the shuttle through the threads.'

The old woman looked at his hand and nodded, yawned, mumbled something about her friend's poor quality ale, then stumbled to her usual place by the fire and fell instantly asleep.

Without a word the three of them gathered by the loom. Geoffrey pushed a small stool for her to stand on, explaining he would soon make a taller version and with whispered commands, he taught Annie how to weave.

During the following days he showed her how to set up the threads and tie them to the frame of the loom and within a fortnight she was weaving, albeit slower than he, but nevertheless competently enough to produce a piece of fine cloth.

On the eve of their departure they waited until the old woman had fallen asleep and then met Annie outside the dwelling where they huddled together close to the monastery wall.

Geoffrey patted the old handcart beside him. 'We shall travel with Graeme in this, sleeping by the wayside until we reach a town or—' he shrugged '—any place that feels good for us to stay a while.'

Annie asked, 'And you have your story ready to tell anyone who asks who you are?'

Geoffrey replied, 'We are brother and sister—we decided that's safer than husband and wife. Jennifer is my sister who fell from a cart and was badly hurt and I am devoted to caring for her.'

Graeme pulled a bundle out from the cart and held up a woman's bodice and skirt made of plain linen. He took a white cap and put it on his head, saying with a grin, 'I think this will complete my transformation.'

The sight of him, looking like a younger version of herself, was too much for Annie and she burst into tears.

After a while, feeling calmer but dejected, she hugged them both and wished them good fortune in their new life. She walked to the door of the dwelling and looked back at their silhouettes moving about in the darkness as they prepared to leave, then, knowing she might never see them or hear of them again, she went into the dwelling and prepared for bed.

The following morning she awoke to find her mother standing over her, demanding, 'Where is my boy?'

'I think he and…'

'Think! Don't pretend you don't know what they're up to. You've been whispering together for day after day. Do you think I haven't noticed? Do you think I'm so stupid that I have no knowledge of their sin?'

'If you love your son, Mother, you'll not mention this to anyone…'

'Son? What son? I have no son, so what is there to tell anyone?'

'You could say that the two young men who used to live here have gone off seeking work in—' she struggled to think where men might go for employment '—I don't know, a bigger town perhaps.'

'Leaving you to work the loom?'

'That's right, Mother. We'll get by with you spinning and me weaving.'

The old woman sank down beside her and said, 'What they do is a sin.'

'So they say, Mother.'

'Don't you believe they are breaking God's law that the joining of man and woman is for procreation only and not for their pleasure and therefore it follows that any other form of coming together is not permitted?'

'I don't know, mother. I only know that I love my brother and he already lives with the pain from the injuries he suffered in the fire, therefore I think he deserves some happiness.'

The old woman crossed herself. 'If any of the neighbours ask where they've gone, I'll say they went off to visit someone far away and I don't know when they'll return.' Her mouth was misshapen as she fought her emotion and her fists were clenched tightly, 'I'll pray for his soul and I'll do penance for him every day for the rest of my life.'

Annie put her arm around the dejected shoulders and the two women sat in silence for a long while.

❖ ❖ ❖

Time passed. The seasons changed. The old woman grew frail and walked with a limp when she went out, which was not often in summer and never in the winter. There was no way of knowing how Graeme and Geoffrey had fared and she never mentioned her son's name.

Whenever Annie went to church she prayed for her brother. While there she dreaded the mention of Sodom and Gomorra, for then she would feel the tension in her mother's body as she stood rigidly beside her while the priest railed against sodomites.

Eight years after Graeme and Geoffrey had left for their new life, Annie, although no longer young, was now a handsome woman with strong arms from the weaving and highly respected for the fine cloth she sold in the market. One man who showed his liking for her was a portly widower, with whom she had often exchanged banter while selling her cloth to him. When this man, known as 'Joseph the cloakmaker', came to pay court to her she almost rebuffed him, but her mother insisted that his suit should be encouraged, saying, 'This will be your last chance, Daughter. We have no child to follow you and there's no possibility of—' she paused, unwilling to say her son's name '—anyone else producing one.'

Knowing her duty was to marry and prevent their line from dying out, Annie accepted the offer and went to live with her husband on the far side of the monastery. Once installed in his house and now known as Mistress Allen she was surprised to find that sleeping with her chubby man was a very pleasurable experience, and, not only that—he made her laugh. And so, later than most and just when she had thought such happiness had passed her by, she fell deeply in love with her husband.

The only cause of worry in her domestic happiness was the resentment of three grown stepsons who had been angered by their father's second marriage and who made clear their fear that she was after his money. On frequent visits to her mother she kept the loom in good order as an insurance against the possibility of being left a widow in need of an income.

She thought of her brother every day and named her firstborn son after him and her second born after his friend so that their names were constantly on her lips and she could be reminded of them amidst the daily life of children's games, tears and merriment.

When a little girl was born, her husband was overjoyed with his first daughter. He insisted she should be named Anne and spent hours sitting beside her, singing lullabies while rocking her wooden cradle. A few days later he was celebrating her birth with his friends in a tavern and suddenly said, 'I fear I may...' and dropped to the floor like a stone.

After his burial the sons from his first marriage came to claim their inheritance and made clear to Annie there was little left for her and she was not welcome to stay in the house. So with two small boys and a tiny baby, she returned to the dwelling where she was born.

Her mother, who was now very frail indeed, lived long enough to know there was a new generation to follow her and to see little Anne scampering merrily with her older brothers, then, one cold January night, she passed quietly into death

When Annie removed her mother's clothes to prepare her for burial she found a hair shirt beneath which the skin was red raw and covered in suppurating sores. Tears blinded her as she realised that, while never once saying her beloved son's name in the years since his departure, the old woman had been constantly reminded of him and had done penance for him every day.

Annie taught all her children to weave and spin and told them tales of long ago when there were three sacred wells, one red, one white and one black. And so she gave them a skill with which to earn a living and handed down the history of their ancestors.

When Geoffrey, her younger son, wished to join the monastery, she was sad, but did not attempt to dissuade him from following his dream. She was delighted by her daughter's marriage to a young farrier and looked forward to the children to be born from their union.

Although loving the grandchildren that came to give her joy, she was disappointed to find that neither the two girls nor the boy, showed any sign of having inherited the gift of sight.

Graeme, her older son married in due course, but when his wife had not conceived in ten years, Annie gave up hope. She assumed the guardians of the dark well from long ago, of which her mother had spoken, should have descended through her brother and must now be extinct.

On a cold day in early spring, when her joints ached and every move-ment caused searing pain in her hips, Annie was longing for death to set her free from physical affliction until Graeme came and told her his wife was with child. With renewed joy in life she struggled through the following months determined to see the baby before she died.

When the time came and the baby girl was safely delivered, Annie limped slowly through the heat of summer sun to see her. On looking into the newborn's eyes she felt her whole being glow with happiness and exclaimed, 'The next one has arrived!'

A few moments later a cold shiver ran through her. Closing her eyes she saw her brother lying dead on a bed with a fatter and balder version of Geoffrey weeping beside him. She had no way of knowing where they were, or how he had died, but although grieving, she was comforted by the fact that he had spent many years with his beloved and had left life at the same time as his successor arrived to take her place in the long line of guardians of the dark well.

Chapter Thirteen

Louisa heard a giggle and a voice say, 'No, it's alright, she's asleep.'

Opening her eyes she saw a young boy in a sailor suit standing in front of her and smiled at him as she said, 'Did you think I was dead, young man?'

'My mother got worried, lady. She wanted me to make sure, on account of you being so still for such a long time.'

Louisa thanked him and said he and his mother were very kind. She stood up and began walking towards the house, until, hearing the church clock strike three times and realising there was still time to call on her Aunt Rosemary, she turned and walked out of the grounds onto the street and then followed the abbey wall around into the narrow lane in which she lived.

On reaching the old cottage she rang the large brass bell beside the front door.

'My dear Louisa,' the old lady said, when the door was open, 'how lovely to see you.' They embraced and then walked along the stone floor to the small parlour where a teapot covered in a knitted tea cosy and prettily flowered cups and saucers were laid on a small round table. Louisa said, 'Are you expecting a guest, Aunt Rosemary?'

'Yes, my dear, I thought you would come today.' The old lady's smile showed the pretty girl she had once been. 'I must have the second sight!' She laughed and poured two cups of tea.

Between sips of her drink Louisa gave a short description of the vision she had recently experienced.

'I am very impressed, my dear. You must have witnessed the fire in twelfth century. I think it took many years to rebuild the church and then later it was destroyed completely after the dissolution of the monasteries.' Her aunt shook her head sadly, then added, 'I felt sorry for the girl who pretended to speak French. I suspect she would not have a happy life married to an old man, but then I suppose that would be better than being sent to a nunnery.'

Louisa said, 'I forget which king was on the throne at that time.'

'He would have been one of the early Henrys—the second I think; he would have spoken French, as did the whole court.'

Louisa felt a sudden tingling in her hands and heard a woman laugh overhead. 'Do you think this house is very old, Aunt?' she asked.

'The back part, where the scullery and the pantry are now, is very, very old; the walls tell me stories of the people who lived within them and I often hear the rhythmic sound of a loom and singing and laughter too. There has been great happiness here and tragedy too of course, life is never without some pain. The rest of it—' the old lady patted the wall beside her '—was probably added on after King Henry the Eighth's men sacked the monastery and the abbey church. I think our forbears, like many local people, used stone from the ruins to build their house. I believe some of the stone has held memories of that time, I often see monks walking through here with their heads bowed and hands clasped in prayer, as though on their way to church.'

Louisa said, 'I am pleased to know you also have had some strange experiences in the ruins of the abbey.'

'And I am delighted you have experienced the dark well. I have long hoped and believed that it still existed.'

'You knew about it?'

'My grandmother told me stories about the three sacred wells, the red, the white and the black. We all know the whereabouts of the red and the white near the foot of the Tor, but the third has been hidden for a long, long time. My grandmother said it had been poisoned, but one day it would be found again.'

Louisa heard a clock chime four times and said she must leave.

Rosemary went with her to the front door and said, 'I'm sorry I haven't had time to read the tea-leaves for you. Shall I take a peek next time you come to visit me?'

'Yes please, Aunt Rosemary, I'd love to know what you see, but only the good please, I don't want to know the bad.'

'Very well, dear Louisa.' She kissed her cheek and added, 'I look forward to seeing you again soon. We have a lot to talk about. I have many more tales to tell and I want to hear about all the visions you have seen.' With a smile she added, 'Please give my best wishes to Agnes. I believe she is involved in a deception of some kind.' Seeing that Louisa open her mouth with a gasp of surprise, Aunt Rosemary said, 'Do not deny it, my dear. I have seen it in the cup, but am sure there is good reason for it.' She kissed her cheek and bade her goodbye.

Louisa hurried along the narrow lane beside the abbey wall looking up at the Tor ahead until she reached the main gates of her Aunt Agnes's house.

After she had told her aunt about the vision of Annie and the fire in the abbey, Louisa said, 'I saw Aunt Rosemary; she sends her love to you.'

The old lady was quiet for a few moments before saying, 'The prettiest of us all.' She then closed her eyes, which was her way of ending the conversation.

Louisa was relieved to keep silent regarding any reading of the tea-leaves and began a painting from the sketch she had made of the well.

Two days later a letter arrived in the post to Louisa from Emily thanking her for the care of her mother and enclosing an envelope addressed to the old lady. When Louisa took out the card on which were painted tiny cherubs cavorting among pretty flowers, she handed it to her aunt, explaining it was sent from Emily with love. Although the old lady appeared very calm, almost disinterested in the card when it was shown to her, she nevertheless kept it close to her all that day and it was placed under the pillow that night.

The following morning Louisa said, 'I could put the card from

Emily on the table where you could see it.'

The old lady agreed and when it was in place she sat gazing at it with her face contorted into a sad smile.

Louisa said, 'I believe Emily is a good hearted soul and loves you very much.'

The old lady nodded. 'I know and I love her—but I always say— the wrong thing and—' she shook her head '—so does she.'

Louisa smiled sympathetically. 'I hope she will come to see you soon.'

'She would not—be welcome when—George is here. They have— a terrible feud.'

Louisa wanted to say, 'It is your house, Aunt. George is a bully and he does not have the right to dictate who visits you.' But she was now sure her aunt's pretence that she had not recovered from the stroke was in order to foil George's plan to either cut Emily out of her will, or make a change that was not in Emily's best interest. She therefore said, 'I think very highly of Emily and will support you in every way possible. Would you like me to write and ask her to come and stay while Edwina and George are in Brighton?'

'I will think—on it.'

Seeing how tired her aunt now looked Louisa decided to leave the subject for a while.

When Monday came around Louisa was eager to get to the abbey and once there could not settle to sketch but sat and waited with closed eyes for another adventure.

Soon the peace was disrupted by familiar voices and opening her eyes she was not surprised to see the exotic group of people approaching. When they stopped a few feet away holding out bent sticks she decided to leave, until, seeing Edward Francis striding towards them, she sank back on the bench.

'Good day, my friends,' Edward said in a cheerful voice. 'I am so pleased to see you all. I wonder if you would like to come and feel the energy over the other side. I think it is very strong there.'

They followed him, still talking loudly to one another, apparently oblivious of their disturbing effect on the tranquil atmosphere.

Louisa closed her eyes and in an effort to ignore the jarring sounds of their harsh voices, concentrated on a robin singing in a nearby bush. Her mind was soon filled with the bird's song, which after a while became the sweet sound of women's voices singing. She strained to hear the words and could make no sense of them then recognised that one or two were Latin …

Chapter Fourteen

As the Office of Prime drew to a close, Veryan kissed the cross on her rosary and left the chapel then walked through the cloister to the infirmary at the far side of the priory. She paused behind a pillar to loosen her girdle and find relief from the chafing around her waist. Sister Bernadette the Infirmarian had assured her she would soon become used to the rough wool next to her skin, but even after four weeks, this had not yet happened and she was still very uncomfortable.

Remembering how she had often complained about the homespun linen woven on her mother's loom, she gave a wry smile and admitted how fortunate she had been in her childhood. In fact her life had been without strife until she fell in love with Robin. Thinking of the handsome young ostler made her bite her lip so hard it hurt and the salty taste of blood reminded her of the tears she shed when he laughingly said he had changed his mind.

She had truly believed his promise of marriage when she went with him into the stables and lay with him in the hay, while he, so callous, so cruel, had told the other men who worked with the horses that she had lain with him. And so the farrier, the saddler and even the driver of the cart who collected the cloth from her mother, all sniggered on seeing her walk past.

Hearing footsteps on the tiled floor and not wishing to be found loitering, she continued on to the infirmary then stood looking at the neat and clean room lined with eighteen straw mattresses, only four of which were presently occupied.

'Did I see you adjusting your clothing again, Veryan?'

Turning to face the Infirmarian, she replied, 'I'm sorry, Sister Bernadette, I do try to accept the discomfort with humility as you said I should.'

'I suggest you try harder if you wish to become more than a novice.'

'Oh, I do, I really do, Sister. I will try harder,' she said, desperately trying to ignore the itch under her right arm.

'Tell me, young Mistress Veryan, why did you come to join us?'

She repeated the words she had said when entering the convent, 'I felt the calling to give my life to Our Lady and Christ and God...'

'And to have food and shelter?'

This had never been suggested before and she was taken aback by the direct question. A red blush was hot on her face as the old woman's ice blue eyes met hers. 'I admit I was hungry and tired when I came, but that was because I'd lost my way walking here and had fallen into one of the new ditches the monks have had dug to drain the flood lands.'

The nun looked unconvinced. 'Where was your home?'

'At Glastonbury.'

'You know the house of the Benedictines?'

'Yes, Sister. My mother's house is by the monastery wall.'

'Does she know you have come here?'

'I'm not sure—' she fidgeted with the fabric rubbing against her neck '—at least, no, in fact she does not know.'

'And why is that?'

'I left without telling her. I...um... I thought it was the best thing to do in the circumstances.'

'And what were those circumstances?'

Veryan recalled her own voice screaming with rage and her mother's tearful pleas for calm. 'We had an argument about something and ...' she broke off with relief as a nun ran into the room crying, 'Sister Bernadette, Sister, oh dear Sister. What shall we do?'

'I have no idea and will not have one unless you explain why you are so agitated, Sister Angelica.'

'A man has left three of his family by the entrance—' the nun wrung her hands and grimaced with anxiety '—he banged on the door and then drove his cart away as fast as the old horse would go.'

Veryan followed the two nuns to the main entrance of the nunnery and then helped them carry the woman and her two children to the infirmary. She could see all three were feverish and knew from their limp bodies and dull eyes that they were desperately ill. When told to undo the woman's bodice she unlaced it and on seeing a large swelling under her arm, said, 'That's strange, is it not, Sister?'

She watched as Sister Bernadette knelt down and peered at the woman's body for several moments, then stood up and made the sign of the cross. 'I have never seen such a thing before,' the old nun said, adding with a tremor in her voice, 'we are in God's hands. And also—' she looked at Veryan '—in yours, young novice. You will sit and watch over them. Call me when, or if, there is any change.'

'Veryan watched over them that night and although sleeping a little from time to time, she mostly sat in the dark thinking of the way she had run away and wondering if her mother would forgive her. There was also Jacob to think of. He had asked for her hand, despite knowing all the gossip spread by the ostler. She had thought he was being kind because they had been friends since childhood and he was sorry for her in her shame. He was that sort of person. 'Too nice for his own good,' as her mother used to say, when he tried to mend a squirrel's broken leg or was willing to take the blame when Veryan had led him into mischief.

Her mother had said it was a good offer in the circumstances and being a baker's wife would mean she'd never go hungry; both of which were true. She liked Jacob. Indeed, she had to admit she loved Jacob! She had always loved him, but she had not wanted to be the squirrel with a broken leg, she had wanted to be the passionately beloved and desperately adored princess of the stories that Jacob had learned from his father and told so well when they had sat by the fire in the evening while her mother spun her wool or flax.

The princess in the stories always lived in a tall tower surrounded by impenetrable forest, or a huge castle protected by warriors; she was always virtuous and virginal, she was demure and docile, she span golden thread and she wove beautiful tapestry.

The beautiful heroine did not live in a cottage by the monastery wall, helping her mother to spin and to weave ordinary cloth for ordinary people. There would have been no drunken old man next door trying to grope her whenever she passed by and no gossiping women at the well sneering at her for her stupidity. And above all, definitely, very definitely, the princess would not have given herself to a sweet-talking philanderer before the handsome prince could come to claim her for his bride!

She was exhausted when the bell sounding for Lauds at five o'clock the following morning awoke her from a short doze. The remembrances and thoughts of the night had left her feeling utterly miserable and consumed with guilt for leaving her mother, who would, she was sure, be desperately worried and imagining a terrible fate had befallen her daughter.

Having been excused from the service in order to watch over the invalids she did not, as was usual, hurry to the chapel, but instead knelt beside the youngest child to see how he fared. She heard him take the same shallow rasping breath as he had all night, but this time only silence followed and knowing the little boy had died, she felt a cold stone in her chest. His sister lived only minutes longer and finally, just as the singing of the nuns ended in the chapel, the mother also died.

She was removing the bedding after preparing the three corpses for burial when a nun came running in saying, 'There's two more outside, looks like the same sickness!'

When they had brought the two young men into the infirmary and placed them gently on clean bedding, Sister Bernadette opened their shirts and found black suppurating swellings in their arm pits and also, on further investigation, in their groins. With a deep sigh, she said, 'Christ be merciful, I think a plague has come among us.'

Within a few days many more sick people had been brought to the door and left there until the infirmary was crammed with them lying on straw-filled mattresses. Veryan worked day and night, putting cold wet cloths on foreheads to reduce fever and giving drinks of water to those who would take it.

The infirmary stank of death; the stench hung on the air all around the priory. The nuns kept praying while mostly keeping away from the sick people.

Sister Bernadette collapsed during Matins in the early hours of the morning and was carried into the infirmary. On removing her clothes Veryan found the telltale swelling under her arm and burst into tears. 'Don't weep, little novice,' the old nun whispered. 'I go joyfully to meet my saviour.' Then she screamed and gabbled of devils with forked tails and how she was burning in the fires of hell until, suddenly lucid and with her aged face lit up in a smile, she said, 'I hear the bell for Sext. It is noon, time we must go to chapel for the third of the Little Hours of the divine office. Hurry, hurry ...'

Veryan, watched the joyful expression fade away and was thankful the old nun had escaped into death.

The only people now working in the infirmary were Veryan and one lay servant, who was obviously terrified by the sickness and did little of any use. When a woman came with her dying child and said, 'I had hoped you would know of herbs that would cure him.'

Veryan replied, 'I know of nothing that would fight this sickness. There are plants I know of that will cure a cough or heal a wound, but even my mother, who is wise in the ways of nature's remedies, even she could not make your son well.'

Thinking of her mother, Veryan wondered if she had caught this vile sickness and longed to get news of her. Realising she had not been listening to the woman who was now asking her to care for the child, she agreed and said she would also pray for his cure, while feeling sure he could not recover.

The woman said, 'I think this is God's judgement on me. I once took pleasure with a boy on May Eve and have never done penance for my sin.'

Veryan wanted to comfort her and also, thinking of her own mistake, said, 'I'm sure God would forgive you.'

'I don't feel sure he would. I know you mean to be kind, but there's so much sinful lust in us all, we need punishment to cleanse us and I think it's happening now.'

'You think we're all being punished?' Veryan asked.

'We have been struck with God's wrath. You're safely hidden from it here. You don't realise how bad things are outside these walls. There's no one to be seen out and about, people are either dead or hiding indoors afraid of catching the vile affliction. Coming here I walked past untended fields and neglected animals. My man returned from Bristol a sennight since and he said this plague is spreading everywhere. He heard it called The Black Death.' She began sobbing and rocking the boy in her arms then sank to the ground in a faint.

Veryan laid mother and son on a mattress. She knew without looking there were swellings under their arms and was sure their corpses would soon be buried together.

The room seemed smellier, more stifling and hotter than usual. She walked towards the door hoping to catch a breeze and breathe in fresh air, then the walls began spinning around her and she fell into darkness.

After this she inhabited a strange dream world of weird forests in which trees walked and tried to trip her up, while all manner of terrifying dogs and creatures chased her, slavering at her heels as she ran, but never quite catching hold of her because her mother was flying overhead, holding her up, just high enough to keep above the ravening beasts.

When the ghost of her mother came down and hovered over her, she whispered, 'I love you, Mother.' Although wanting so say she was sorry, truly sorry she had run away and she had felt unable to face Jacob in her shame, she was too weak to speak further.

'And I love you, Daughter dear. Drink this water.'

She sipped from the cup, feeling the hard rim on her lip and the cold water run down her throat, which was strange when it was only a dream.

'Sleep now, child, you've come through the worst of it and now we must get you strong again.'

Sleep seemed a very odd thing to do when she was already asleep. She tried moving her hand and with a great effort managed to grasp the old woman's arm, which felt warm and strong. 'Am I alive, Mother?'

'You are, Daughter.'

She heard her mother's sobbing laughter before falling into a deep and fever-free sleep.

The next day, not that she knew how much time had passed, but her mother said it was so; she drank some gruel from a spoon. Later, with her mother's help, she sat up and looked around the infirmary. Seeing only one figure lying on the straw bedding, she knew the mother and son had died. Then, thinking the lack of sick people might be a good sign, she asked, 'Is it over?'

'No, my dear, it's not done with us yet. The plague is still out there, but there's no one left to bring the sick here and if they did I'm the only person here to care for them.'

'The sisters are all dead?'

'Many have died, the servant who was helping you disappeared when I arrived and the rest keep their distance — they're doing the only thing they can — praying for the end of the sickness and for the salvation of the souls who succumbed to it's vileness.'

When she asked her mother how she came to be in the nunnery, the old woman gave a wry smile. 'I have my ways of knowing. What's more, when I heard about the vile illness spreading all around the area, I knew you'd be in the infirmary caring for the sick, so I came asking after you.' She sighed. 'They told me you were dying and indeed I felt the angel of death's wings beating around me when I saw you, but—' she made the sign of the cross '—heaven be praised, I managed to get the fever down and you are young and strong and here we are!'

Veryan said, 'I wonder how many others survived it.'

'Not many, that's for sure,' her mother replied sadly. 'Most of those who remain alive are lucky like me and somehow did not take in the vile poison that made people sick.' She looked at the only other occupant of the room. 'That poor nun is sinking fast and will soon be gone to meet her maker. She's a rich lady, I believe, who was sent here by her family for lying with a servant and giving birth to a bastard.' She shook her head. 'All last night she was calling for her child and her lover, but never once did she cry for her mother, whereas other's I could mention ...'

'I dreamed of you, Mother.'

'I know, child, I know.' She smiled. 'I heard you calling for me and my heart was glad, so glad.'

When the nun, who had once been a rich lady, had died, Mother and daughter prayed together for the unhappy woman's soul. Then Veryan said, 'I think perhaps I'm not suited to the nunnery, Mother.'

The old woman nodded. 'I'll take you home now. There's no more I can do here.' She helped her to stand and said with mock solemnity, 'Your carriage awaits, well, actually I have the old handcart outside—if you're not too proud?'

'I'll never be too proud to go with you, Mother.'

When they reached the dwelling by the monastery wall and she was safely inside lying on a bed beside the fire, she found the courage to ask,

'Did Jacob catch the plague?'

'He had not a fortnight ago, but since then I don't know.'

'Was he still willing to take my hand when you last spoke with him?'

'He was.'

'When I have recovered my looks and if he still lives, I will try to explain my reason for running away.'

'I think you'll find him understanding. To him you are his beautiful princess who needs never apologise, nor explain.'

A while later, awakening from sleep, Veryan heard a knock on the door and the nervous tremor in Jacob's voice as he asked if she had come home yet. Raising herself on one elbow and trying to tidy her unruly hair with the other hand, she asked him to enter.

Chapter Fifteen

Louisa could still feel the strands of hair between her fingers when she opened her eyes. As the memory of being Veryan faded she remembered the exotic people who had been in the ruins earlier and turned to look for them. To her surprise she found her Aunt Rosemary standing nearby, resplendent in an outfit designed for bicycling, which included a divided skirt and a wide brimmed had tied around her head with a silk scarf. Edward Francis was a few feet away wearing his distinctive hat and next to him was an elderly man, whom she had not seen before and who, on meeting her gaze, lifted a conventional panama hat from his bald head.

'We have been divining, or, as Edward would have it, dowsing,' Aunt Rosemary explained. 'And we have been brought to the wall behind you.' She gave a surprisingly girlish giggle. 'My hazel twig tells me we might have found that dark well of yours.'

Louisa looked at the eager faces of the two men and back again at her aunt. 'That would be so wonderful. I had assumed it was lost long ago.'

Edward said, 'We can't promise anything. But I, for one, would like to know what is bringing us all to this spot.'

The old man stepped forward saying, 'And so would I.' He held out his hand. 'My name is James Overton. I am fascinated by the history of this place and good friends with both Edward and the owner of the abbey ruins. I'm especially interested in the legends of King Arthur. I wondered if you've seen any visions of them?'

Louisa shook her head. 'I'm afraid not.' She told them a brief summary of Veryan's story, adding, 'One never knows, perhaps the Knights of the Round Table might appear on another occasion.'

James Overton said, 'The monks found King Arthur's and Queen Guinevere's tombs and the bones were reburied in the abbey, so I expect you'll see them in due course.'

Aunt Rosemary said, 'And don't forget Joseph of Arimathea.'

'That's right,' Mr Overton agreed. 'He was Jesus' uncle and the story is told that he came here and founded the Christian church and...'

'Some say he brought Jesus here as a boy when he came to buy Cornish tin—' Edward grinned at Louisa '—just thought I'd mention it.'

Aunt Rosemary asked, 'Have you seen him, Louisa?'

Louisa gulped and replied, 'I don't think so. The man who came with the wooden cross and built the little church must have spoken English because I understood him, although I did struggle with his accent.'

Mr Overton said, 'I wonder if you'll see what happened later here—' he gestured around him at the ruined walls and lumps of stone covered in ivy and surrounded by brambles '—this was a huge monastery with an enormous and incredibly beautiful abbey church before King Henry the Eighth's men closed it and murdered the Abbot and two of his monks.'

'Hanged them on the Tor,' Edward said shaking his head.

Aunt Rosemary spread her hands hopelessly. 'All because the King wanted to make himself head of the Church so he could divorce his wife and marry again.'

'And, don't forget, Aunt,' Edward suggested, 'the monasteries were beyond his control.'

'Also they were very, very rich,' Mr Overton said. 'They owned vast tracts of land and often collected tithes from the population. I'm afraid the King wanted their wealth—it's as straightforward as that.'

Edward said, 'The abbot's fishpond at Meare is a good example of how far the abbey lands stretched beyond the monastery itself.' He shrugged, 'I know the abbey was a rich landowner, but the monks did a good job of draining the land didn't they?'

Mr Overton nodded. 'Oh yes indeed! They instigated the digging of the rhynes that crisscross the levels; the land around was covered in water until then. The Romans did some drainage further towards the sea, but you are correct, Edward, we have the monks to thanks for the landscape as we now see it. Although,' he added with a smile, 'The Isle of Avalon, as it is often called, was aptly named, and the island is still to be seen rising above the flood water during excessive and prolonged rain.'

Aunt Rosemary pursed her lips before saying very politely, 'I do find all this fascinating, but could we not continue with the investigation?'

Edward walked purposefully towards the place where Louisa had been sitting, climbed over the bench and pulled a plank out from the wooden barrier behind it. He then climbed over the barrier and disappeared from view.

After a few moments Aunt Rosemary said anxiously, 'He is very quiet, I do hope all is well.'

Sounds of rubble being disturbed and a loud exclamation of, 'Damnation!' caused an intake of breath by Aunt Rosemary, which made Louisa want to laugh, despite being worried about Edward.

'Can you see anything?' Mr Overton called out.

'It's dark and murky down here, I can see steps where monks probably went in and out,' Edward replied. A few moments later his head appeared over the wooden barrier and he added, 'There's a big flat stone under an arch that I think might be covering something interesting—a well possibly. I ran out of matches so I couldn't see any more.'

Mr Overton punched the air and exclaimed, 'Well done, Edward, well done, old chap!' Then he laughed like an excited boy.

After Edward had climbed out and replaced the plank of wood on the barrier, everyone agreed that nothing more could be done that afternoon.

Mr Overton said he would return the following day with a lantern and Edward agreed he could meet him at three o'clock then looked questioningly at Louisa.

'Unfortunately—' she swallowed hard '—I shall be unable to join you. I must attend to my aunt.'

Edward said, 'By the way, Mrs Wendon, you may have seen me with some acquaintances earlier.'

Louisa wanted to say, 'Are you referring to the exotic people with loud voices,' instead she replied that she had indeed seen him.

'They were making rather a lot of noise and I therefore suggested they might walk up the Tor to give you some peace. They are interested in dowsing, not for water as we have today, but for the energy lines that some of us believe link up sacred sites.'

Louisa instantly understood. 'Is that like a kind of pull on one to go to a place or tingling in the hands when you draw near?'

Edward spread his hands in the air. 'How fascinating! Is that what you experience?'

'I had not thought about it before,' Louisa replied. 'It was something I accepted without question, but yes, that is indeed what I feel.'

'I think you will not be in need of any dowsing rods, Mrs Wendon, you will find energy lines without such instruments.' He grinned and added, 'I am sure those people from London will want to meet you and hear of your gifts. I know this is the last day of their stay here, but they assured me of their intention to return in the near future. Would you be willing to meet them next time they visit Glastonbury?'

Louisa frowned and fingered her black skirt while remembering the beautiful clothes worn by the two women. How could someone like her mix with people like that? She saw her aunt smile encouragingly and then found the courage to say, 'I would be delighted to meet with them.'

After they had all bade one another goodbye and Louisa had walked a short distance away, she was pleasantly surprised to hear her aunt calling her name. Having turned and walked back to meet her Louisa was surprised to hear her say, 'I would like to visit my old friend Agnes tomorrow. Would that be convenient, do you think?'

'I would be most grateful, Aunt Rosemary; you are evidently making it possible for me to come here during that time, but I fear you will miss …'

'I will be happy to miss the investigation, Louisa dear.' The old lady gave a loving smile. 'That hat suits you, as does the lace. I'm so glad you are coming out of mourning.'

'I shall need to stay in black for a year, Aunt.'

With a sigh the old lady said, 'Surely you have been mourning long enough, dear child!'

They agreed that Aunt Rosemary would come to the house at fifteen minutes to three the following day and went their separate ways.

While walking back to the house Louisa wondered if Aunt Agnes would be agreeable to having Aunt Rosemary call on her the next day. On arrival she thanked the housekeeper who had been sitting knitting in the chair beside the bed and waited until she had left the room and well out of earshot before mentioning the proposed visit.

When Aunt Agnes heard of this arrangement she was delighted, much to Louisa's relief. 'I shall have—to pretend I—am unable—to speak,' the old lady said. 'But you could—tell her I—have regained—some hearing and—would enjoy the telling—of a little—gossip. I do miss knowing—what is going on—Louisa dear.'

'It is the price you pay for this secrecy, Aunt Agnes,' Louisa said, hoping to hide the irritation she sometimes felt when keeping up the pretence and also wondering, not for the first time, if perhaps her aunt was either senile, or her brain had been affected by the stroke.

Seeing her aunt looking sad, Louisa said, 'You wished me an adventure today and your wish came true. I'm afraid it is distressing, however. Would you like to hear about it?'

'Oh yes—my dear. We—cannot always—have a—happy ending.'

The following day seemed longer than usual until Aunt Rosemary arrived and settled herself down in a chair, saying, 'Well, Agnes, I'm so sorry you had the stroke. I'm told you can hear, but not speak.' She raised one eyebrow. 'For one with the gift of the gab that must be a torment, my dear!'

When Aunt Agnes snorted with suppressed laughter Louisa grinned, knowing the old lady had the perfect person to keep her company. While leaving the room she chuckled on hearing Aunt Rosemary say, 'Well, my dear! You will not believe the rumour I heard recently...'

Five minutes later, having hurried out of the house and through the garden, she made her way through the burgeoning undergrowth to the ruins where she found Edward and Mr Overton, already there waiting for her.

Looking behind the spot where the visions had come to her she was amazed to see the undergrowth flattened and the top of a ladder sticking up from inside the crypt.

'We've made it secure, Mrs Wendon,' Mr Overton said. 'The next thing will be to lift the lump of stone to see if it is indeed covering the well. As you know, I've been keeping the owner informed of our progress and one of his men will come and help another day. But for now we thought you could go down and see the stone with Edward, while I wait up here and keep guard.'

Edward climbed down into the crypt carrying a lamp and then steadied the ladder for Louisa as she descended thinking how easy life must be for men whose legs were not constantly hampered by layers of petticoats and skirts.

On reaching the bottom she stood looking at the carved stone arch in the alcove then at the large slab of stone on the ground beneath it and knew with absolute certainty she had found the dark well of her visions.

Edward lit the lantern and placed it beside the stone then said, 'Shall I go out and leave you for a while?'

She agreed and while watching him climb away from her, wondered whether they might have become romantically involved if he had not been married. He was an attractive and interesting man who had travelled to Africa, a kind of buccaneer in a way: but he was married and besides that impediment, she was a penniless widow who must accept her courting days were done.

Looking under the arch she dismissed her thoughts of romance. Nothing was important, nothing that is but the stone and whatever it concealed....

Chapter Sixteen

'Tobin, you miserable ingrate, where are you?'

Hearing his stepmother calling, Tobin stopped collecting the nuts from under the tree and picked up the sack. As he swung it onto his shoulder he was pleased to find how very heavy it was and then gave a rueful smile, knowing that no matter how great was his harvest it would never be enough for his father's wife.

He walked along beside the high stone wall to the dwelling built just outside it and met the angry woman waiting for him. 'What a waste of food and water!' she said eyeing him malevolently. Then, reaching for the sack, she asked, 'Is that all you've got?'

'It is,' he replied, adding in his head, 'You miserable old hag.' He grimaced while remembering the time when very tired after a long day collecting broken branches from the trees for firewood, he had spoken the words that were in his mind as well as the usual obsequious response and she had heard it and beaten him with a stick until he fell unconscious.

When his mild-mannered father questioned him about the bruising and black eyes, he had answered truthfully and then later received another beating from the furious woman. His father was a weaver and wove cloth on a loom in the main room of the dwelling, which meant there was little space for his second wife and their two daughters. While Tobin, who spent most of his time keeping out of their way, slept in a small shack he had made leaning up against the wall surrounding the abbey and rarely stayed in the dwelling longer than was needed to eat a meal.

His father had inherited the small dwelling from his first wife, Tobin's mother. Many generations of her family, so his father had told him, had owned the house before her and a story had been handed down about the first woman to live in it. This old lady had lived by a well, close to where the abbey now stood and she had been given this dwelling in exchange for the one she lived in so that the abbey could be built there.

Once, when he had asked about his mother, his father had looked very sad then explained she had died giving birth to him. After hearing this he liked to imagine what she looked like and how life would have been if she had lived. Perhaps she would have smiled affectionately at him, which would have been very different from the sour looks of his father's wife, or she would have given him the same amount of food as the other children, which would mean he was no longer hungry all the time.

On a day in winter when there was even less food than usual and therefore he was extremely hungry, he returned from collecting twigs and broken branches for the fire and was heaping them beside the door when he was horrified to hear his father begging for mercy. Wondering who could be frightening him so, he lingered to listen and heard his stepmother say, 'I tell you it's what you must do with the monster. That way he'll be fed and we won't have the burden hanging round our necks for ever more.'

'But, wife, I beg you, he is only a boy and he can't help the way he's made.'

'It's not my fault neither. I don't know if it was God or the devil that made him swaybacked and so ugly, but either way he must to go to the abbey tomorrow at dawn. It's all arranged. I've told you my final word on the matter and that's the end of it!'

Tobin touched the purple mark on his cheek and felt tears run down onto his fingers, then hearing his father's footsteps, quickly wiped his face dry and began stacking the sticks against the wall.

'I have good news, Tobin—' his father swallowed hard and averted his eyes '—you have been offered a place as servant in the abbey.'

'I thank you, Father,' he said, knowing from the man's clenched jaw and thin pale lips that this was a painful duty for him. He kept his face set until reaching his bed in the shack and then, feeling utterly miserable and desperately lonely, he wept until he escaped into exhausted sleep.

The following day he tried hard to match the strides of his strong, straight father as they walked to the abbey gates. When a small door at one side was opened and a monk peered at him, he shook with fear.

He was aware of his father and the man speaking, but made no attempt to understand their words. He felt his father's hand giving him a gentle push on his shoulder and heard him say, 'Farewell.' Then he walked through the door and stood on a cobbled yard in the pale light of a cold winter morning.

When the monk turned and walked away, he stood frozen for a moment until, seeing him turn and beckon, he followed him to a building where a large monk was stirring a pot over a fire.

'I've brought a boy to assist you, brother,' the monk said and left him standing on the threshold quaking with fear.

The large monk continued stirring for some time, then, turning to look at him asked, 'When did you last eat, boy?'

'Y-yesterday m-morning, s-sir,' Tobin replied.

'I'm surprised. You look as though it was longer ago than that,' the monk said. He scooped a spoonful of gruel into a wooden bowl and handed it to him. 'Here, eat this and then I'll tell you your duties.'

Tobin stared in disbelief at the bowl then crouched down in a corner with it.

'No, my son. Sit at that table and take one of those spoons—that's the way we eat here.'

Tobin had never been given so much food at one meal before and ate it very quickly. When he looked up from the empty bowl he found the monk smiling gently at him.

'If you work hard for me you'll not starve, nor will you have more than your share, but your share you'll have, I'll see to that.'

Tobin felt warmer and better fed than he ever remembered and stammered, 'I'll d-do y-your b-bidding, s-sir.'

'Brother Bernard is my name.' The monk pointed to a large ladle, saying, 'You bring that and follow me.' He picked up the iron pot of gruel and led the way out of the kitchen and into a room where many monks were sitting in silence at several long tables all listening to a monk reading from a book.

Tobin had never seen a book, nor heard anyone read from one before and was fascinated. He listened in awe to the reading while standing behind Brother Bernard, watching him ladle the gruel into bowls. Then he stood quietly while the monks said a prayer and was delighted to stand listening to the reading until they had eaten, then he collected the bowls and carried them into the kitchen.

When Brother Bernard said, 'You and I are going to get along very well, boy.' Tobin wanted to tell him this was the first time anyone, apart from his father, had said anything kind to him, but dared not say a word.

He continued fetching and carrying, running errands and doing the monk's bidding throughout the day and when night came, he climbed into the bed he was given close to the kitchen fire and smiled as he fell asleep.

As the days passed and he gained in confidence he was given more and more responsible tasks until he could cook gruel and make bread for the monks. While going about his work he often heard the sound of singing emanating from the huge building that the monks filed into for their prayers and one morning when Brother Bernard took his hand and led him to stand at the back of the building he stared in awe at his surroundings.

Looking around him at the red walls decorated with gilded carvings of figures, animals and strange beings, he was enthralled. Then, seeing the window through which the light streamed, making the bright colours of gold, crimson, blue and green shine in unimaginable beauty, he thought angels would soon fly in and he would realise he had gone to heaven.

When no angelic beings had appeared and the monks all filed out after their devotions, he was disappointed in one way, but relieved in another, for now he could come every day and experience the beauty of this wonderful place.

He particularly liked the figure of the Madonna holding the baby Jesus and whenever possible would sneak in and look up at her serene face. The love and devotion for her filled his whole being and he was so happy that he smiled while he worked no matter how dirty or difficult the work he was given.

One pleasurable task was to fetch water from a well inside the abbey church and he would walk down the steps to the crypt and kneel to look into the dark water before dipping his bucket into it.

One morning, just as dawn was breaking, he knelt before the well and was about to draw some water from it when he saw a picture forming and drew back in surprise as soldiers appeared smashing the beautiful windows. Then to his horror he saw an old man being dragged naked from a stone building and tied onto a hurdle. He gasped and closed his eyes to stop this dreadful sight, but on opening them again saw the silhouette of three bodies body hanging limply from gibbets on the Tor, just like the crucifixion of Jesus with the two thieves that he had heard about in the reading in the refectory.

Reaching for the bucket he threw it at the image, causing water to splash all over the stone floor and walls. His heart was pounding as he carried the water to the kitchen and placed it beside Brother Bernard who looked at him and said, 'You look very distressed, Tobin. Are you unwell?'

He shook his head and then to his embarrassment, burst into uncontrollable sobbing interspersed with description of what he had seen.

When he eventually became calm he opened his eyes and found himself lying on the flagstones with the cook from the abbot's kitchen kneeling on one side of him and Brother Bernard likewise on the other. His throat was very sore and he could only whisper, 'I'm so sorry, Brothers. So sorry.'

The Abbot's cook, Brother Sebastian, had always seemed a frighteningly austere man to whom Tobin had never dared speak when fetching and carrying between the monk's kitchen and that of the Abbot, but now there was great compassion in the man's grey eyes as he said, 'You have spoken of dreadful deeds of destruction and unimaginable horror, Tobin. Was this a nightmare while you slept?'

He shook his head.

'Perhaps you have had seizures like this before?'

He shook his head again.

'You kept saying the vision was in the well, do you remember this?'

He nodded.

'Have you seen such things in there before?'

'No,' he whispered, adding, 'I've never seen such things before and never wish to again.'

He saw the two men exchange looks over him and wondered if he was to be punished for this episode and whispered, 'I'm so sorry. I'll do any penance you....'

'No, Tobin—' Brother Sebastian gently pulled him upright '—I think you fell asleep and had a bad dream.' He patted him on the back, adding, 'I suggest we say no more about it.'

Tobin looked from one monk to the other and saw their kindly smiles. If he insisted on saying the experience was real then he would probably be sent away out of the abbey and knowing that would be the worst thing that could possibly happen to him, he agreed. 'Yes, I'm sure you're right, Brother Sebastian. I thank you for your kindness. I shall not mention it again.   '

Later, as he pulled some bread from the oven, he repeated the whole episode in his head and while remembering his last words, he realised with amazement that he had not stuttered for the first time in his life. He no longer cared what the strange experience had been, whether it was a dream or a vision mattered not, for it had left him speaking as others did and he was delirious with joy.

❖   ❖   ❖

The days passed and the seasons changed from one to another many times. Tobin became a man and a respected and useful lay brother. He loved his work preparing food for the monks. If special guests were entertained he would enjoy helping in the splendid abbot's kitchen when fish from the mere was brought in and all manner of delicacies were prepared.

He listened with pleasure to the readings in the refectory while the monks ate and one lay brother, who noticed how enthralled he was, took him into the scriptorium where he worked making the vellum and the inks and pigments the monks used when writing their books and missals. This man, Brother Bertrand, had been a scholar in the Low Countries; he had come to England with his wife and after she died he joined the monastery, offering his knowledge to them as a gift to God.

Brother Bertrand showed Tobin how to make sense of the shapes of letters he drew that made up a pattern corresponding to spoken words and so Tobin, although not able to read fluently, could understand how a monk could look at a book and read aloud to the other brothers in the refectory at mealtimes.

Tobin's greatest joy was to stand at the back of the huge church when the monks were at their devotions. He loved to hear the sound of their voices chanting and singing in a language he could not understand while he prayed to the mother of Jesus, whose loving blue eyes gazed down on him, reassuring him that he would one day be with her in heaven.

Occasionally he recalled the strange vision in the well and always averted his eyes for fear of seeing the horror again when fetching water, but as time went on, he persuaded himself that Brother Sebastian was right and he had indeed fallen asleep and had a nightmare.

When, on one of his occasional forays from the abbey to fetch something from the market, he heard local people talking of rumours about the King being at loggerheads with the Pope in Rome, he assumed this was nothing to do with him and the other lay brothers he talked with also thought the same. He did not dare ask the opinion of any monks, who were mostly silent anyway and were always thinking of higher things than gossip.

Time passed, there were fewer visitors at the Abbot's table and the monks often looked anxious as they walked around the cloisters clutching their rosaries.

Tobin began to feel a tension in the air. He knew in his bones that trouble lurked in the shadows somewhere waiting to pounce, but had no idea what it might be. At dawn one morning, after a sleepless night feeling this apprehension very strongly, he went to the well in which he had seen the strange vision years ago. He took a bucket with him to pretend he was fetching water in case anyone saw him, but instead of dipping the bucket into it and disturbing the flat surface, he knelt on the stone at its edge and gazed into the inky black mirror.

The image that appeared was again horrible beyond his imaginings, but it was not the same. This time a woman's face stared up at him from the water. She had a birthmark on her face very like his and her eyes were as blue as those of the Madonna in the church. Her skin was white, deathly white and as she stared at him she said, 'My blood will poison the well for generations and I will dam its flow.'

The face vanished and he stared miserably at the water knowing he dared not tell any monk about it. Nor could he ask any person for the meaning of either this vision, or the one he had seen when first he came to the monastery. The woman's face haunted him in his dreams at night and fear of the earlier one coming true filled his mind by day.

He sensed disquiet in everyone around him. Monks looked anxious and other lay brothers muttered to one another in quiet corners. Fear was in the air he breathed. Brother Bertrand who had shown him how to read and had become a good friend over the years, came to him one morning while he was making bread and said, 'There are rumours the King will take revenge now that he rules the Church in England. I've heard soldiers have plundered and destroyed churches elsewhere and I feel sure it's only a matter of time before the King's men will claim this, the greatest and most beautiful abbey.' He paused to shake his head sadly and there was a sob in his voice as he went on, 'Death holds no fear for me, nor even the pain of a soldier's sword, but I have heard of books and precious relics being burned and I could not bear to see our library being destroyed.' He grasped Tobin's hand and with tears running down his lined cheeks, whispered, 'Fare thee well, my friend.' He then turned and left the kitchen.

Tobin was more fearful than ever during that day and on the following morning was deeply saddened to hear that the kindly old man had died in his sleep. Everyone around Tobin agreed the lay brother, having almost reached three score years and ten, had come to the natural end of a good life or had taken either a poisonous fungus or plant, but he, Tobin, knew in his heart that the old man had willed his death and taken nothing to hasten his end.

One month later he was about to dip a bucket into the well when another terrible vision of the monastery appeared in the surface of the water. Although longing to close his eyes or look away he was transfixed. In place of the refectory, the monks kitchen, the magnificent library and scriptorium there was green grass and undergrowth. Where the magnificent church now stood there were remnants of the walls, with no roof, no beautiful windows, no red and gold decoration: only a grey and ghostly ruin remained beside the abbot's kitchen that was still standing.

The vision left him stupefied; for how long he had no idea, but the light was fading when he heard shouting and clattering overhead. A young lay brother who was just a boy came hurtling down the narrow steps and fell to his knees beside him. 'We are being cast out,' he said tearfully. 'I don't know what to do, Brother Tobin.' He pointed overhead. 'All the monks and lay brothers have already left. I have no family and nowhere to go.'

A cold hard feeling clamped Tobin's chest as he remembered the earlier vision of soldiers rampaging through the abbey church. 'You may come with me. '

He held out his hand. 'Tell me your name, Brother.'

'Arthur is my name.'

'We can be a family of two brothers if you like, Arthur.'

'But there'll be all those monks out there begging ...'

'I know it will be difficult. We will have to seek work elsewhere.' He led the boy out through the doorway. 'I'll see if my father will help us. He's ruled by his mean hag of a wife so he might not let us stay, but I'm sure he'll feed us and give us clothes to wear instead of our habits.'

They walked around the buildings through an orchard to the far wall, which they climbed onto then jumped down onto the ground next to a small dwelling. Seeing light shining through a crack in the wooden door, Tobin knocked on it and heard shuffling sounds indicating that someone was inside.

The door opened a little and a woman's voice asked, 'Who's there?'

'I'm Tobin, son of Mattius.'

The door opened a little further and he could see one blue eye looking at him, which he assumed belonged to one of his half sisters.

The voice asked, 'How do I know you're who you say you are?'

He replied, 'There can't be many men with sway backs and a purple mark on their face.'

The door opened wide to reveal a young woman with a grey shawl wrapped around her who gave a curtsey then ushered them inside.

When she looked askance at the boy, Tobin said, 'This is my friend, Arthur, who was also a lay brother in the abbey with me.' He looked questioningly at her. 'I assume you heard what has happened at the abbey?'

She nodded.

He wondered momentarily if she was either simple minded or unable to speak. He looked around the dwelling and seeing the loom had no yarn in it he asked, 'Is my father not weaving now?'

The young woman began wringing her hands. 'It's no good, sir. I'll have to tell you the truth of it, of what happened and you may tell me to go and I'll go even though I have nowhere else and I'll die of cold and....'

'Tell me, please,' he said gently. He led her to a bench beside the fire and sat down with her while the boy sank to the floor holding his hands over the embers for warmth.

'I thought you might come when I heard folk say all the monks have been sent from the abbey.'

'Yes, I have come in the hope my father would give us food before we leave.' Then, very gently, he asked, 'What was it you were going to tell me that worried you so?'

'They're all gone, sir.'

'My family?'

'That's right, sir. They caught some bad fever that many folk had. Your father and mother died quickly, him first and then she went soon after.'

'And you and your sister?'

'No sir, I'm not of the family, that's what I have to explain. The daughters had both gone off by then, one with a soldier—heaven only knows what's become of her and the other married a miller then died in childbed so I heard.'

His first feeling was of sadness for his father who, although too weak to stand up to his wife, had been gentle and loving towards him when her back was turned. 'I wish I had known,' he said, thinking he could have said prayers to the Madonna for his safe ascendancy to heaven.

'So you see, sir, I've no right to be here. I sometimes came and helped with sewing the habits for the monks, your stepmother's hands were so stiff and her eyes were too weak to thread a needle and once the daughters had gone they could no longer do the work—that's how I knew about you and the family. I did try to help them like a good Christian, I promise you I did.' She swallowed then stood up and wrapped her shawl tightly round her thin body. 'I'll go if you want, I'm used to making my own way, sir.'

He guessed that her own way would be either from begging, or selling her body. 'No, there's no need for you to leave.' He pointed to the small, roughly made balcony where his stepsisters had slept in his youth. 'You can sleep up there and we will make beds down here as my parents did.'

He walked to the loom and ran his fingers over the wooden frame. He remembered standing by his father, watching him push the shuttle through the lines of thread and knew what he must do. 'I'll get this working again,' he said.

'There's bags and bags of wool ready for spinning up there,' the woman said, pointing to the balcony and then adding, 'I've never spun, but I'm sure I could learn.'

Arthur, who had been sitting staring into the fire, giving no sign of having heard a word of this conversation, turned to face them and said, 'I can spin. I used to help my sister, she hated doing it and I really liked it.' He reached inside his habit and pulled out a round loaf and handed it to the woman. 'Here, take this. We could share it.' He grinned. 'I grabbed it when I left—I thought to myself, at least I won't die hungry!'

The woman laughed and took it from him. 'I thank you, Arthur.'

'You're welcome—' he blushed and bowed ceremoniously '—My

238

Lady. . . whatever your name is.'

'Marta,' she replied. 'My name is Marta.' She turned to Tobin who was still hearing her laughter in his head. 'Now we have all been introduced, I suggest we could sleep a while and then begin the new day with our new life.'

Tobin and Arthur wrapped their cloaks around them and lay down by the fire while Marta went to her bed on the balcony.

Listening to the boy's slight snuffling sounds as he slept, Tobin laid his plans. Firstly they must hide away until having changed from the habits of the lay brothers into nondescript ordinary clothes. They would need to mix in with the local people and not stand out from them.

Thinking through the effects of the day's events he felt sure life would never be the same again. Many local people had depended for their livelihood on the abbey and those that could move away would no doubt go elsewhere to ply their trades. The people who remained in the chaos would struggle to survive and, he hoped, would be too busy worrying about their own affairs to notice two men living in this house.

Lying beside the fire he stared into the strange world of the glowing embers and saw himself weaving at his father's loom. Two children played nearby and, further away, silhouetted by firelight, was the figure of a woman bent over a cooking pot. With a blink of his eye he destroyed the image, reminding himself it could only be an impossible dream.

Returning to the present worries, he wondered what would become of the Abbot and what would happen to all the abbey lands and farms he owned. How would the local people survive without the work provided by the abbey? Where would all the monks and lay brothers go? The questions went around his mind until his head ached and he could no longer think of such great problems. He only knew one simple fact: he would survive somehow.

His last thought before falling asleep was of Marta's laugh and the sound of it echoed through his dreams.

The following day the three of them stayed mostly in the house making clothes for the two men from the fabric of their habits and a few old garments Marta had found stuffed in a gap under the eaves that had belonged to Tobin's father.

Once clothed they took a while to settle into the strange garb, fidgeting in their trousers and easing the necks of their jerkins, while Marta gave words of encouragement, saying, 'I never saw such a pair of handsome fellows!' Then she chuckled and so did they.

Arthur experimented with the new freedom of movement his trousers afforded him, moving his legs around until he was performing a joyful jig. Seeing this, Tobin, who had never before attempted such a thing, did a tentative little hop and skip until he almost fell over and while clinging onto Arthur for support, laughed so infectiously that soon all three were doubled up with helpless mirth.

The need for food was the next important matter needing their attention and Arthur volunteered to investigate whether any of the usual market traders were selling their edible wares. Venturing out into the lane he walked with the Tor in view, past several cottages then around the abbey wall until he reached an inn from which emanated the sound of drunken shouts and singing. He continued on past other noisy, smelly hostelries to the abbey entrance where, to his horror, he saw soldiers strutting around or slumped drunkenly in corners. Feeling very fearful of being asked for his name and abode, he turned into an alleyway only to find a gang of youths he felt sure was lurking in wait for opportunities to loot while the area was in turmoil.

Although now terrified, Arthur kept walking until he reached the market place where no one was selling flour, or bread, or turnips, or any of the usual fare set out on stalls. There was none of the normal noise, no shouts, no laughs, no friendly jibes. In place of the traders a few desperate looking people were trying to sell their possessions and some others were begging for food. With tears in his eyes he continued walking, following the abbey wall around past yet another inn.

While passing a cottage he heard a goat bleating and seeing the door hanging open on its leather hinge, he looked inside and saw a large white goat chewing on one end of a leather boot.

'They'm gone.'

Arthur turned around to find an old woman lying on a bed by the cold ashes of a fire and asked, 'Have your family left you?'

'They'm gone,' she repeated and closed her eyes.

When he knelt beside her to feel her wrist it was clear she had died. 'I'll come back to bury you,' he said, then realising she could no longer hear him, gave a nervous giggle.

As though imitating him the goat made a bleating sound. 'Very well,' he said. 'If you are asking me to take you home with me, I agree.' He picked up a leather strip lying on the floor and looped it around the goat's neck and half led it, half pushed it out of the doorway and along the lane, past another three cottages to the stone dwelling where Tobin and Marta gave him a rapturous welcome.

When he took them to see the corpse, an elderly woman neighbour who knew the family came and explained they were leather workers who had made many things for the abbot and fearing there would be no further work now that the abbey was closed they had left to find work elsewhere.

'I suppose they knew the old lady had not long on this earth and it was kinder to let her die here,' Tobin said sadly. Adding, 'I suppose they left the goat because it would be a hindrance.'

'They never had no goat,' the neighbour said, with a frown.

'Someone must have decided she was too difficult to take with them in a hurry—' Marta smiled appealingly at the two men '—I like goats. They have wonderful eyes and also she could be very useful to us.'

'To eat?' asked Arthur, looking dubiously at the animal.

'Not straight away,' Marta replied, 'We could let her graze on the open land across the lane and if we found a billy to mate with her she'd give us milk and a kid to eat.'

'I suppose she could live with us.' Tobin frowned and added, 'providing she eats no more boots or any other items of clothing.'

Arthur snorted with laughter and agreed.

When Tobin expressed his concern about the burial of the corpse, the neighbour said, 'I'll speak to the priest at the church where she worshipped. We never got on, never good friends, so to speak, but I want her to have a Christian burial nevertheless.'

When they had returned and the goat was tethered at the back of the house, Arthur said, 'I have an idea for food which may keep us until things have settle down.' He led them outside and pointed to several pigeons sitting in the trees nearby and on the thatched roof above them. 'They have come from the loft in which they were kept to grace the Abbot's table. I suppose they are no longer being fed by the monks and have come looking for other sources of sustenance.'

Tobin was impressed. He knew his own lack of mobility made catching animals to eat impossible and was grateful to know they would not starve. He did fetch some plants and roots for them to eat, but his main preoccupation was the loom he wished to reinstate.

Marta did not venture far, fearing attack by lingering soldiers and a few local young men taking advantage of the situation to rape any unprotected female. She was glad to help Tobin rebuild the loom and do any other tasks in the house.

Putting the loom together took several days and in that time Arthur began spinning the wool into yarn with one of several spindles he found in the dwelling. He also surprised Tobin when he made a rudimentary spinning wheel using pieces of wood attached to a broken cartwheel he found lying in a heap of rubbish by the abbey wall.

The three of them were soon comfortable in each other's company and in the evening, while sitting by the fire for a while before going to bed, they told each other the story of their lives. So it was that Arthur explained that he had been left orphaned and destitute after his mother died of birthing fever and then his father was killed when their house burned down.

When Marta asked what had become of the sister who hated spinning, the boy gave a dry sob before explaining that the uncle who had taken him to the abbey to be a lay servant had taken the sister to be his wife.

Both Marta and Tobin sat in shocked silence for a moment until Arthur said, 'I content myself with the thought that she is well fed and warm although—' he grimaced with suppressed emotion '—I fear she will still hate him as much as she did before.'

When Marta's turn came to tell her tale she was slow at first, explaining that life had been hard for her and her mother after her father disappeared one morning never to be seen again. Then she told of the years spent as a maid in an ale house where men often took the girls by force, throwing them backwards onto the tables and pulling their skirts over their heads, thereby trapping their arms and holding them fast.

Tobin was so horrified he covered his face with his hands and wept for her.

Arthur said, 'I suppose my sister is better placed than that,' and sucked his thumb like a small child.

The following evening Marta told them of the child she bore as a result of this debauchery. 'He was a poorly little scrap,' she said. 'I wanted him to live, although I had no idea how I'd manage, but he never took breath. They buried him by the church wall. I go and pick flowers to put on the spot, pretty little bluebells and primroses when they're in bloom and I planted some forget-me-nots too for all the babies like mine that are buried there.'

Tobin asked how she came to live in the dwelling and she explained that while delivering some cloth to the alehouse keeper, a man had commented on the fine stitching in her bodice. 'I thought he was being like the other men at first and took offence, but then he explained about his wife's failing sight and so I went with him and spoke to her. After a while I just became like one of the family and they let me sleep in the little shed outside until it snowed and then they said I could use the daughter's bed.' She smiled at Tobin. 'And that's how I came to be here.'

Arthur cried in his sleep that night and called out, 'She's but a child I tell you!'

Hearing this Tobin ached for him and for the girl. Also he ached in another way for Marta, but knew his feeling must remain a secret— for no woman, he was sure, could ever love a man who was sway-backed and marked with purple.

One morning when Marta was milking the goat outside the dwelling, a woman who lived nearby came to her and with excitement in her voice, said, 'The Abbot has been taken.'

'Taken!' Marta exclaimed.

'Aye, to London so I heard.'

'Why would that be?'

'On account of the King wanting him tried.'

Marta was horrified. 'Tried! Whatever for?'

'Treason I suppose. I heard as he'd not given up all his treasure to the King's men.'

'But the abbey and all the lands have been taken from him. What more could they want?'

'Folks are saying as he hid some valuables. That's all I know.' The woman saw another neighbour coming along the lane and she hurried towards her eager to impart this information to her.

When Tobin heard news of the Abbot's impending trial he was horrified and recalling the terrible vision of an old man being tied to a hurdle he knew the Abbot would be found guilty.

A few weeks later, when Marta heard from the same neighbour that the Abbot had returned and was being tried in The Tribunal that day, she ran to into the dwelling with the news.

Tobin immediately said he would go into the town and find out if

244

this information was true.

'No, I must go,' Arthur said firmly. 'You are remembered as a lay brother and would be at risk if a drunken mob of local youths turned against anyone who was involved with the abbey.'

Tobin argued for a short while, but had to admit the truth of Arthur's words and with a heavy heart watched him leave the dwelling. He then sat at the loom and while weaving thought of the sights he had seen in the well.

Several hours later he heard shouting outside and although knowing the Abbot was being dragged to the Tor, he did not move from his seat. He heard Marta open the door then quickly close it again. He was glad when she brought her stool close to him and sat silently with her hand on his arm until Arthur burst in then immediately sank to his knees weeping.

Tobin and Marta knelt either side of the boy, quietly waiting for him to speak. Eventually the sobs subsided and the lad said, 'It was so horrible. You cannot imagine what they did to the poor Abbott and his two assistants.'

Tobin ached in his heart, feeling sure he knew what had been done.

With his face screwed up as though in pain, Arthur said, 'Hung drawn and quartered they were on top of the Tor.' He groaned. 'Their heads were cut off and the mob were taking them to put on the Abbey gates when I came home.' He shuddered. 'There was talk of taking the parts of their bodies to other places for people to know what has been done, Wells was one, I don't know the others.'

Marta wiped tears from her eyes as did Tobin, who said, 'The King has had his way.'

Arthur nodded. 'I wonder if the treasure they sought was ever found.'

'They would have found him guilty whether they did or not,' Marta said, 'so I doubt we shall never know.'

The seasons passed. Life around the empty abbey gradually settled down. Many people left the town and if any of those remaining knew that Tobin and Arthur had once worked as lay brothers they did not speak of it.

While politicians and rich nobles were given the lands and property once owned by the abbey, the local people made the best of their situation, earned a living where they could and took stone from the monk's living quarters and the great abbey church to build their houses.

Some folk talked in private of the good old days when the land was well run and there was much employment for the local people, but in public they touched their forelock to the new owners of the abbey lands and carried on with their lives.

Although life was a struggle for many months, Tobin, Arthur and Marta worked hard making fine woollen cloth, which they sold in the market.

After the third winter of their sojourn in the dwelling, Arthur, now grown into a handsome young man, went courting a girl who was struggling with her widowed mother to look after a small plot of land. By the following spring the girl was great with child and after they were married he went to live with her, taking the goat and two of her kids with him.

On their first night alone Tobin and Marta sat by the fire talking as they had always done until she stood up and held out her hand, saying, 'Come Tobin my love, let us go to my bed together.'

He looked up at her incredulously and then, feeling as though his heart would burst with joy, he stood up and put his arms around her. 'If I come to your bed I'll never want to leave it,' he said.

'And I'll never want you to,' she replied.

Chapter Seventeen

Louisa sat looking at the carved arch and the slab of stone beneath it wondering if the black water was still there as it had been when the abbey was sacked. The well might have been blocked up, or the water could have been diverted. If it was dry, for whatever reason, she might be connecting with the memory of it, just as she was with the people who had been involved with it in the past.

She picked up the lamp and climbed up the ladder to where Edward and Mr Overton were waiting for her. Having accepted their help to climb over the barricade onto the bench and then down to the ground, she thanked them and told Tobin's story.

Both men listened intently and Mr Overton made little exclamatory noises from time to time, sounding, Louisa thought with a secret smile, more like an excited child listening to a Grimm's fairytale than an elderly gentlemen hearing the description of her vision.

When she had finished, the old man rubbed his hands together while saying, 'Fascinating! Absolutely fascinating! The whole town, indeed the whole area would have been affected by the closing of the abbey. So many local people would have made their living from it, or have been employed by the monks in some way. It must have been devastating for them.'

Edward said, 'I agree. Also I doubt if elderly monks with little experience of the outside world would have survived long afterwards.'

Mr Overton sighed thoughtfully. 'That is true. There must have been great hardship and poverty for them.'

He looked into the distance for a few moments, evidently imagining the scene, then turned to Louisa and said, 'I hope we will get the tackle for lifting the stone next Monday. I had thought we could do it sooner, but it's not possible.'

247

'That would suit me very well,' Louisa said feeling glad she would not have to miss the event. Seeing the two men exchange glances, she wondered if they had connived at this delay for her benefit and gave them both a big smile before wishing them a good day.

Edward raised his hat, turned to leave and then looked back at her, saying, 'I took tea with Aunt Rosemary after our adventure yesterday. A remarkable woman!' He then strode away whistling a tune she remembered her father singing. 'I saw a lady caught my eye. I did but see her passing by, yet shall I love her 'til I die.'

She walked to the house humming the song and remembering the many times she had accompanied her father on the piano in the music room overlooking the Thames.

The two old ladies were dozing when she tiptoed into the room. 'Oh my goodness, Louisa!' Aunt Rosemary exclaimed on awakening, then added, 'I was just resting my eyes, dear.' She reached for her hat and while pushing the black jet topped hatpin in place, she said, 'I am longing to hear what is under the stone. I hope you will come to tea after the next adventure in the abbey.'

'I should like that, Aunt, although I may have difficulty getting away once cousin Edwina returns from Brighton tomorrow.'

'I would have thought—' Aunt Rosemary gave a disapproving sniff '—you should have more free time when Edwina is available to sit with her mother.'

Aunt Agnes muttered, 'Never liked him,' then snored loudly.

Aunt Rosemary gave a knowing smile and took her leave.

Later, after settling her aunt for the night, Louisa said, 'I am so glad you enjoyed the visit from Rosemary.'

The old lady's eyes lit up. 'Such a dear girl—and so pretty!' She smiled while looking back into the past. 'The times we—had you—know. Such—laughter and such—happiness! The young—of today—don't …' she yawned and closed her eyes, then a moment before her breathing fell into a regular rhythm, she said quietly, but clearly and crisply, 'I'm sure she loved him, you know.'

Louisa went to bed wondering which man Rosemary had loved long ago when she was young. Could her father have been the object of her affection? And if so, how did her mother come to marry him?

While finding the most comfortable place to lie on the lumpy mattress she wondered what Aunt Rosemary might see in the tea-leaves for her future. Most likely, she thought, there would be a few years minding Aunt Agnes, followed by another old lady in need of care, preferably in Glastonbury near the abbey so that she could feel close to the dark well. It would be good to know if she might make a friend. A woman in similar circumstances of about her own age with whom she could go for walks would be nice. They could read to one another perhaps and go on drawing and painting expeditions.

A moment before relaxing into sleep she thought of Edward and quickly dismissed him as married and unavailable, even if there was any possibility of sharing her life with a loving man, which was out of the question. She had known one love, that was surely all she could hope for in this lifetime—was it not? This thought led her to question if she had actually lived the stories in her visions, or had she merely experienced them as someone like her aunt would see such things in the tea-leaves?

Recalling the shame of Veryan and the feel of the wool chafing her skin, she knew it had all seemed so real. She had breathed in the terrible stench of the infirmary and heard the sweet singing from the chapel as though she had been there and yet … and yet, was this possible? Then there was Annie whose love for Graeme her brother had felt so real. And Raven too, and Luna, White Bird, Windflower and Willow; she could remember how it felt to be each one of them. Could she really have been all of these people? Could she have even been Tobin, a man, was that possible? Also, now she came to think of it, were other people around her living new lives and would this explain the reason some people seemed familiar, as though previously known long ago?

She fell asleep wondering.

The following morning, while dressing, Louisa heard two maids giggling in the corridor outside the door to her room. 'I warn yer keep yer distance when he passes by and never be in the room alone with him. Worse than the handyman he is and that's saying something I can tell yer.'

The other maid laughed and said, 'Reckons he's Prince Charming, does he?'

'Maybe he does, but he's really a Demon King,' and they both went off giggling.

Louisa felt sure the maids were having a problem with menservants and was worried about them. In the days when she was a mistress of her own house the maids would have come to her with such problems but, feeling sure Edwina might not wish to be troubled with these matters, she decided the housekeeper would be more appropriate in this house and resolved to mention it when a convenient moment presented itself.

The house was in turmoil while preparations were made for Edwina and George's return. When Louisa explained the reason for the maids running along the corridors, Aunt Agnes looked anxious and began fingering the sheet with her good hand.

Louisa walked to the window and suggested, 'A walk in the garden would be nice on such a wonderfully sunny morning. The red roses are glowing on the pergola and they have such a wonderful scent.'

The old lady agreed with a nod, but neither smiled nor spoke while being made ready to go out and was much more subdued than usual when she had been carried downstairs an hour later.

While guessing her aunt was worried about the return of Edwina and longing to ask the reason for this concern, Louisa made no mention of it. She maintained as cheerful a manner as possible as she pushed the Bath chair around the garden, stopping to admire the flowers and listen to the birds.

Having spent almost an hour outside, they returned to the front steps where the gardener was waiting to carry the old lady into the house. At that moment the horses pulled the carriage through the gates, along the drive and came to a standstill beside them.

Edwina said she was pleased to see her mother out in the garden, but her husband made no attempt to hide his bad humour and strode past her and up the steps with the slightest of nods.

'George is tired after a very trying journey,' Edwina explained to Louisa.

'We understand.' Louisa beckoned to the gardener to come and lift her aunt, then added, 'Your mother is weary after this exertion and you will need to rest after travelling so far. We will not trouble you in any way.' Louisa followed the gardener as he carried Aunt Agnes up the stairs to her room. Wondering as she walked behind him if he could be the handyman the maids had spoken of.

Later in the day, when her aunt had insisted on going back to bed instead of her usual sojourn by the window, Louisa looked at the bowl of fading roses on the bedside table and asked, 'Shall I pick some fresh flowers, Aunt?'

The old lady gave a slight smile and whispered the words, 'Scented, please.'

Feeling encouraged by this reaction, Louisa picked up a basket and hurried out of the house to the garden. Having picked enough to make an attractive arrangement, she turned and seeing the pale cream climbing rose growing up against the house, decided to add a few of these blooms to her collection.

While passing the sitting room window to reach the roses she heard raised voices emanating from within; one was a man shouting and the other a woman, whose shrill tone was easily recognised as that of Edwina.

She stopped and stood behind a large buddleia bush in full bloom with a butterfly on every purple flower. Breathing in the scent of honey and watching the exquisite creatures fluttering around her, she strained to hear what was being said inside the house.

'And I'm telling you I won't do it!' Edwina whined.

George shouted, 'You promised to obey me—remember?'

'I remember you've spent all my money and I don't want to…' she screamed as though in pain.

Louisa stood frozen in horror. She heard a loud bang and assumed it to be a door being slammed. Then, wondering if her cousin had been hurt, she walked to the French windows around the corner of the house and, peering through the glass, saw Edwina, lying curled up like a child, on the chesterfield.

Her first impulse was to rush in and comfort her, but then she hesitated, knowing her cousin might well reprimand her for snooping and tell her to mind her own affairs. When she saw Edwina get up and go to stand in front of a mirror, Louisa decided to pretend she had heard nothing and walked around to the front door and then up to her room.

While arranging the flowers she found the sound of a scream and the door slamming constantly reverberating in her head. Eventually, having ensured her aunt was sleeping, she ran downstairs to the sitting room door. Taking a deep breath and straightening her shoulders, she knocked and when told to enter, walked in to find her cousin sitting by the window with her back to the light and holding a handkerchief to her cheek.

'I'm so sorry to trouble you, Edwina,' Louisa said, trying not to look at her face. 'I wanted to explain that we borrowed the Bath chair and I have taken your mother to church several times and also for little walks to enjoy some fresh air. I hope that meets with your approval.'

Evidently taken aback, Edwina relaxed her grip on the handkerchief and revealed a half closed eye and cheek that was already swollen. 'How kind of you, Louisa.' She quickly covered the eye. 'I thank you.' With a nod of her head she repeated, 'I thank you, that is most kind.'

Feeling relieved to know her cousin was not mortally wounded, but very angry with George for hurting her, Louisa returned upstairs where she found her aunt awake and looking brighter.

'I have been thinking, Louisa.' The words were still slowly spoken but without any slurring or difficulty in enunciation. The old lady paused to take slightly wheezing breath then continued in the improved manner, 'Although unable to come with you to the abbey ruins for your visions.' Pause for a breath. 'I am most grateful to you for telling them me about them.'

Despite attempting to remain calm, Louisa could not control her emotion as she sat beside the bed. 'Your speech has improved beyond all measure, Aunt. That is so wonderful!'

'I do not understand the reason for it.' Wheezing breath. 'I dreamed I could speak and so I can!'

They sat looking at each other in wonderment for a short while and then the old lady said, 'I also dreamed about Tobin last night. He is very real for me.' Wheezing breath. 'I believe he and Marta would be happy together, don't you?'

Louisa agreed.

'A happy marriage is not always the result of falling in love, I'm afraid.' She gave a cough and then her breathing was laboured for a while. When recovered, she said, 'One does not know what beast might be lurking in a man, does one?'

Louisa nodded while wondering if this was a reference to her aunt's husband or her cousin's.

'I think you were lucky, my dear, were you not?'

'Oh yes Aunt, I count myself very fortunate to have known such happiness with my dear man, before—' Louisa remembered the miserable latter years of her marriage and fought back her tears '—before the illness.'

'Some people never know that kind of love, my dear. And I hope—' the old woman reached out and touched her hand '—you will know it again.'

'No. I'm afraid that's not possible. I've had my share of love and now

I'll learn to live alone. I could never fall in love again, I'm sure of it.'

The old woman smiled and said, 'Never say never, my dear.' She looked into Louisa's face and added, 'You're a beautiful woman, although I doubt you know it.'

With a shy laugh Louisa insisted, 'I was never good looking at the best of times and now I am too old for romance, so there is no need for beauty.'

'Nonsense!' her aunt exclaimed. Then, with a sad shake of her head she looked towards the table on which was a photograph of Edwina and George taken on their wedding day, twenty years earlier. 'I would rest easier in my grave if I knew you were watching over my daughter after my demise. I know she's not an easy person. I'm afraid my husband treated her like a little princess and she's still inclined to behave like one to this day, but she is not happy and never will be with that—' she clenched her good hand into a fist '—that ...'

'Bully?' Louisa suggested.

'Yes, that's what he is. They don't realise I hear what goes on. Did you know he hits her?'

Louisa admitted she did know.

'So, my dear, will you promise to watch over her for me?'

Louisa hesitated, knowing a promise made now would mean she had to live in, or near to the town, for many years to come. But then, deciding she had no reason to go elsewhere, she agreed, 'I promise, Aunt.'

'That's such a relief! It means I can go in peace.'

'You might live for ...'

'No, my dear, don't pretend—' she paused to take a rasping breath '—we are not immortal. I have reached my allotted span and am ready to meet my maker.'

Louisa sat waiting while her aunt rested for a few minutes, knowing from the breathing pattern that she was not asleep.

'I hear the maids talking when I am alone.' The old lady plucked agitatedly at the sheets with her good hand. 'They said George's brother is coming to visit …' She gasped and struggled for breath.

Louisa sat her up with pillows behind her and fetched a glass of water.

When her aunt had recovered, she went on, 'He is a lawyer. He is ruthless. He is also unkind; especially to women.' With a yawn, she closed her eyes and this time was soon asleep.

The following morning Louisa and her aunt were sitting by the window while a young maid changed the sheets on the bed. When the girl left the room to fetch a clean towel, Louisa looked at the raindrops running down the glass and said, 'I'm afraid it will be too wet to take you to out this morning, but I shall ask Mrs Thorpe to arrange for you to be carried downstairs after luncheon if it is fine.'

The old lady was delighted and at the same moment as the maid returned through the door carrying clean towels, she said excitedly, 'How wonderful! I am so grateful to you …' realising her mistake, she began wheezing and gasping for breath.

While helping her drink some water Louisa saw the maid scurry away carrying the bundle of used linen and wondered if she would tell the other servants, or, worse still, tell Edwina that her mother had made a miraculous recovery and could speak.

When the old lady had recovered her breath and tears were running down the furrows in her lined cheeks, Louisa put her arm around the dejected narrow shoulders, saying, 'It is possible the maid did not hear you speak, Aunt.'

'If —' the old woman gave her lopsided smile '—I should say *when*—' she gave a rasping laugh and paused to take a breath '—I die.' She grasped Louisa's arm with her good hand. 'See Mr Merriot.' Adding urgently, 'Promise me. I beg you.'

'I promise,' Louisa replied, assuming this man was an old friend. 'I will see Mr Merriot. Does he live nearby?'

Her aunt gave a weary nod and muttered, 'High Street,' then her eyes closed and her head fell forward.

For a moment Louisa thought death had claimed her, but on hearing the slightly rattling breath, knew she had fallen asleep.

Later, when offering her aunt some supper, Louisa was distressed to find the old lady struggled to open her heavy eyelids a little and waved the food away before closing them again. Knowing something was seriously wrong, she went downstairs hoping to speak with her cousin and warn her there had been a change in her mother's condition, but found the sitting room deserted.

She went to the housekeeper and was told the mistress and her husband had gone out to dinner. When she explained her fears for her aunt's condition, Mrs Thorpe sent a footman to the doctor's house requesting him to visit as soon as possible.

Louisa returned to sit at her aunt's bedside and listened to the rasping breath getting more and more laboured. From time to time she heard mumbled words and names as though the old lady was reliving her life. *Wilfred* and *Will* were discernible as were *wrong* said several times and a very definite repetition of, '*No! No! No!*' Also *George* was muttered as were her daughter's names and also, she thought, her own father's name, *Ernest*, was said, but it was not clear enough to be sure.

The doctor arrived at ten o'clock. He listened to the rhythmic rasping breath and felt the feeble pulse then said there was little that could be done and departed, leaving the odour of cigars and brandy in his wake.

Soon after midnight Edwina arrived wearing a blue silk evening dress and sat by the bed. When Louisa tried to tell her what the doctor had said she waved a hand encased in a white kid glove in silent dismissal and turned away from her.

Louisa went to her room and sat dejectedly on the narrow bed. She could hear her cousin wailing in the next room, saying how much she loved her mother, over and over again, interspersed with something about George that was not loud enough to understand.

Eventually, at four in the morning, Louisa went into the bedroom and found Edwina lying asleep on the bed with her arms around the cold corpse of her mother.

The house was dark and very quiet the following day, which was Sunday. All curtains were drawn, all blinds were down and everyone whispered solemnly as though speaking in a normal voice would be disrespectful to the corpse lying in the bedroom.

At nine o'clock in the morning Edwina made a great deal of noise when locking the door of her mother's room and could be heard opening cupboards and dressing table drawers as though checking to make sure nothing has been stolen.

An hour later, when Louisa greeted her politely in the corridor, Edwina, dressed in black sateen with a black lace mantilla on her head in the style of the late Queen Victoria, ignored her words of condolence and behaved as though Louisa was both invisible and malodorous. Although deeply hurt, Louisa maintained her composure then went and sat on her bed wondering what to do next.

There was little to occupy her alone in the tiny airless room and feeling in need of fresh air she left the house to walk in the abbey grounds, despite a grey sky threatening rain. While approaching the ruins she decided it would be impossible stay in the house for long now that her cousin made her so unwelcome and therefore she needed to leave as soon as possible.

She longed to talk with her Aunt Rosemary and was glad she had arranged to visit her in two days time. The old lady might either know of someone with a small room to rent while she looked for employment or, better still, would offer her sanctuary in the old stone house for a short while.

On arrival at the ruins she considered ignoring the bench by the wall and waiting until the following day when Edward Francis and Mr Overton would lift the stone in the crypt, but the desire for a vision was too strong to be ignored. Feeling as though drawn to the bench she sat down and, ignoring the spots of rain landing on the mackintosh over her knees, she closed her eyes...

Chapter Eighteen

'I've brought you up here because I want you to make a promise, my dear child.'

Sara pulled up her hood and turned away out of the wind to save her face from the hair whipping against it while trying to hear her grandmother's voice. Watching a bird below them swoop down and then rise again with a small creature in its beak, she longed to ask her if angels could spread their wings and fly like that, but, aware of her serious expression, thought she might be irritated and say, as she often did, 'Heaven bless me child! Doesn't your mind ever stop wondering *why*?'

Seeing her grandmother's mouth moving, she leaned closer to her. 'You will take over the secret, Sara. Others have forgotten, but we shall remember it was the dark well of old—the most sacred of the three wells on the sacred island and—' the old woman paused to put her hand on her heart '—the very reason the abbey was built on that spot, to keep it hidden from view and so....' Most of her words were blown away towards the hills, although she did catch, 'Promise to tell the next one...' and clearly heard the word, 'secret.'

'Well!' The old woman pressed so close Sara felt warm breath on her cheek. 'Do you swear on all the ancestors who walked this sacred hill?'

'Oh yes, I swear.' Although not absolutely sure what she was promising to do, she knew it was important enough for her grandmother to struggle up the Tor when her back and all her joints were hurting as they always did in the freezing cold and especially, as she so often complained, with rain in prospect.

The old woman hugged her and then led her down the slope to a sheltered spot where she said, 'I'll not be long on this precious earth, dear child. You're too young to take over yet, but I'll show you what I'm talking about and then, when you're older you'll know what to do.'

They walked further down the slope then along the lane past a farmhouse on their left and the large orchards on either side until they reached the wall enclosing the abbey ruins, then walked beside it to several small cottages, in one of which she could hear her mother singing while spinning and the steady clunk and whizz of her father's loom. To her surprise they continued on past her grandmother's dwelling and then around the back of it where the old woman went into a small shed leaning against the wall and squeezed through a narrow gap in the back of it. Sara followed apprehensively, knowing they were going into the grounds of the abbey that she had always been told was private property and must never, ever enter.

When they emerged behind a large bush Sara watched as her grandmother peered through the foliage before signalling that there was no one about and then followed her as she walked from tree to tree through the overgrown grounds until they reached the great walls of the ruined abbey.

'Look here—' she stopped and touched one of the slabs of stone in the wall beside her '—remember this spot.' She looked around anxiously before bending down and climbing through a gap.

Sara could hear her heart thumping as she followed and seeing her grandmother below, jumped down onto a square flagstone. She watched as the old woman knelt down, lifted a flat piece of stone and put it to one side, before beckoning to her. She went and joined her then peered down into the darkness.

The questions immediately rose up in her mind. Why were they doing this? What was the black stuff in the round hole? Until, seeing a beautiful face and unable to contain herself, she asked, 'Who is that lady looking up at me?'

Her grandmother made a sound that was either a sob or a laugh and then quickly put the stone back over the hole. She pulled herself upright with great difficulty and a moan of pain, then, after giving Sara a wonderful smile, led her back through the ruins to the bush and back into her little dwelling.

Once inside the old lady said, 'I knew you had the gift and that's...'

'Who was that lady?' Sara asked.

'Don't interrupt me, dear child. I knew you had it and that's why I've shown you our secret—that's what it is, *our secret* and no one else's. You must never tell anyone, you understand?'

'Yes, Grandmother.'

'Now, you tell me what you saw in the dark well.'

'A well! Is that what it was?'

'That's right. Now what did you see?'

'I saw a lovely lady with blue eyes and fair hair curling under her hat.' Sara wrinkled her nose while recalling the lady's clothes. 'She had dark clothes with lace high up under her chin and a shiny thing hanging on a chain around her neck.' She paused to remember how beautiful and yet extraordinary the woman had looked.

'Anything else?' The old woman asked eagerly.

'I think she had been crying, she held a piece of white cloth up to her eyes. I don't know why exactly, but I think her little boy had died. I think she had wanted to die with him, but she had to look after someone else and so she decided to live and she was sad, that's all.'

'That's wonderful, dear child. I now know that there will be a woman in the future who will make the well live again.' The old woman looked sad for a moment. 'I've seen the path set out for you, dear child. Take note of what I say to you now and remember this very important fact.' She grasped Sara's hand tightly. 'Remember that if the water is contaminated with blood it will be sullied for many generations. What did I just say?'

Sara felt a shiver run down her spine. 'You said I must remember that if the water is contamin—something with blood, it will be...' she looked hopefully at her grandmother.

'If ever blood should flow into the water of the black well it will be sullied for many generations.'

Sara nodded. 'Oh I understand. Yes. If ever blood flows in the well it will be sullied for many generations.'

'That's it, dear child.' The old woman sighed and sat down on a wooden seat beside the fire-pit then looked hopefully at the grey ashes.

'I'll fetch some kindling, Grandmother,' Sara said.

'There you are! I said you had the gift. You saw what was in my mind before I could ask you,' and she laughed so merrily that Sara joined in despite not knowing what was so funny.

The following morning, when she had swept the floor and fetched fresh water from the nearest spring, she went as usual to collect her grandmother's bucket in order to fetch water for her. When there was no answer to her knock she tried pushing on the door and when it swung open she found the old woman lying on the floor close to the fire. Moving closer she saw her grandmother's eyes staring fixedly at the wall.

The shock seemed to suck the air out of her and she stood frozen, unable to move or make a sound for a long moment. Then she opened her mouth and screamed long and loud until her mother appeared and slapped her face.

She went home and did not speak again for a long time, so long that she was considered simple by everyone who knew her, apart from her father who taught her how to use his loom and never gave up hope that she would speak again one day.

Her mother seemed to think she could mock her into speech, saying frequently how quiet and pleasant it was without silly questions being asked morning noon and night, but Sara remained obdurately silent. Inside her head she still talked and also she listened and learned a great deal, because people often assumed she was deaf as well as dumb and relaxed in her presence.

Where once the women would have stopped their gossip to one another when she approached to fill her bucket at the well or to wash the clothes in the washhouse, they now continued talking about their problems and each other's without any inhibition. And so the time passed until she reached womanhood.

On a morning in spring, when the floor of the forest was covered in a haze of bluebells, she walked along a narrow path through the trees towards the Tor with a basket on her arm in order to pick wild garlic leaves. Although she still never spoke to anyone, she did sometimes sing to herself when alone and feeling sure there was no one around to hear her, she sang a song her grandmother had taught her long ago.

'As I was going to Glastonbury Fair, I met a man so handsome and fair with eyes of blue and golden hair. ....' She broke off hearing a deep voice joining in and continuing, 'There's none I know that can compare with the maid I met at Glastonbury Fair.'

She stood still looking for the owner of the voice, but could see no one. She had heard a song about a fairy man called Jack o' the Green who beguiled maidens in the spring and wondered if this was he. With her heart pounding so loud she thought he must hear it, she walked through the bluebells to a clump of white flowers and picked the pungent green leaves around them.

A voice said, 'I always think the bluebells and the white ramson flowers make such a wonderful combination at this time of year.'

Now realising that the voice came from overhead, she looked up and saw a man perched precariously on a branch of the oak tree a short distance away. 'I do agree,' she replied, wondering why her voice sounded unfamiliar.

The man jumped down, landed awkwardly and lay groaning in a bed of nettles.

She dropped her basket and ran to him, asking, 'Are you hurt?'

'Well, I'm not sure if I'll live—' he grinned up at her '—but I might be persuaded to try, if you'll help me out of these damned nettles.'

She had never heard anyone use the word 'damned' before and hesitated, wondering if he was one of the heathen infidels she had heard the priest talking about one Sunday.

'I won't bite,' he said, holding out a hand towards her.

She took a few steps and stood close to him. 'I think you can get out of there without my aid,' she said, trying to contain the laughter bubbling up inside her.

'Well bless my soul! What a miracle! I believe you're right. Mistress— er—what was your name again?'

'I didn't say,' she said, laughing.

He stood up and walked through the nettles to stand a pace away from her and bowed low, saying, 'I'm Barnaby the weaver at your service m'lady.'

She gave a small curtsey. 'And I'm Sara Weaver, sir.'

'There! I knew it! We are both from the same trade, although I doubt you have travelled so far from home as I.'

'From whence have you come, sir?'

'Barnaby.'

She struggled to keep her face straight. 'From whence have you come, Barnaby?'

'I have travelled many days from the uplands to the North where many sheep are kept and therefore much wool is available, but I had the urge to seek my fortune and now I'm on my way to a port in the South where I can take a ship to the New World.'

'Where is that?' she asked, thinking he was probably teasing her and there was no such place.

'I don't exactly know where. I just know it's far away across the seas. I met a sailor who had been there and he told me of sea monsters and wild animals and dragons and people with feathers growing from their heads and all manner of strange beings that made me want to go and see them for myself.' He went and pulled a sack from behind a bush and swung it over his shoulder. 'You could come with me, we could have an adventure together, what do you say, Miss Sara Weaver?'

She shook her head. 'No, I thank you. I have to go home and cook a hare with garlic for my parents and brother.'

He rubbed his stomach. 'Mary Mother of God! I haven't eaten for two days and this beautiful girl tells me she's going to cook my favourite meal!'

'I don't think the Madonna should be taken in vain,' she said primly.

'You're right of course. I apologise to her and to you.' He wagged his forefinger at her and added, 'We shouldn't be mentioning her at all these days, don't forget.' He indicated with his head towards the ruined abbey. 'I see the king's soldiers did their worst back there.'

She nodded. 'It happened in my grandmother's father's time, he was a servant to the monks. The Abbot and two of his men were hung drawn and quartered on top of the Tor.'

He shook his head sadly. 'I want to get away from such evil, that's why I thought I'd go to this new place where I can be free from religious prejudice and control.'

She had never heard anyone dare to say such a thing and stared at him incredulously.

Her father's voice could be heard calling her name and she said, 'I must go.' Moments later, when he appeared on the path, she called to him, 'I'm here Father.' Watching him walk towards her with his mouth open in shock and realising she had been talking again, she felt dizzy and steadied herself on the trunk of a tree.

'My dear, darling, girl,' her father put his arm around her shoulder. Then looking at the young man with the sack on his shoulder, he asked who he was and where he was going. When he had heard Barnaby's plans he said, 'You have performed a miracle for me. My daughter,

who has not spoken a word since very young, now talks with ease.'
He held out his hand. 'Please, Mr Barnaby the weaver, I beg you join
us for a meal before you go on your long journey.'

They walked back to the dwelling beside the abbey wall and soon
the men were discussing the loom, the quality of wool, the poor price
paid to the weavers and spinners, while Sara helped her mother
prepare the meal.

Barnaby charmed every member of the family and was invited to
stay in the small lean-to beside the house that had once been her grandmother's, but was now a store for wool and fabric. He stayed the next
night and the one after and many after that.

By the time he asked her again to go with him Sara was deeply in
love and agreed. That night she went to lie with him in his bed and
the day after they asked her father for his permission to wed, but he
refused, saying she was too young to leave and besides he could not
manage without her.

Barnaby stayed for a full turn of the moon. Each night he made
love to Sara and every day he tried to persuade her to run away with
him. Finally, when the moon was full, he said he would leave at dawn
whether she would go with him or no.

Sara walked to the Tor in the moonlight and sat on a rock, remembering the promise she had made to her grandmother. A sacred oath,
the old woman had called it, one that could not be broken. With tears
blurring her vision, she sat and waited for the first bird to give warning
of a new day approaching. Then, as more and more awoke and began
their chorus in the cool light of dawn, she knew her lover was loading
his sack on his back and leaving for his new life.

When the sun revealed the green fields below her, she stood up and
straightened her shoulders. Barnaby had gone, unaware of how much
she loved him, nor would her grandmother ever know how great a
sacrifice she had made to keep her childhood promise, but keep it she
would.

With a heavy heart she walked back to her parents' house and into the place where Barnaby had slept. Desperately controlling her tears, she pulled away several bales of wool and found the gap in the wall. This was the first time she had dared to go into the abbey grounds and was surprised to see others carrying their bales of cloth to the building that had once been the abbot's kitchen. No one looked at her or appeared to notice when she slipped down into the gap in the remains of the huge thick wall.

Her fingers shook as she nervously lifted the stone as her grandmother had done years before. Then, with a deep breath, she looked down into the inky black circle of water. For a while she thought nothing would happen and then she saw a group of very angry women, one of whom was wielding an axe. The picture quickly faded and she replaced the stone, feeling disturbed by the strange image.

When a voice behind her said, 'Can you see in the well, mistress?' she looked round and saw a woman wrapped in a brown cloak.

She swallowed hard before backing away.

'Don't worry, Mistress. No harm will come from it, I won't tell anyone. I saw you come down here and I guessed you were the girl your grandmother told my grandmother about. My gran used to tell me to look out for you because you had the gift of sight just as she did and you could get the guidance from the well.' The woman held up a coin. 'I'd pay you for your trouble.'

Sara picked up the stone slab again and looked into the pool. The picture came quickly and she said, 'I see you holding a child with dark hair and brown eyes. You are carrying him away from here. I see a big house in the distance and a man coming to greet you with open arms.' She looked up and saw the woman smiling at her as she handed her the coin.

'God bless you! God bless you!' she said and walked away out of the ruins.

A short while later, on arrival at her parents' house, she picked up a bucket and went to fetch some water. Then, having returned with it, she told them of Barnaby's departure and also, with a tremor in her voice, that she was carrying his child. To her surprise, they accepted the situation quite calmly and when she asked if she could live in her grandmother's old house in order to have her own home for the baby, her father readily agreed. Looking into his eyes she saw that he thought she had stayed for his sake and although longing to explain her reason, kept the secret as her grandmother had wished.

A few days later a young woman came to her door and asked nervously if she would look into the well for her. Despite trembling with fear, she agreed; it was as though the well was pulling her towards it and she was helpless to refuse.

❖   ❖   ❖

And so it began. At least once a week a woman would come to ask her for guidance. She told them what she saw, unless it was too terrible to describe, and then she found a way of warning them to be prepared for something that might not be quite as they wished it to be, but in general she was able to give good news rather than bad.

No one in the family mentioned Barnaby again, at least not until her daughter was born and then her mother muttered several thoughts against him, but Sara defended him, saying, 'I loved him and am glad I have my baby to remember him by.' She called the girl Bryony and took great delight in her.

When the child was three years of age, a charming and handsome young man from a neighbouring town courted Sara. This time her father approved of the match and so they were wed and he came to live with her in the little house built by the abbey wall.

Her new husband soon gave her cause to worry about his gambling and drinking and she was deeply unhappy within weeks of their marriage. When she gave birth to a son she thought he would calm down and be a responsible parent like her own father, but he continued his philandering ways and left her alone night after night as before.

When he had not returned one morning she assumed he was either asleep in a ditch at best, or in a prostitute's bed at worst and would arrive dishevelled and repentant by the afternoon as he usually did. The day wore on and there was no sign of him. By the next morning she was anxious and went to the alehouse to ask if they knew his whereabouts. No one had seen him, either in that or any other tavern in the town. She was now distraught with worry.

Days went by and still there was no word of him. Some neighbours thought he had been press-ganged into the navy and others said he had been seen with a woman at the fair shortly before his disappearance and others still said he owed money to a man in the local tavern, but she never ever heard news of him.

She continued to live her life alone looking after her parents as they grew older and doing her best to keep spinning and weaving as they had done while also caring for her daughter and son.

Bryony grew into a lively young woman who soon married a merchant's son and had her own babies, most of which died and of those that survived, not one was interested in making cloth, which was a cause of great disappointment to Sara, especially after her father died and she struggled to keep weaving.

Sara's son was a handsome young fellow who had inherited both his father's charm and his weakness for gambling. On the day his body was pulled out of the river and brought to her on a cart by two fishermen she laid him out in his best clothes and felt a grief beyond tears.

Suddenly she was old; too old to bear such pain. She had tried so hard to teach him how to use the loom and to breathe into him the enthusiasm for weaving, but to no avail and now there was no point in continuing the pretence. She would never spin or weave again.

Time passed and although she never wept for him, she grieved every day with a dry ache in her heart for the boy who had made her laugh and charmed her and everyone around him. Sometimes she thought he had reminded her of Barnaby and sometimes that he had reminded her of his father and sometimes, in the quiet of the night, she admitted with a wry smile that she had married the second love because he was like the first and so one mistake had led to the other. But then, with another smile, she accepted that at least she had had the boy to love for his short life, despite his weakness.

One day, several years after her son's death and while thinking of her father, she uncovered the loom then ran her gnarled fingers over the wooden frame knowing there was no hope of working it even if it were still usable. She was feeling the cold this winter more than ever and had made up the fire to warm the house, but her back still ached and her hands were too stiff and painful to card the wool let alone spin it ready for weaving.

With a sigh she remembered when the whole family was engaged in making the cloth they sold in the old abbot's kitchen beside the ruins of the abbey, but that was long ago in the good times. Now, it was the worst of times. The local women rarely came and paid for her guidance and therefore she had no money to buy food. She had no husband and no son to help since the former disappeared without trace and the latter had squandered all her savings before he fell into the river while drunk and drowned. Admittedly she still had her daughter Bryony, who had invited her to go and live with her family to help with the children, but she had politely refused. She belonged in her little dwelling by the abbey wall—not that the walls kept the populace out any longer and many of them took stone from the monastery ruins to build houses of various sizes all around the growing town.

This was where she was destined to be, living close to the secret well and ready to give guidance when asked, which happened rarely since the arrival of a priest who railed every Sunday against all kinds of sorcery and was particularly antagonistic towards witches. She had never met a witch, who, so it was said, cast evil spells on people and used her magical powers to control them; while believing such beings existed, she had neither seen, nor had she heard of one, in the locality.

When a milkmaid from the farm nearby sidled up to her one day and speaking from the side of her mouth, said, 'I warn you there is talk of you being in league with the devil. Beware!' She had been too shocked to respond at the time, but later, after thinking about it, she understood that her own gifts would be seen as sorcery by some and that was the reason no one came to her for guidance from the well.

She now knew the reason her grandmother had taken her to the Tor and made her swear she would never, never ever tell anyone about her gift to read the dark well except to the one who would follow her and take on the task of guarding it. And with this knowledge came the realisation that she had broken the promise; she had looked in the well for many women in need of her gift and a cold hard feeling of foreboding lay heavily within her heart.

Death was suddenly beckoning to her and before she could go willingly towards it she knew that, while unable to change her failure to keep the promise, she must impart her knowledge to the one who should take over the duty of guarding the well. The only person who had the gift of second sight was her daughter's youngest girl who must be shown how to look into the dark water, but the child was not yet ready for such knowledge and she must therefore hold on to life for a year or two longer.

She heard a thump on the door and her daughter calling 'Mother! Mother! Where are you?'

When she opened the door her daughter dived through it and sank onto a wooden bench by the fire, wringing her hands in obvious despair, while saying, 'We are doomed! My children are all ailing, my darling boy is near to death and so is my husband. And on my way here I've heard it's all over the town.' She stared with wild feverish eyes while screaming, 'A plague! A plague!' Then she held her head moaning piteously.

Sara said she would go with her and do what she could for the family. She packed some dried herbs into a sack and followed at a slower pace while her daughter ran to the house in which she lived and then collapsed.

Throughout the next three days and nights Sara tended to the family. She brought down each invalid's fever with cloths dipped in cold water and then, to her relief the youngest girl regained consciousness, followed a few hours later by the boy, then the father and finally her daughter opened her eyes and smiled weakly at her.

Later that day, while she was feeding them with a gruel made of oats and herbs, a neighbour's child came to ask for help and so, when she had settled her family to sleep, Sara went with the girl and tended her mother and three remaining siblings, the youngest two having already died.

Soon more and more people were waylaying her as she went from house to house tending to the sick. Whenever there was a member of the family who had escaped the illness she gave them instructions on how to care for their kin and moved on to the next stricken household.

Eventually, when the epidemic had run its course, she returned to her dwelling and slept the deep sleep of exhaustion.

Some time later she became aware of a thunderous knocking on her door. While struggling to bring herself fully awake, she thought this would be someone in need of help and was pulling back the covers when the door burst open and a large woman ran in wielding an axe.

The small dwelling was suddenly full of people shouting accusations, either to her, or about her. 'Miserable mean witch! Saved your own didn't you? What about my man?'

'Yeah, what about my children, didn't save them did yer?'

'Look at her! What a witch! Look at the bunches of plants by the fire, if you needed any proof, there it is.'

Suddenly in the midst of this chaos one voice was heard above all the others. 'She did magic in the abbey. I know she did it in a well in the ruins. My sister told me.'

All other sounds stopped with a shocking suddenness and all eyes were on the middle-aged woman standing by the door. Finding she was now the centre of attention, her face turned a bright red and she looked behind her as though about to leave.

'Wait!' The first woman to arrive went and closed the door, then, with a menacing smile, she said, 'Tell us more, mistress.'

'I er—I don't know more than that,' the now frightened woman swallowed and looked as though she regretted having spoken.

'Tell us more!' a woman standing by the loom shouted.

'Yeah, what wicked spells did she do?'

'And curses, what curses did she…'

Sara stood up, pulling her night shift down to hide her bare legs and tried to explain she did neither of those things and also she had helped people recover from the sickness as best she could, but no one was listening.

'Why didn't she catch the plague? That's what I want to know and what's more, what was she doing in the abbey ruins?'

'Putting curses on all of us, that's what!'

'Yeah, she's the one that gave us the plague!'

Sara was trying to form the words to ask if having survived the plague meant that they also were witches, when a hand suddenly thwacked the side of her head and she saw bright flashing stars for a moment before another blow knocked her unconscious.

When she awoke all she could see was a sliver of light at first and then as the one eye opened a little more the light became the sky above her. Figures were moving around her. A voice kept muttering, 'It must be here somewhere.' And then the same voice cried out triumphantly, 'Here it is! I'll move the stone.'

She saw faces made ugly by hate staring down at her. Someone said, 'Let's see what she does now!'

She felt her arms gripped and her limp body pulled across the stones then her face was thrust over the dark well. For a moment her swollen and bleeding face was reflected in the black water. She saw a drop of blood fall and cause the image to break up. Her grandmother's voice echoed down the years, 'Remember, child, if the water is contaminated with blood it will be sullied for many generations.'

She reached out and grabbed the side of the well and felt a piece of loose stone come away as she fell forward. Suddenly, knowing her life would be one of pain and misery if she survived and it was too late to show the well to her little granddaughter, she threw her head forward into the water and dived down the hole clutching the piece of stone. Going down into the tunnel of stone she felt a gap and in her last living moment she pushed the fragment into it.

A while later, finding she was looking down on the group of women arguing about what they should do with the corpse, she knew her spirit had left her broken body. She watched as the others backed away nervously, one weeping and wringing her hands, while the largest woman pulled the corpse out of the well and dragged it away.

Looking deep into the well and seeing the lump of stone she had pushed into a drainage hole that carried the water to an outlet in the town she knew the water would no longer stand still in the dark well, but would run out over the top of it for a very long time. Her last thoughts before leaving were to wonder how long the well would be contaminated and who would be the one to look into it when it was healed.

Chapter Nineteen

Louisa found her face wet with tears when she opened her eyes. 'It has been contaminated!' she exclaimed while wiping her eyes.

For several minutes she sat in rigid shock while trying to accept the recently seen horror. On eventually moving her hand, rivulets of water ran from the cape down her arms onto her lap and she stood up cautiously before shaking as much of the rain off her as possible.

Seeing the large dark shape of an umbrella approaching she waited until Mr Overton reached her and held it over her.

'A bit too late to be of much use, I'm afraid.' He said, adding with a smile, 'I almost didn't come out today in this dreadful weather, but then I saw you from my study window and wanted to make sure you knew I've arranged for help with lifting the stone over the well tomorrow. Also I wanted to tell you, if you were here, that is, that I've been to luncheon with an old friend of mine who has connections with the great and the good of the town. He's heard rumours that the abbey lands are to be sold.'

'Who would buy them?' she asked.

'The Church I hope,' he replied. Then he asked if she had seen any visions that day. On hearing the story he shook his head sadly, then said, 'I think I read someone's description of the Lady Chapel in the early eighteen hundreds. No, I'm sure it was earlier than that, more like seventeen hundred or so and the crypt was described as being flooded.' He scratched his chin thoughtfully then added, 'I'm not sure if it was the same man or not, but I also remember reading that when the crypt was cleared of rubble, many coffins were floating in water.' He shook his head. 'Sorry, I'll have to look it up in the records, but nevertheless you've hit on something there.'

The following day the sun was shining with not a cloud in the sky.

She packed most of her belongings in readiness for departure until lunchtime. Then, having eaten in her room as usual and realising she had some time to wait before meeting Edward and the historian at two o'clock, she left the house and walked to a spot in the abbey grounds where she could see the remains of a church on the green summit of the Tor rising up above the trees.

She was thinking that if she had neither known anything about it, nor seen it in the past, she would say it was merely a strangely shaped hill with a tower on top, but feeling the pull from it, admitted there was no denying its power and also its connection with the ruins. Allowing her eyes to go out of focus she could imagine the shape the Tor had once been before earthquakes and human destruction and suddenly she was Willow again, seeing the huge dark shape of The Great One silhouetted against the pale morning sky.

She remembered how her mother had explained that the huge earthwork had been made to represent two figures joined as one, a gigantic kneeling man, with his head crowned in a circle of tall stones on one side and a voluptuously curved woman on the other.

Her mother had said that, before it was made in this form, the ancestors had worshipped only the female side of the divine because people had not understood the vital part in procreation played by the male. Once they had learned this fact, they saw how nature had created this huge great mound in a wonderful manifestation of balance; and how each spring the suns rays shone between the two figures, symbolizing their conjoining and impregnation of the female for new life to be born.

On blinking and finding she was once more in the present gazing at the Tor, Louisa wondered if the memory of its glorious past lingered in people's hearts and this was the reason they were still drawn to it so many generations later. Even now, she thought, the sacred symbol of oneness in creation was still relevant. In this time of imbalance, when women, who had been suppressed by men for so long, were calling for equality, it might be time for the spirit of The Great

One to be recognised again.

Turning around to look at the ruins of the abbey, she thought that, although the church had been built for Christian worship, there were some similarities with the Tor; both were now a mere shadow of their former glory and both had been used to celebrate the seasons and all the important times in life, including birth and death.

She saw Edward and Mr Overton standing with another man at the usual spot by the ruins and hurried to meet them.

When all three men had expressed their sympathy and sorrow that her aunt had died, Edward said, 'We've got the lifting tackle in place ready to lift, but we'll have to take it away again and replace the barrier as we found it.'

Mr Overton said, 'I've heard some good news. There is hope that the Church of England will take over the ruins. The rumour is that a benefactor is likely to buy the property and give it to them.' The old man looked anxiously around the grounds before adding, 'I'm sure there'll be clerics and land agents all over the place very soon and we don't want anyone finding us tampering with the building, do we?'

They all nodded and then agreed that the old man would keep watch while the other three went down and the two men could lift the stone while Louisa looked under it.

When she descended the ladder Louisa found two metal bars already in position on either side of the stone and a rope in place leading to a winding wheel. She quickly knelt in the tiny space while the men turned the handle and slowly winched the stone up several inches.

Peering under the stone she saw the round hole, then, when the stone was winched a little bit higher, she gasped on seeing the inky black circle that seemed like the fabric of Edwina's mourning dress, but was, she knew, the water of the dark well.

Edward said, 'We can't hold it for long.'

She wanted to reply, but was transfixed when a young woman, little more than a girl, she thought, gazed up at her. She seemed familiar, her face was similar in appearance to her own, but with a rounder nose and fuller lips; reminiscent, she thought, of Willow. With a smile of understanding she realised there was a similarity also to Wind Flower and White Bird and to all of the people she had seen in the visions, including Tobin.

The young woman was looking into her eyes. Her expression was a mixture of wonder, delight and astonishment. Louisa leaned closer, longing to communicate and find out her identity and the time in which she was living, but although she asked her name, it was clear the words could not be heard.

When the girl turned away, as if speaking to someone behind her, Louisa strained to see who was there, but without success. All that was visible were several strings of brightly coloured beads hanging around her neck and the long auburn hair flowing loose around her shoulders.

Edward said, 'I'm sorry, I think we'll have to let it down now.'

Louisa reluctantly moved back to let them replace the stone and watched as the well was covered once more. She climbed the ladder and emerged into the sunlight to stand with the three men beside the great wall of the old abbey and said, 'I'm so grateful to you all.'

When Edward asked if she had seen anything in such a short time, she replied, 'Oh yes, a great deal more than I could have hoped for.'

'What did you see?' Mr Overton asked.

'Just a young woman,' she said.

'That's all?'

'It's more than enough,' she said with a contented smile. 'The well is healed and there will be another guardian at some point in the future, that's all I need to know.'

After thanking both the young man with his lifting gear, and the elderly Mr Overton for their help, Louisa and Edward walked back towards the house.

'I'm very sorry your Aunt Agnes died so soon after your arrival,' he said, then asked, 'will you still come to Aunt Rosemary's tomorrow?'

'I see no reason to cancel the arrangement,' she replied. ' I am not being considered as one of the family. My cousin, who is in deep and, in my opinion, ostentatious mourning, does not treat me as one of the family, in fact she ignores me and does all she can to make me feel unwelcome; therefore I'm free to come and go as I please.' She shook her head sadly before adding, 'I am grieving for the loss of Aunt Agnes, but I think she was ready to pass on. She had a good life until the last few months, which really were not very comfortable for her. Also, I need some advice from Aunt Rosemary. I can't stay in the house for long so I'll have to find somewhere to live very soon and also another position. I'm hoping my, I beg your pardon, I should say *our* aunt, will know of someone in need of nursing care for a relative, or a room to rent.'

He suggested they should meet by the front gate of the house at three o'clock the following afternoon. 'We mustn't be late,' he said with a grin. 'Our Aunt Rosemary will have been baking today in readiness for this great occasion. She's like a young girl going to her first grown-up party and is more excited than I've ever seen her.'

Louisa chuckled. 'I'm surprised you know how excited young girls get when going to parties.'

'Oh yes, I'm an expert on young girls and older ones too, come to think of it.' He grinned mischievously before explaining, 'I grew up with four sisters, so I'm well acquainted with giggling and gossiping, and what's more, I am adept with curling tongs and ribbons. Also I can listen to lengthy discussions as to whether bonnets are out of fashion and hats are the thing; and most important of all, who should wear what, on which occasion, to attract which unsuspecting admirer.'

'You don't sound very impressed with us!'

'On the contrary, I would love to have daughters and experience it all again. I'm making do with two nieces at present and it's not enough.'

Louisa remembered the woman and children with him in church and said, 'I think I may have seen you in church with them one Sunday.'

'Yes. I am godfather to the older girl and feel obliged to accompany my sister-in-law from time to time.'

'Your sister-in-law?' She asked in surprise.

He kept his face straight, but his eyes smiled momentarily before he replied solemnly, 'Yes, my brother's widow.'

Wondering how she had come to believe he was married she quickly tried to remember what her aunt had said about the wedding in the cathedral but failed and then, to cover her confusion, she said, 'I'm so sorry he died.'

'A riding accident, I'm afraid. '

Her heart was thumping so loudly she feared he might hear it. In an attempt to sound calm, she asked, 'And what of your sisters now, are they still silly and excitable?'

'Far from it! Well, if I'm honest, I must admit the youngest one is still inclined to be quite giddy, but the others are terrifyingly sensible women who believe in women's franchise…'

'That's wonderful. So do I!'

'I had a feeling you would.' He doffed the wide-brimmed hat, revealing his sparkling eyes. 'I look forward to discussions on the subject tomorrow, but for now I must leave you at the mercy of your cousin's husband and his brother.'

'You know George?'

'I know his reputation hereabouts, which is not good; and I have heard rumours about his brother, which are even worse. I confess I made some enquiries at Aunt Rosemary's behest because she worried about your Aunt Agnes. I am on very good terms with Mr Merriot, who I have discovered is your aunt's solicitor and I have recently taken the liberty of speaking with him regarding your aunt's affairs. I suggest you keep your wits about you and sign nothing unless Mr Merriot agrees to it.' He strode away and disappeared behind a large tree.

Louisa walked through the garden and then up to her room thinking of the beautiful young woman in the well and wondering if she would be of the next generation, or the one after that, or even further into the future.

On arrival in her tiny room she smiled at her reflection in the small mirror and admitted to a conviction that great happiness awaited her in the future. She knew deep in her heart that the auburn haired young woman bedecked with beads would be her descendant and for that to be so she must bear another child.

Remembering her planned visit to Aunt Rosemary the following day, she hoped the old lady would read her tea-leaves as promised and wondered whether she would tell her of a marriage in the future and even, perhaps, of a baby waiting to be born.

The following day at two o'clock Louisa was sitting on the bed in her room ready to go out and meet Edward in one hour. She was remembering their conversation when he talked about his sisters and how his eyes had sparkled when saying, 'I had a feeling you would.' Did that mean he admired her for supporting a cause with which he agreed, or did he think the opposite and was laughing at her?

Feeling her heart racing at the thought of seeing him, she realised the revelation that he was not married had changed everything. Despite having assumed for so long that she would continue to pay no attention to other men, as she had while her husband was alive, she could now admit to being attracted to a man with a shaggy auburn moustache and laughing eyes.

Taking the locket from around her neck she opened it and looked at the picture of her husband she had cut from a photograph and pushed in behind the lock of her son's hair. The image seemed boyish and bore little resemblance to the shrunken gaunt man she remembered in the latter years of her marriage.

After closing the locket she held it for a moment and tried to visualise what he would look like had he been healthy and alive. He would be handsome with a hooked nose and blue grey eyes, much taller than her and slightly built.

Edward on the other hand was of a sturdier build; broad of shoulder and chest, and short enough for their eyes to meet on almost the same level. With a start she reminded herself there was no point in thinking about the man who was very kindly accompanying her to see their mutual Aunt Rosemary and could not possibly be romantically inclined towards an impecunious widow—or could he? She had noticed him looking at her ankle once or twice, and the fact that he appeared so frequently when she visited the abbey might not have been mere coincidence—or could it?

Hearing a knock on her door she opened it and was surprised to see a maid looking red in the face with excitement. 'I'm very sorry, Mrs Wendon. You are required in the drawing room immediately.'

Louisa was surprised to hear this and said she would go.

The maid looked down at her feet while adding, 'Beggin' yer pardon, Mrs Wendon. Me an' all the staff loved old Mrs Govern. Ever so happy we were with her. And I'd like ter be so bold as ter tell yer that we all appreciated how kind you were to her, takin' her out in that chair an'all. That's why I'm sorry.'

'Sorry about Mrs Govern dying?' asked Louisa.

'No, that is ter say, I am sorry the old mistress died, but I'm also sorry the new girl's got yer into trouble.'

'Trouble, what kind of trouble?'

'She didn't mean no harm.' The maid swallowed. 'She told Mrs Thorne the housekeeper as how she heard the old mistress speak when she was changing the bed linen and Mrs Thorne went and told the new mistress what she'd said, so she's 'aving a fit of the vapours and the handyman—' she gasped and struggled to keep her face straight '—beggin' yer pardon, I meant ter say the *master*, threw a vase through the French winders.' She bent over and covered her face with both hands for a moment, then gave a quick bob and ran away along the corridor either sobbing or laughing.

Louisa went downstairs, trying to breathe deeply to stop her heart pounding. After knocking on the door she entered the room to find Edwina lying on the chaise longue, a man whom she assumed must be George's brother sitting in one armchair, George sitting in an another, holding a brandy glass, and a maid sweeping up fragments of a Chinese vase and shards of glass by the French windows.

Edwina looked scathingly at Louisa and said, 'I've been told the most extraordinary tale that I really have great difficulty in believing. I'm hoping there has been a misunderstanding and you can explain it to me.' She stretched her neck forward, reminding Louisa of a chicken, then went on, 'One of the maids said she heard my mother conversing with you—is that true?'

'Yes, cousin, it is.'

'And had she spoken to you before yesterday?'

'Yes, cousin, she did.'

'Would you please explain your reason for not informing me of the dramatic improvement in her condition?'

Louisa kept her eyes focused on Edwina as she replied, 'Your mother begged me to keep it a secret.'

'Keep it a secret!' Edwina exclaimed. 'Why did she do that?'

Louisa was aware of George walking towards her. 'I don't know exactly. She was frightened of ...' she broke off hearing voices in the hall. The door opened and a familiar tall figure stood in the doorway.

'Emily!' Edwina exclaimed. 'Thank heavens you've arrived, at last!'

'I came as soon as I could. I did not receive the telegram until dawn this morning when I found it on my desk under some papers. I'm afraid the porter took it while I was in the operating theatre and forgot to tell me until today. Fortunately I had just come off duty at the time and could catch the next train here.' Emily looked at Louisa and said, 'I'm sorry she died so soon after you came....'

'Sorry!' Edwina exclaimed. 'You sent us a viper into our—' She waved her hand in the air. 'I don't know....'

282

'Bosom?' George's brother suggested.

Emily frowned and looked at Louisa then back at Edwina, who said, 'We thought Mama had been left deaf and dumb after the stroke, remember?'

Emily nodded.

'Well, she wasn't and this, this unspeakably vile witch, knew and didn't tell me.' Huge dry sobs emanated from Edwina's throat and she buried her face in her hands.

Emily went and knelt beside her. After a few moments, when the sobbing had subsided, she said, 'There must be an explanation.'

Edwina whined like a little girl, while saying, 'She said Mama wanted her to keep it a secret.'

Emily looked at Louisa. 'Is that so?'

Louisa said it was.

'And can you give the reason for this secrecy?'

Louisa saw George's hands clench into fists, but she was determined to keep calm and not show any fear of him. 'I don't know exactly what had frightened her, but I think someone wanted her to change her will.'

Edwina said, 'George!'

Everyone else in the room froze, including the maid on her knees by the window.

Edwina turned to look at her husband. 'She had the stroke that day when you brought your brother to see her, you said he….'

'You can't blame…'

'Yes I can! She was perfectly all right until he arrived. She was pleased to see us when we arrived the day before and was looking forward to our visit. She had been talking about going for a walk in the abbey ruins with me and the next thing I knew you were calling for the doctor because she had collapsed.'

George shouted, 'I was only thinking of *you*, you stupid *fool*!'

'How dare you call me a….'

'Because that's what you are! As stupid as your silly, foolish mother!'

Emily held up her hands and commanded, 'Be quiet, both of you!' She turned to George and asked, 'Why did you bring your brother to see Mother on the day she collapsed?'

George swallowed and looked at the Turkish carpet as he replied, 'He's a solicitor, as you know.'

'But why, when we have our usual man, Mr Merriot?'

George took a step towards the door. 'I don't have to stay and listen to this.'

'Yes you do!' Louisa went and stood with her back to the door. 'I don't know what went on, but I think Edwina and Emily deserve an explanation.' She could feel her hear thumping, but was determined to show no fear.

George sneered at her. 'You're not so stupid as I thought, little meek and mild Cousin Louisa in her shabby old mourning clothes. Not the poor bereft little widow now are you?' He turned to Edwina. 'I told you I was looking after you, stupid cow! You didn't understand the will when it was read to you after your father died, did you? Well I did and I heard loud and clear what he said should happen when your sainted mother went to join him in the graveyard.' He paused to look at his wife whose mouth was hanging open.

'And so did I!' Emily said. 'I both heard and understood and that is the reason I suggested Louisa should come and help care for Mother.' She went and put her arm around her sister who was now sitting bolt upright. 'You see, dear Edwina, I knew our father had wanted to put right a wrong when he died, but he loved our mother so much he couldn't bear to think of her losing her beloved home and so he made sure it would happen after she died.'

George loomed over Louisa and demanded she should let him pass.

Emily said, 'Let the bully go, Cousin.'

Louisa stepped sideways and allowed him to wrench the door open and slam it behind him.

His brother gave a weak smile and left the room.

Edwina wailed, 'I don't know what's happening,' and burst into tears.

Emily beckoned to Louisa and she went to join her cousins on the chaise longue. When Edwina had dried her eyes and all three were sitting quietly, Emily said, 'Edwina dear, our father persuaded Uncle Ernest, Louisa's father, to put money into a business venture that failed.'

Louisa said, 'I knew he had lost money, but I didn't know it was his brother who persuaded him.' She shrugged and added, 'I expect it was a gamble and they could have made a fortune if they had won and then they would have been heroes, but they didn't win. It's what happens to people when they take risks — they lose sometimes.'

'That's true, Louisa, but on an earlier occasion my father borrowed money from your father to buy this house and he never paid him back.' Emily sighed. 'I expect the intention was to do so when they had made their fortune.'

The shock of this revelation took Louisa's breath away and she stared in speechless amazement at her cousin.

Edwina said in a small, girlish voice, 'Are you saying this house will go to Louisa?'

'I am not saying that,' Emily replied. 'I am saying that the money...'

Feeling unable to bear the sight of Edwina's face contorted with childlike petulance, Louisa stood up and walked to the window overlooking the garden. She could hear her cousins talking; one whining about losing her inheritance and the other pleading in a placatory tone, but the words floated away over her head as she recalled the events since her arrival twelve weeks earlier.

The time spent with her Aunt Agnes had been very precious and she would always be glad she came to be with her during those last months of her life. She had enjoyed the old lady's reminiscing and thought their talks and laughter had brought a little joy into the poor woman's barren life.

She was aware of Edwina saying, 'But he'll leave me if I don't have …' and stopped listening. Focussing her mind on Aunt Rosemary she felt sure their lives would now be entwined for as long as the old lady lived. There was so much to learn from her, the history of the house and the family and also to hear of her gift of the second sight. Maybe she would show her how to read the tea-leaves; that would be a lot simpler than looking into the well!

Thinking of the well she wondered if others also felt that the small circle of water hidden within the thick walls of the abbey was the most sacred of the three sacred wells close to the sacred mound on the sacred island. Also, remembering the lives she had experienced in her visions, she was certain that the dark well was the reason for the abbey church to be built where it was. It seemed ironic to know that a small spring could have generated so powerful an effect on humans that they were driven to contain it within such an enormous building.

She had learned that the feelings she experienced of being drawn by the well was called dowsing and this was of interest to others, such as the noisy, exotically dressed, intellectuals; which was absolutely fascinating and a little daunting, but it also gave her courage to believe in her own intuition. When taking tea with Aunt Rosemary and Edward later she would now dare to ask if they agreed with her that the invisible thread she felt between the well and the Tor was the source of power that had made the island sacred to their forbears long ago.

Edwina's shrill voice suddenly broke into Louisa's mind and she heard her cousin say, 'Oh Emily, are we obliged to do this?' Thinking the will was still being discussed, she returned to her own thoughts.

What an extraordinary collection of lifetimes she had seen in her visions! Some might say they were no more than dreams, or possibly the products of her lively imagination, but who could have imagined Windflower and the shining man? Then there was White Bird in love with Damon the Bard, presumably a Druid, although she had not heard that title used at the time. And Luna the half Roman slave girl; now that was a strange story! Raven's tale of lost love and also loss of the well was sad. Annie the serving maid and her brother Graeme who was hurt in the fire and suffered for forbidden love was a story so far outside her own knowledge of life she could never have imagined it. Veryan and her involvement with the Black Death ended happily, as did Tobin who experienced the sacking of the monastery by King Henry's soldiers. Finally there was Sara, whose tragic ending contaminated the well with her blood and who dammed its flow with a stone in her dying moments. All these visions would stay in her heart, especially and most importantly, the beautiful young woman in the future, yes, that was the best sight of all!

Emily's calm voice drifted back into her consciousness, '.... however much it is, will be paid back.'

Hearing Edwina's shrill pleas against selling the house and giving *her* anything, Louisa closed her mind again and looked out of the window to find a man in a floppy hat standing on the lawn. Seeing Edward was holding his pocket watch out in front of his chest in a demonstration of the time, she realised the servants had told him of the meeting being held in the sitting room. She waved her handkerchief to him and smiled when he lifted his hat in response.

Then, as a heron flew gracefully overhead, casting a large shadow on the grass beside him, in a perfect imitation of her vision in the carriage window after her father's funeral, her smile broadened and she almost laughed aloud.

With her face alight with joy, she turned to look at the ormolu clock on the mantelpiece and seeing it was fifteen minutes past three, she said, 'I'm afraid I cannot stay any longer, I'm late for an appointment. I shall wait until we hear about your mother's will from the solicitor, Mr Merriott, to be sure of the facts and now I must go and visit my Aunt Rosemary.'

Edwina said, 'Oh Louisa! Oh dear! Oh dear! Oh dear!' She wrung her hands. 'Emily has persuaded— I mean *explained* it to me. I don't know what to say. I had no idea…' She dabbed at her red eyes with a lace handkerchief then, in a falsely bright tone, asked, 'Will you join us for dinner this evening?'

Louisa swallowed a surprised laugh and graciously accepted the invitation. She walked slowly out of the room, feeling as though floating across the Persian rugs. Out in the hall, with no one to see her, she picked up her skirts to run upstairs to her room and hastily put on her hat and cape.

A short while later, on reaching the front gate with her hat askew and her cape unbuttoned, she said breathlessly, 'I'm so sorry for keeping you waiting, Mr Francis.'

He raised his hat and then, offering her his arm, he said, 'Please don't apologise, Mrs Wendon. If our aunt's reading of the tea-leaves is to be believed, you are well worth waiting for.'